THE NEXT GIRL

A C.T. FERGUSON CRIME NOVEL (#8)

TOM FOWLER

Published by Widening Gyre Media.

Cover Design: 100 Covers

Editing: Chase Nottingham

For Lisa and Isabel, as ever.

CHAPTER 1

"You know you'll have to make a toast at some point, right?"

My cousin Rich, pale beer in hand, said this to me as we stood at the bar of Morton's Steakhouse in Baltimore. I held an IPA—a much more interesting brew—and watched my girlfriend Gloria Reading mingle with the guests at her birthday bash. She was twenty-eight today and showed no signs she would soon be staring down thirty. "I don't think a toast is formal enough," I said.

This realization was surprising. Gloria loved extravagance. I was surprised she chose Morton's for her gathering because it was nice but not swanky. Gloria and I both came from wealthy families. I thought of myself as a man of the people, and some of it rubbed off on Gloria in the time we knew each other. She'd loosened up quite a bit, and the change had been refreshing to see.

"Nervous about talking in front of a crowd?" Rich said with a smirk.

I rolled my eyes. "I've never been nervous about talking in my life."

Rich's girlfriend Jeanne sidled up to him and put an arm around his waist. He mirrored the gesture. They looked good together, both dark-haired and strong, though Rich's few extra trips around the sun showed in the gray creeping in at his temples. "Nice party," she said. "Thanks for the invite."

"Anytime," I said. Most of the people here were Gloria's friends, many of whom I knew. She met Rich and later Jeanne through me, and we all liked each other enough for them to be here tonight. With both working for the Baltimore Police Department, getting them anywhere together proved a challenge. Perhaps evildoers in the city worked a light schedule tonight.

I downed the rest of my beer, ordered another IPA, and asked the bartender to make a vodka martini for Gloria. "A fine drink," Rich said.

"It's on the list of reasons I love her," I told him. I collected the beverages and carried them to the private dining room we enjoyed. Morton's had set up two large tables for our use, each seating eight. The area featured enough square footage for more--and charged for it accordingly--but Gloria wanted to keep the event manageable. She remarked she'd been to enough outsized fundraisers and fancy dinners over the last year or more.

I handed Gloria her drink, and she slid her arm around my waist. She chatted with a man and woman I met once but couldn't remember. I did my best not to wear a blank expression until reintroduced to Wendy Potter and Cullen Weis. Like most in Gloria's circle of female friends, Wendy was pretty and around the same age. She wore her blonde hair pulled back and capitalized on the warm evening with a great sundress. Cullen attired himself like he just stepped off the world's preppiest cruise ship. I thought about asking him to tie his favorite knot but figured it wouldn't go over well.

A few minutes later, we all sat down to eat. I thought back to Rich's earlier words. Would I need to make a speech? Shouldn't Gloria be the one to stand up and say a few words? Her parents weren't here--we were doing dinner with her folks and mine another night--so third-party speaking responsibilities fell to me by default. Still, I hoped we could simply enjoy a meal, dessert, coffee, and a few adult beverages before retiring to a hotel for the night.

True to its name and reputation, Morton's served a good steak. We all got some cut or another, and the servers dropped off an assortment of sides to share. Being a simple man, I helped myself to a bunch of fries—or *pomme frites* as the menu called them. Naming something in French allowed for a two-dollar upcharge. Gloria fed me a bite of her New York strip, and I returned the favor with my filet. Rich rolled his eyes at us, and then he and Jeanne did the same thing a minute later. I shook my head at him, and he shrugged.

Once the meat and most of the accompaniments were gone, the wait staff collected diners' plates. We all worked on our drinks and fell back into the rhythm of group conversations. Cullen sat at the other table looking mighty impressed with himself for buying out the J. Crew catalog. When the din quieted, I grabbed my wine glass and stood. The hall quieted, and fifteen pairs of eyes drifted to me.

"Hi, everyone," I said. "Thanks for helping us celebrate tonight." I regarded Gloria, who beamed up at me. "I've known Gloria for a couple years now. I'm surprised she's put up with me as long as she has." Polite laughter filled the room. "She's made a big difference in my life. I don't always have the easiest job . . . there's some weirdness and odd hours sometimes. It never seems to try Gloria's patience, though.

"She's the best person I know, and she has the biggest heart." I felt my eyes well up. Gloria wiping away a tear almost gave me pause, but I pressed on. "I love this woman, and I'm glad all of you came out to celebrate her tonight." I raised my glass. "To Gloria!"

"To Gloria!" came the response from the gathering. My wonderful girlfriend dabbed at her eyes while waving thanks to everyone. The servers rescued us from any awkwardness by circulating dessert menus. A round of sweets and coffee later, and I felt ready to leave. Others had the same idea and said their goodbyes. Wendy and Cullen bid us adieu. I thought about asking Cullen where he was sailing to next but didn't. Turning thirty recently softened me. Or maybe it was Gloria's fault.

Rich and Jeanne were our last guests. The women hugged, and Jeanne surprised me by pulling me in for one, too. Rich and I did the handshake plus one-armed embrace thing many men do. I walked them toward the door. "You guys staying anywhere?" Jeanne asked.

"Yes. It's a surprise, though."

Rich grinned. "Any other surprises?"

"Like what?"

"Did you bring a ring?"

The corner of my mouth turned up involuntarily. "Piss off," I said.

* * *

From Morton's, we took an Uber to The Inn at Henderson's Wharf. It sat on the water in the Fells Point neighborhood of Baltimore. Reaching it required driving over the city's cobblestoned streets. They are not the most pleasant roads to traverse after consuming too much food and a few adult beverages. We carried our bags inside—which is to say I did all the carrying—and got our keycards from the chipper lady at the front desk.

Once in the room, I threw open the curtains. We enjoyed a great view of the Baltimore Harbor. Gloria joined me at the window. "Beautiful," she said.

I put my arm around her. "Yes. The view isn't too bad, either."

She smiled, and we kissed. "Did you just choose this place because you used to live across the street?"

"It helped," I said. When I arrived in Baltimore after my eviction from Hong Kong, I rented an apartment across Fell Street from the Inn. We couldn't see it from our window, but it was off to the left. My unit didn't offer a view of the water, but I frequently went running along the streets and pier. "I always wondered what this place was like. Turns out it's a great boutique hotel."

Gloria nodded. "I like it." I wondered if her opinion would have differed a couple years ago. The older version of Gloria may have turned her nose up at anything less than five-star accommodations.

The hotel left us a bottle of champagne in the room. I popped the cork and poured some bubbly into each glass. We clinked glasses again. "I liked your toast," Gloria said. "Simple and heartfelt."

"Thanks. I'll have to come up with something good for your thirtieth."

"Next year will be my last birthday." Gloria downed the remainder of her champagne in one drink. "I'm going to remain twenty-nine forever."

I drained the rest of my glass, too. "Let me know how it works out for you."

She smiled. "I will." We were both tired after an evening of celebration. Such a thing never would've happened in our early twenties. Gloria adjourned to the bathroom to take a shower and get ready for bed. I knew I had plenty of time to wait, so I read the news on my phone. I kept it light to start, perusing sports headlines and shaking my head at the Orioles' most recent loss. At least they were trending up long-term.

From there, I made the mistake of going to local stories. I ignored the writeups of a couple shootings which were sadly all too typical. A different article caught my eye. *Search Continues for Local Missing Girl.* When I tapped on the story to read it, I did a double take at the young woman's picture. She was pretty with bright blue eyes and long, straight blonde hair. It all gave her a strong resemblance to T.J., a local girl rescued from a bad life by my friend Melinda Davenport. I'd even used T.J. to help me close a case once—over Melinda's strenuous objection, of course.

The article mentioned how seventeen-year-old Brittany O'Connor vanished yesterday. The police were described at various points as puzzled, baffled, and overworked. Brittany remained missing over a day, and her parents were concerned. They offered a reward for information leading to her safe return, and the police commissioner assured everyone their best people were working the case. I wondered if Rich got called in. He normally worked homicides, but kidnapping victims had an unfortunate habit of ending up dead.

I found a couple other stories about the disappearance on other sites, but none offered any new details. Before long, Gloria emerged from the bedroom wearing a negligee whose picture could accompany the word "scandalous" in the dictionary. I watched with interest as she sashayed to the bed, crawled onto it, and planted a kiss on me. "Why don't you get ready?" Her minty breath felt hot against my neck.

"You don't have to tell me twice." A few minutes later, having showered and brushed my teeth, I emerged from the bathroom in a pair of boxers. I tried to put on a seductive walk. Gloria's giggles told me how effective it was. She pulled down the sheet and blanket to reveal she'd doffed the negligee. "I was looking forward to taking it off you," I said.

"I figured I'd save you the trouble," she said, her hazel eyes fixed on me. "You don't mind, do you?"

"Not at all," I said. I walked to the bed to show her exactly how little I objected.

* * *

THE NEXT MORNING, Gloria and I threw presentable clothes on and walked to the lobby for breakfast. I made two cups of the strongest coffee I could find while Gloria perused the food options. She carried a plate of assorted fruit and three croissants to the table. I added two containers of yogurt and a plate of bacon. "Very continental," I said as we sat down to eat.

Gloria nodded around a mouthful of pineapple. "I think I need a danish to really make it."

I glanced at the plate of buttery croissants. "Should we speak French?"

"Can you?"

"I can ask where *les toilettes* are," I said. "It's not much good to us, though, because I can see them from my seat." The men's and ladies' rooms were immediately along the hall to the right of the lobby.

"Maybe we should skip French, then," Gloria said with a smile.

We each required a second cup of coffee, but we finished breakfast and returned to our room. I brought one duffel bag, and once I changed out of sweats and into a T-shirt and jeans, packing it was simple. Gloria brought a purse capable of holding a laptop with ease, a medium-sized suitcase, and an overnight bag whose contents could supply a beauty salon for a month. If we'd driven in her coupe, trunk space would have been tight. When we went to Hawaii last year, she brought five pieces of luggage. Whoever dreamed up bag fees for airlines held Gloria in mind when he did it.

I was about to order an Uber when my phone rang. The nature of my job means numbers I don't recognize besiege my phone, often at odd hours. I took the call. "Our daughter is missing," a woman said before I could even get out a hello. "We haven't seen her since yesterday, and she doesn't answer her phone. This never happens. Can you help us?"

It took me a second to realize she paused in her rapid-fire delivery. I needed to answer before she launched into another diatribe. "Have you been to the police?"

"Why does everyone ask that?"

Her question meant I wasn't the first PI she called. I felt sure I was the only one who worked for free, however. "Because they should be your first call. Did you make it?"

She sighed into the phone. "Yes."

"And?"

"They said it hadn't been long enough yet. We know something's wrong, though. She's never not returned our calls or texts. Can you find her?"

If I declined, she seemed likely to call back every hour and plead with me anew. "Can you come to my office later?"

"I can go there right now," she said.

"I can't, so it'll have to be later." She wasn't pleased, but I didn't care. We agreed on noon, which would be about ninety minutes from now. I ended the call and slipped my phone back into my jeans pocket.

"New case?" Gloria asked.

"Maybe," I said. "The woman's daughter has been missing for twelve hours. It could be nothing."

"But she really could be gone."

"Yeah . . . she could. I'm going to meet the parents at noon to talk about it."

I summoned an Uber, and a few minutes later, we were off on our short jaunt back to Federal Hill. I wasn't looking forward to my twelve o'clock appointment.

CHAPTER 2

I stepped off the elevator at two minutes past twelve to see a couple waiting outside my door. The husband appeared to have about a decade on his wife, though as I walked closer, I noticed dark circles under their eyes and a general disheveled look. I didn't expect anyone to dress up for a meeting with me, but these two could've slept in their clothes and only recently bothered getting out of bed. Considering what they were dealing with, it may well have been the case.

Both had blond hair. The husband stood about six feet even, making him two inches shorter than me. He sported a dad bod, all the rage with the earlier generation. The wife frowned at me as I moved toward the door. She might have been pretty once but lost it in a state of constant worry. She also looked maybe only a few years older than me. I pegged her as the type who always wanted to speak to the manager. Good thing I worked for myself.

"You're late," she said as I slid my key into the lock.

"Elevator delay." I opened the door, and we all walked from what passed as a waiting area to my inner office. I sat in my leather executive chair, and they took the two guest numbers. "Anything to drink? Water? Coffee?"

"No," the wife said.

"I'd love a coffee," the husband said. It earned him the hairy eyeball from his spouse. I added water to the Keurig sitting atop my file cabinet and brewed two single cups, handing him one and keeping the other. We were barely a few minutes into the meeting, and I already wanted some whiskey to add to my java.

"Are you the O'Connors?" I said after a sip.

"No," the woman said as if I'd asked if they were cannibals. "We're the Swains. Why did you think we were the O'Connors?"

Another missing girl. Interesting. I didn't want to worry them about someone else's daughter. These people had enough on their plate. "Must have gotten you confused with someone else who called me," I said. "Let's start from the top."

"I'm Karen," she said, "and my husband is Jon."

"Short for Jonathan," he added, and I wondered if he always chimed in with this because he loathed an extra H in his name. "What's C.T. short for?"

"Cinnamon Toast," I said. "My parents' favorite breakfast."

"That can't be true," Karen said, her brows pulled down.

"Of course it isn't. It also doesn't matter. We're not here to talk about me or compare names. Tell me about your daughter."

"Ashleigh is wonderful," she said. Then, Short-for-Jonathan added how the last syllable was spelled L-E-I-G-H, and my dislike for this couple deepened. If I discovered her friends were Hayleigh and Kelseigh, I was out. We all have our limits.

"You haven't heard from her since last night," I said, and they both shook their heads. "What time?"

"About ten-thirty," Jon said. "She was with a couple of friends from school. She usually stays at one of their houses on Saturdays, so we didn't expect her to come home. She normally texts us good night, though."

"She could have fallen asleep."

"But she didn't tell us good morning, either," Karen said.

"She could have stayed asleep. How old is she?"

"Seventeen."

"Teenagers need a lot of rest."

"Something's wrong. Mothers know these things."

I bit down on my counterpoint. It wouldn't be a productive conversation. "I presume you tried calling and texting her this morning?"

"Yes," Jon said. "No answer to either."

"What about the friend she stayed with?"

"Says she saw her last night before bed. They have a downstairs guest room. She didn't see Ashleigh this morning and just figured she left early."

"There's no one else she could have stayed with? Another friend? A boyfriend?"

"No." Karen shook her head so hard I wondered if it would unscrew from her neck. "Ashleigh doesn't do things like that."

"I did a lot of stuff I shouldn't have when I was seventeen," I said.

"Is that why you're a private investigator today?"

I narrowed my eyes at Karen. Jon was about to interject, but I silenced him with an upraised index finger. "I know you're worried about your daughter. I get it. You came to me. I let you in . . . and I'll toss you right back out if you keep giving me your attitude."

Jon spoke now. "We're sorry. We're . . . dealing with a lot right now."

"Fine," I said. I ignored Karen, who studied her poorly-painted fingernails. "Why are you so convinced something's wrong?"

"She's a good kid. Hasn't always been, though. We went through a real rough patch with her when she was thirteen and fourteen. She almost got expelled from school. It took us a little while, but we got her straightened out. She's been on a good path for a while now. Honor roll every semester of high school."

"Boyfriend?"

"Not at the moment."

"Why do you keep coming back to the boyfriend angle?" Karen asked.

"Is she pretty?" I said.

"What does that have to do—"

"Yes," Jon broke in.

"I've been in high school. I'm sure you both were, too, but I've done it more recently. We didn't quite have iPhones then, but texting was definitely a thing. I know how high school boys and girls behave, especially when it comes to seeing each other when they shouldn't."

"Ashleigh wouldn't." Karen set her jaw, and her head wagged side-to-side.

I drank some more coffee. It wasn't enough to get me through this meeting with this couple. "Look . . . I'm skeptical she's missing. I'll entertain the possibility for now. If I'm going to look for her, though, I'll need information. Her friends, a school schedule, a recent picture . . ." I could gather a lot of the same information illicitly, but it was much easier to have someone hand it to me.

Karen wrote out a list of Ashleigh's friends while Jon texted me a photo. I forced myself to hide my surprise at seeing it. She bore a very strong resemblance to Brittany O'Connor, the other girl who disappeared recently. And was also seventeen. "All right," I said once they'd given me everything they could, "I'll get started."

"You'll keep us updated?" Karen said.

"When I have something."

"You make it sound like you're doing us a favor."

I sighed. The woman found herself in a bad situation, but she still managed to try my patience. "Am I charging you?" I said.

"No."

"Then I *am* doing you a favor. Why don't you leave while I still feel up to it?"

Jon offered another apology, and they left. I was glad to be rid of them. Hopefully, I'd find Ashleigh at a friend's house soon and not have to deal with them much.

A bad feeling tugged at me, though. Ashleigh Swain and Brittany O'Connor. Both seventeen, blonde, blue-eyed, and pretty. Both missing within about a day of each other.

Two girls didn't make a pattern, but I didn't like where the situation was headed.

* * *

I CALLED Rich to see if Ashleigh found her way onto the BPD's radar yet. "Haven't heard of her," he told me. "Doesn't look like there's an open case." He paused. "Couldn't you have found this out yourself?"

"Yes." Rich provided me an in, though he didn't do it on purpose. During my first case, he left me alone at his computer for a few minutes. It was more than enough time for me to snag its networking information. Since then, I've maintained a virtual machine the Baltimore Police Department thinks is part of their system. I check it on the regular. Rich complains about it every now and again, but I've never seen an indication anyone in power knew or cared about my foothold. "Sometimes, I like to get data from the source."

"What's this girl's story?"

"I don't know yet, but I'm hoping it doesn't turn into a sad one. Seventeen, pretty, disappeared . . . parents say from a friend's house."

"Huh. Sounds similar to what I'm staring at."

"You caught the O'Connor case?"

"Yep."

It wasn't a good sign. "She dead?"

"Not that I know of," Rich said.

"I thought you worked homicides."

"This has turned into something of a red ball. All hands on deck."

Brittany O'Connor vanished a couple days ago. The longer she remained gone, the shorter the odds she'd be found alive. Or at all. While I'd expect the BPD to want her found, it still seemed quick to bring in someone like Rich. I heard chatter in the background on his end of the call. "You at work?"

"Yep."

"On a Sunday?"

"Justice doesn't wait for Monday."

"I'll meet you at your desk in a little while," I said, and I hung up. Twenty minutes later, armed with two iced coffees, I walked into the precinct and found Rich at his desk. The building got an overhaul a couple years ago, and it went from gray and dreary to modern and bright. I still thought the open-concept floor plan was absurd, but it became a trend before the BPD remade the place. I dropped one cold beverage in front of my cousin and plopped into a guest chair.

"Thanks," he said, sipping the coffee without looking away from his monitor.

"Reading up on Brittany O'Connor?"

He nodded. "A lot of similarities. Same age, same city. Your girl blonde with blue eyes?"

"She is."

"Pretty?"

"Yes."

"I keep trying to tell myself two doesn't make a pattern."

"Me, too," I said. "It's not much to go on, but it could be the start of a disturbing trend."

"It could. Or both these girls might turn up later today."

"I broached the possibility with Ashleigh's parents."

"They weren't receptive?"

I shook my head around a drink of coffee. Today marked my first time visiting the precinct on a Sunday. It didn't sound any quieter. Cops still worked all around me. Most offices would be ghost towns on the weekend. To paraphrase what Rich told me, however, justice doesn't take weekends off. Even if I wanted to. "They admitted they'd had a rough patch with their daughter," I said. "They think she's come through it and is basically an angel."

"You're not convinced?"

I shrugged. "She's barely been gone twelve hours. Kids her age are always doing things they shouldn't, often with people they shouldn't."

"I know. This O'Connor case feels different, though. She's been gone longer and not a peep. No one's seen her since sometime after school Friday."

"You know we're working the situation together, right?"

"We're not," Rich said.

"We are. You'll see. I'll have some piercing insight as usual, and Leon Sharpe will tell you how smart I am, and then he'll direct you to work with me."

Rich rolled his eyes. "Good to see you've planned out the progression." He paused for a sip of cold caffeine. "I could use a win here."

"Then you'll find no better partner," I said."

"My last case didn't go well." I frowned. This was the first I'd heard of it, and I couldn't recall a time Rich didn't bring a case home . . . even the ones he worked without me. Between his time in the army and his years with the BPD, he's turned into a damned fine detective. If he couldn't crack something, I doubted anyone could.

"What happened?" I asked.

He waved a hand. "Doesn't matter. Everybody fails at some point."

"Speak for yourself."

"You will, too. It's inevitable. The important thing is what you do after."

"This is turning into an after-school special," I said.

"Let me see what I can figure out here. I may want to bring you in at some point since you're already working something similar. They could end up being related."

"OK. I'll look over the O'Connor file at some point." Rich started to ask me how, then realized the futility of his question. I left him to his iced coffee.

CHAPTER 3

I hoped Rich's case and mine weren't connected. He tended not to believe in coincidences, and I shared the sentiment. Two young girls could disappear within a couple days of one another without the incidents being related. What nagged at me happened to be how much Brittany and Ashleigh looked alike. It went beyond hair and eye color; the girls could easily pass for sisters if standing next to one another.

Ashleigh's parents weren't very helpful in my office, and I didn't think they'd know anything about Brittany. I drove to their house in Fullerton, which is about as far northeast as one can go and still be in Baltimore. They lived off Belair Road on a one-way street called Fleetwood Avenue. Their modest brick two-story house was squat and narrow but deep. The white paint of the shutters needed to be redone years ago, and the exterior begged for a good power washing. The porch was clean by comparison with a spotless welcome mat and new--if tacky--plastic lawn chairs.

When Karen answered the door, her eyes widened at seeing me on the porch. "Mister Ferguson, this is . . . a surprise."

It was for me, too, but I didn't need to go down such a rocky road with her. "I'd like to see Ashleigh's room if I could."

"Why?" She crossed her arms.

"Whether someone snatched her or she ran off, details in there could tell us about it."

"Do you still think--"

"For Christ's sake, let him see the room." Jon appeared in the door a second later. "What if he learns something important?"

"It's not like she has a diary," Karen said.

"She may have a blog," I said, "or an online journal."

"We'd know about it."

I smiled. "Sure you would."

Jon invited me inside while Karen stewed in the entryway. "Her room's upstairs," he said. "Do you think you can discover anything in there?"

It tended to work in Hollywood, but this answer would not prove reassuring. "I'd rather try and come away with nothing than wish I'd stopped by later," I said.

The logic seemed to placate him. For her part, Karen remained indifferent. The cynic in me wondered if Ashleigh ran away simply to escape her mother. I wouldn't have blamed her if she did, and I'd only spent twenty minutes with the woman. The upstairs hallway was long but narrow. Ashleigh's bedroom was at the back of the house, the opposite of her parents. Jon opened the door and let me in. "Take as long as you need," he said.

"Thanks." I'd been a seventeen-year-old boy thirteen years ago. I spent time in the bedrooms of girls my age. Not much changed over the years. The most notable differences were the updated technology and lack of heartthrob posters. There was no need to hang a picture of Dreamy McDreamerson on the wall when he could be the background image on your cell phone.

I looked around the space. Gone were the landline phones and computer monitors I remembered from my time. Ashleigh's room looked about medium in size. She slept in a double bed still neatly made. Her two bookshelves held an eclectic mix, ranging from fantasy classics to programming manuals. I wondered how many of these books she read for pleasure versus for school.

Her desk held a few framed photos of Ashleigh with some friends. I noticed three other girls in the various shots. Jon told me to take my time, so I removed each picture from its frame and snapped them with my phone before replacing them. An Android tablet lay on the desk. I hit the home button, and a password prompt stared back at me. Ashleigh's parents gave me her birthday, so I tried it. No dice. It featured a micro SD card slot and a mini USB port.

I couldn't do anything with the former at the moment, but I carried a solution to the latter. I connected Ashleigh's tablet to my phone via cable, then used my mobile to open a connection to my server. One script later, the data on her Android traversed the cellular network to where I could look at it later. It would take a little time to complete, so I continued nosing around. Desk drawers contained office supplies and a graphing calculator. No booze, pills, weed, or condoms. Atop it were Hydro Flasks in five different colors. I've always thought myself a huge proponent of drinking water, and even I didn't own so many bottles.

Not much else stood out to me. Ashleigh's closet held more clothes than I thought it could handle, plus a bunch of shoes and some shabby sports equipment. I didn't find a secret panel anywhere nor anything interesting she hid from her parents. Maybe she saved such things for her tablet. Between whatever data I could pull from it and the pictures of her friends, at least I had something to work with.

When everything finished copying, I disconnected my cable and walked back downstairs. Karen stood nearby, her arms still crossed. "Find anything?"

"Maybe. Do you know the other girls in the photos on Ashleigh's desk?"

"Of course we do," she said, doing her best to sound offended.

"Great," I said, summoning considerable willpower to maintain a professional tone. "Can you send me their names? I could find them, but it might be faster this way."

"We will," Jon said before his wife could comment.

"Thanks." I looked at Jon. "You were a big help." I left without offering an opinion of Karen.

* * *

By the time I arrived home, Jon sent me the names of the three girls in Ashleigh's photos. They were Sally Hager, Nina Reilly, and Marie Victor. He added a note telling me Sally was the girl at whose house Ashleigh was supposed to spend the night when she disappeared. I wondered if Karen would have been anywhere near so helpful.

I began with the hostess of the evening in question. A simple search told me Sally and her parents—Sue and Carl— lived not far from the Swains. I called and reached the dad, who sounded very put out to be contacted by anyone on a Sunday. It wasn't even football season. He said I could come by, and I told him I would. I wished I'd tried to do facial recognition or reverse image searches while I stood in Ashleigh's room. It would've saved me a round trip from Federal Hill to Fullerton.

Later, about two blocks from the Swains', I parked near the Hagers home. It was larger and looked both more modern and better maintained. Rich's Victorian in nearby Hamilton was probably a little bigger, but Sue and Carl's house was plenty large. It would comfortably hold more than two of mine. Every blade of grass in the yard looked to be the identical length. Maybe the owner sounded salty on the phone because I interrupted a vigorous landscaping session.

When he answered the door a moment later, I realized I guessed wrong. He was short and round and not at all the kind of man who would cut his own grass or sculpt his own foliage. The house was plenty nice, and I figured the BMW parked nearby was his. He could afford to pay someone to handle the grounds. "You the detective?"

"I am." I showed Carl Hager my ID and badge.

"Ashleigh's really missing?"

"So far as anyone knows. I'm hoping you and your daughter can shed some light on the whole mess for me."

He invited me in to a large living room. A TV measuring at least sixty inches hung on the wall. The hardwood floors looked like someone polished them recently. All leather furniture was clean. Either Sue Hager was a hell of a housekeeper or they hired maid service out, too. If my place were bigger—and if I had any yard to speak of—I would have paid someone, also. "I'll get Sally." He disappeared up the stairs, which creaked under his weight.

A minute later, Carl returned with his daughter. She was short, also—probably five-four at most—but athletic and pretty. If I were to harbor a guess, I would say she played guard on the high school girls' basketball team. Sally wore her dark hair in a ponytail, and her deep brown eyes stared at me with trepidation. "Hi, Sally. I'm hoping you can help me."

"Ashleigh's gone?" She sat on the edge of a sofa.

I parked myself at the opposite end and faced her. "It looks likely, but it's still early. There's a lot I probably don't know yet."

Carl took a seat across from us on a loveseat. He seemed content to let his daughter speak for herself, something I couldn't imagine Karen Swain doing. "However I can help," Sally said. "Ashleigh and I are good friends."

"Did she stay here last night?"

"Yeah." She paused and frowned. "Well . . . I thought she did. She was here. This morning, though, she was gone."

"Were you surprised?"

Sally's head bobbed. "She sleeps downstairs in the guest room. I always go down and wake her up for breakfast."

"But when you did, she wasn't there?" She shook her head. "Any sign she'd been there?"

"I'm not sure."

"You want to see it?" Carl asked.

"When we're done, yes," I said. "Sally, tell me what happened last night."

"It was pretty normal. Ashleigh walked over after dinner. It was . . . like, seven, I think. We hung out for a while." I imagined them both on their phones despite sitting a few inches from one another. "I had a headache, so I went to bed early."

"What time?"

"About nine-thirty, I guess."

"And then Ashleigh went downstairs?"

"Yeah."

"She sleep here often?" I said.

"Why?" Carl asked.

I kept my focus on Sally. "You said, 'she sleeps downstairs.' To me, this means it's something she does with some regularity."

Sally wrung her hands and studied the leather of the couch. After a few seconds, she said, "Ashleigh didn't always get along with her parents."

"You meet them?" Carl said.

"A couple times now."

"Jon's not bad." He snorted and shook his head. "Poor guy married a bitch, though."

"They only argue," I said, "or are we talking something worse?"

"Ashleigh . . . had some problems a few years ago," Sally said.

"Her parents mentioned something about it. No specifics, though. Do you know what kind of problems?"

"She was seeing a boy. Her parents didn't want her to, of

course. He . . . got her into weed. I'm pretty sure she was sneaking out to have sex with him, too."

"The girl was fourteen," Carl said. "I get being stern with her afterward, but I think they took it too far. Barely let her do anything."

"She was depressed for a while," Sally added. "Like, seeing the counselor pretty often. Anyway, she started spending Saturday nights here. Her parents didn't seem to mind. We've been friends for years."

Carl said, "I figured she could use a night away from there. We got a room downstairs almost never gets used."

"Can you show me?" I asked. They both walked to the basement with me. A family room took up half the space. Unlike the main level, linoleum covered the floor. The TV was smaller here and the furniture much more pedestrian. In the back half, a queen bed and two nightstands sat atop plush carpeting. A powder room sat off to the side. French doors obscured by Venetian blinds bisected the back wall.

"She definitely came down here," Sally said.

I pointed at the doors. "She could have walked out here, and you'd never know."

"She could have," Carl chimed in.

I looked around the space. The sheets and blanket were pulled down on the bed, but it didn't appear slept in. A small book bag rested against the nightstand. I picked it up. "Is this hers?" Sally indicated it was. I opened it. Its contents consisted of a change of clothes and a phone charger. I searched all the pockets but found nothing else. She had her phone with her when she left. "Can you text me Ashleigh's cell number?" I handed Sally a business card.

"Sure." She grabbed her mobile and sent the number to me.

"You need anything else?"

"I don't think so. Thanks . . . you've both been really helpful."

Carl showed me out. I got back into my Audi and checked the message from Sally. If Ashleigh carried her phone with her when she walked out of the Hagers' basement, she could still have it with her.

And I could track it.

* * *

I USED my phone to connect to my server again. A program allowed me to use cell towers to find any mobile, either where it was or where it last made contact. It proved accurate to about a hundred yards, which wasn't bad for code I found and tweaked. I entered Ashleigh's number and waited while the software did its thing.

A few seconds later, it displayed a result. The location lay a couple blocks off Belair Road across the county line. I put the S4 into gear and headed toward it. The drive wasn't far, since I was already close to the edge of the city. I made the left at Taylor Avenue, then pulled to the curb at Highview, the first cross street. It put me within the radius for Ashleigh's device.

Highview was a narrow side street, and three others crossed it before its terminus. I got out of the car and fired up a version of the phone finder on my own mobile. With a second data point, I could narrow down my search. The radius shrank. I hoofed it to Fuller Avenue, the first intersection. To my left, it continued to Belair Road; to the right, it ran for about eight houses on either side before reaching a dead end. A couple larger homes sat at the end of the cul-de-sac. I didn't want to knock on twenty doors, but if I needed to, I would.

I started to the right. Ashleigh's phone lit up as a red dot on my screen. If the display were accurate, it wouldn't be far ahead. A couple houses later, I pulled even with the dot. I knocked on the door and showed the woman who answered a picture of

Ashleigh. She told me she'd never seen her before, and I didn't have any reason to doubt her.

As I reached the sidewalk again, I noticed the sewer grate. My stomach tightened. The level of accuracy built into my app meant Ashleigh's mobile could be in one of the nearby homes. This would be much better for her future survival than if I found it discarded. I couldn't see much below street level, so I turned on the small LED flashlight I always carry with me. It lifted the blackness.

"Shit," I said to the empty street. Under the grate, atop a few bits of random detritus, lay an iPhone case covered in stickers.

CHAPTER 4

I COULDN'T REACH THE PHONE EVEN WHEN I LAY IN THE gutter and reached as far as I could. My arm would need to be at least twice its length. I rummaged through the trunk of my car to see what might help. A rope would easily reach but lacked a way to grab anything. Without any better options, I lashed a rag into the end of it, making the crudest basket in human history.

A few attempts also revealed it to be the least effective. My improvised carrier would hold the phone but didn't have a means of lifting it. I scoured nearby trees but didn't see a stick long enough to raise or nudge the device. A face popping up in a window reminded me this was Sunday afternoon, and any random actions I took may attract attention.

I put the rope back in the trunk. As usual, technology would solve the problem. I fired up a Bluetooth hacking app on my phone. It blew through the woeful security on Ashleigh's and began copying her device. It finished a couple minutes later. I could download it onto a spare at home. I got back into the S4 and pulled away before I drew any further undue scrutiny.

While I drove home, I called the Swains. They needed to know about my discovery, even though it torpedoed the odds of Ashleigh running off on her own. Thankfully, Jon answered. I couldn't have put up with Karen lecturing me about my theory not being correct. "I have some news for you," I told him, "and I don't think it's good."

He sighed, long and slow, and it sounded like he deflated. "What is it?"

"I found Ashleigh's phone."

"Where?" he asked before I could tell him.

"At the bottom of a sewer."

He didn't say anything for a few seconds. When he found his voice, it was quiet and small. "You're sure it was hers?"

"She have a case with stickers all over it?" I said. Silence again. "I was tracking its location. I think the odds of hers beaconing in the area and me finding someone else's are remote."

"I get it. I'll tell Karen."

"I'll let you know if I find anything from it."

"You have the phone?" he said, hope strengthening his voice.

"No. I have the data from it."

"How did you—?"

"Don't worry about it," I broke in. "Whatever's on there can only help my investigation."

"You'll let us know what you come up with?"

"I will." Which I intended to . . . eventually. Knowing didn't help most people in these situations regardless how much they thought it would. The phone clone gave me two devices of Ashleigh's to sift through once I sat at my desk. Between them, I hoped to find an indication of where she went in the very unlikely event she disappeared of her own volition or a line on who might have taken her.

* * *

I DROVE to my office rather than my house. An earlier case blurred the line between home and business when a man walked into my house with a gun. Since then, I've rented an office in the CareFirst Building in Baltimore. They took over from the previous owner, and I remain one of the few non-medical tenants —if not the only one. One of these days, they'll probably realize it and get rid of me.

I maintained a powerful server here which hosted a few specialized virtual machines. While I waited for my data dump from Ashleigh's tablet to load, I fetched a spare unit and down-loaded the captured image onto it. Both crunched for a few minutes. I texted Gloria and told her I'd be working from the office for a while. She replied she'd handle dinner, which meant carry-in. Gloria could not be trusted past the very basics in the kitchen, and I would only let her cook dinner if the fire depart-ment parked two trucks at the end of my street.

When everything was ready for analysis, my phone rang. I looked at the caller ID: Gabriella Rizzo. We'd known each other since we were kids, though the last time I saw her was more than a year ago. "Hi, C.T.," she said when I picked up.

"It's been a while, Gabriella. How are you?"

"Doing well. I'm in town."

"Oh. Welcome back to Baltimore. Drive with your windows up."

She chuckled. "I remember that much, at least."

"What brings you back to our fair city?"

"Dad wanted me to come home." Gabriella's father was Tony Rizzo, a longtime friend of my parents. He also happened to run organized crime in Baltimore. My parents spent the last few years avoiding him. I guess they figured it out after years of cluelessness.

"He's finally realized you're the best person to take over for him?" I said.

"We're working on it," she said, her voiced tinged with

sadness. "Right now, he wants to buy some city land and turn it into a park with his name on it."

I spent a few seconds staring at the wall in my office. "A park?" I eventually said. A paragon of conversation, I am.

"It's something he says he's wanted to do for a while."

"And he thinks you're plugged in to all the unused plots in a city you haven't lived in for years?"

"I told him I'd help," she said.

Why would Tony want an eponymous park? Anyone who didn't know him by reputation knew his restaurant—*Il Buon Cibo* was a mainstay of Little Italy's restaurant scene. "Is he all right?"

"Sure. Why?"

"This seems like a legacy move . . . something you do when there's not much time left."

"You know he had the flu and pneumonia earlier this year?"

"Mm-hmm."

"He's a lot better now," Gabriella said. I didn't detect conviction in her words. I wanted it to be there.

She didn't seem interested in elaborating, so I said, "Good. I'm glad to hear it."

"He told me you two had a bit of a falling out."

"Things were a little frosty for a while." Tony was pissed I helped a potential rival escape his goon squad. We talked about it afterwards, and once the chilly period passed, I thought we were OK again. Perhaps I'd been presumptive.

"Maybe we could all have dinner one night."

"Sure," I said. "Sounds good. I know a great Italian restaurant."

"Me, too," Gabriella said after a brief giggle. "How about we not invite the lawyers?"

"What lawyers?"

"Dad's working with a firm. McLelland . . . something or

other. I forget. He wants to make sure everything goes through like it's supposed to."

"I'm surprised he doesn't have someone in the city on the payroll," I said.

"Not much value in a parks employee, I guess."

"Probably not."

"I have to run, C.T.," Gabriella said. "Good to talk to you."

"You, too. Keep in touch." We hung up.

After I set my phone down, I spent a few more minutes gaping at the wall wondering what it all meant.

* * *

Teenaged girls' text conversations were insipid.

I hated to generalize. My sample size of one constituted the smallest statistical base possible. Ashleigh's texts held nothing meaningful or incriminating. I would have been happy with either one. Most of the threads I read were about classes, home-work, boys, teachers, other girls, and similar things most people didn't care about.

I combed through Ashleigh's chats with her parents. As I expected, her conversations with Jon were more normal than the ones with Karen. Those held an edge of latent hostility, like they didn't get along and papered over it in case someone else happened to read the messages. *Are you staying with your friend again? Nothing's wrong with your bed here. Did you forget to get back to me again?* Both Ashleigh's parents and Sally's father mentioned she went through a rough patch. Whatever it was, it didn't appear she and Karen put it behind them yet. I would need to ask Jon about it if I wanted to learn anything.

Her photos included a lot of shots with Sally, Nina, and Marie. The girls wore clothes matching so closely they could have been uniforms. Long shirts were common, shorts in all but the coldest winter months, hair scrunchies, and Hydro Flasks. Ashleigh owned five different colors of water bottles so she could accessorize. "They're VSCO girls," I whispered to my empty office. It didn't answer me. It never does.

Clothing choices and an affinity for a popular photo app weren't reasons to disappear. I sifted through other data on the phone but didn't find anything to catch my eye. My server held a virtual image of the tablet I uploaded from Ashleigh's room. It felt weird using a keyboard and mouse to operate apps not designed for them, but the setup worked well enough.

Even though Ashleigh's phone was Apple and her tablet Android, they both had many of the same apps installed. Much of what I looked through at first proved redundant with the data on her mobile. I moved onto the web browser. It opened to a blog Ashleigh maintained. I scrolled through the posts; all were set to private. The material was strictly for her, a diary of sorts for a 21st-Century girl.

Fifteen minutes into my reading, I concluded Ashleigh wasn't happy.

I knew people like her. They could fake it well enough. The smile fooled enough folks, and when it didn't get the job done, an easy laugh sealed the deal. Underneath, however, was a girl who didn't know much about whom she was or whomever she ought to be. A few posts dealt with the pressure of going to college. The specter of huge student loan debt, probable separation from friends, missing home . . . how many teens dealt with these issues regularly now? Ashleigh and I were only about half a generation apart, but things were different when I was a junior and senior in high school.

Even though these thoughts made me feel old, they were true. My parents pushed me to achieve, and Ashleigh's writings indicated hers did, too. The only reprieve I got was for the death of my older sister when I was sixteen. It took a while, but I rallied and finished high school strong. My parents weren't ogres, but they wanted me to do well and go to a good college. Of course, they could afford to write a check for six years of a quality education.

Jon and Karen weren't in the same boat. Ashleigh could qualify for some minor scholarships, but she still needed to get through her senior year and not lose any academic ground. She wrote about wanting to go to a community college for two years, which struck me as a sound financial decision. Her parents—especially her mother—hated the idea. Karen wanted her daughter to spend four years at a good school, graduate with honors, and save the world, according to Ashleigh.

No pressure.

She could have been exaggerating her mother's expectations. Karen struck me as the less reasonable of the duo, however. Their texts indicated a polite but strained relationship. The blog posts expanded on it. *My mother doesn't trust me. Even though all the shit I did was a couple years ago, she can't get past it. I'll always be the girl who needed saving. I wish Jon could get through to her. I hope he still tries, but I couldn't blame him if he gave up.*

Karen wouldn't consider the possibility Ashleigh ran away. Maybe it was personal—her daughter would be fleeing *her*, after all, and what mother wants to admit she's the cause of driving a child away? Even though Ashleigh's blog rarely painted her mother in complimentary terms, I couldn't presume Karen did something to make her leave.

I couldn't ignore the possibility, however. Ashleigh could have been abducted. Her phone could have fallen into the sewer in a struggle, or whoever snatched her may have thrown it there. Or she could have done it herself. Spike the mobile down the drain and disappear.

My problem was I didn't know which was more likely.

CHAPTER 5

Next morning, I left a sleeping Gloria in bed and hit the mean streets of Federal Hill for my morning constitutional. We were well into May, and warm weather meant I opted for shorts and a thin running shirt. I sweated before my first lap and was covered in it by the time I finished four miles and walked home. Gloria was awake when I arrived, and her wrinkled nose told me I needed a shower right away.

Freshly clean, I came downstairs a short while later and worked on breakfast. My refrigerator reverted to its default state of not holding many options, so I went simple with blueberry pancakes and sausage. Gloria joined me as the pancakes finished. She covered hers in enough butter to alarm a cardiologist, then added enough syrup to give me diabetes from the fumes. How she maintained her terrific figure puzzled me.

A short while later, I nursed my second cup of coffee when Rich called. "I think we have a problem," he said.

I watched with interest as Gloria bent over to pluck a book from a low shelf. "No problems here." She half-turned and smiled in profile.

"I mean about our case."

"It's 'our' case now?"

"Norton just told me about a body in Frederick County. It's a girl who's been missing a few days. Want to guess her age?"

I frowned. Another young woman, and this one was dead. Things looked much worse now for Brittany and Ashleigh. "Seventeen."

"How about hair and eyes?" he said.

"Blonde and blue?"

"She makes three. You said two wasn't a pattern, and I agree. But three is different."

"What are we going to do about it?" I said. "Considering it's *our* case."

"Norton is meeting me here soon," Rich said. "We're going to ride out to Frederick County and see what's going on. Probably good if you came along."

"I'll be there," I said and broke the connection.

"You have to go?" Gloria asked.

"Yeah. The case is taking a turn." I summarized the conversation for her.

"Are you dealing with a serial killer?" She clenched the book tightly enough to whiten her knuckles.

"It's way too early to tell," I said. "Serial killers are rare. This looks like it might be a pattern."

"Be careful." She got up, sat next to me on the couch, and rubbed my back. "Rare or not, I don't want some psycho setting his eyes on you."

"What if it's a woman setting her eyes on me?"

Gloria's concern turned into a smile. "Even worse."

* * *

I OPTED to drive separately from Rich and Norton. My alternative was to ride in the back of the latter's state police car. Between my arrest in Hong Kong over two years ago and a couple of trumped-up bookings here, I figured I'd spent enough time in the rear of cruisers. My Audi offered a much smoother ride, anyway.

My familiarity with Frederick County began and ended with the namesake city. It held a couple restaurants I liked plus a charming minor-league baseball stadium. Apart from a few scattered pockets of civilization, most of the county consisted of grassy fields and farms. One of those was our grim destination today.

We turned onto a narrow dirt road. Recent rain moistened the surface and minimized the dust our tires kicked up. A two-story house lay ahead of us. To the sides, green stretched as far as I could see. The farmer planted a bunch of crops I couldn't identify in some of the fields. Others lay fallow for now. As we approached the residence, another state police car waited for us.

We stopped where the road widened to resemble a parking pad. Norton and Rich got out to confer with their uniformed colleague. Off to the left, another trooper kept watch in a fallow field, standing over what was obviously a body covered by a white sheet. I joined Rich and Norton for the walk.

"Farmer's wife saw it this morning and called it in," the state police captain told us. "A couple deputies responded. We've seen the other two cases and requested to be brought in."

"Where are the locals?" I said.

"They left."

"Your guys chased them off?"

"Their choice," Norton said. "We didn't insist on taking over or anything."

"And now?" Rich said.

"Now, we think we'll work with the Baltimore Police on the two similar open cases."

"You'll also ally yourselves with any brilliant private investigators who might also be working this," I said.

"Sure," Norton said. "Soon as we find one." He and Rich

enjoyed a chuckle. I let them have their fun. We would need all hands on deck, especially with one of the girls being found dead. I've always gotten the impression Norton tolerated my presence more than he valued my input, but he wasn't shooing me away and locking things down.

Tilled dirt covered the ground. Maybe something would be planted here soon. The only thing marring the brown landscape was the white sheet. We stood around the body. The trooper standing over it, a squat Latino whose name tag identified him as Cabrera, gave us the few details they'd gathered. "She was found earlier this morning. We're waiting for the ME." He stared at me for a couple seconds before crouching to pull the sheet back.

I took a deep breath and turned away. A blonde girl had been shot in the back of the head, and the bullet did a considerable amount of damage. Other than a couple streaks of blood, her face was intact, and I noticed the resemblance to Ashleigh immediately. "Almost no blood at the scene," Norton said, inspecting the dirt. "Looks like she was killed somewhere else and dumped here."

"Looks like it, Captain," Cabrera said. "Everything here is full of tire tracks, but we'll see what we can do." Our cars recently added another pair. I didn't think the cops would figure anything out the way things were going, and the pursed lips on Norton's and Rich's faces told me they shared my skepticism.

"How long has she been dead?" I asked after a few seconds of silence.

"Can't tell yet," Norton said. "Body still looks pretty fresh, but we won't know for sure until the ME gets here." From behind us, tires drove over the dirt road. "Speak of the devil. You talk to the farmer and his wife?"

"Yes, sir," Cabrera said.

"Anything useful?"

"Didn't see or hear anything beforehand, no."

"We heard your ME from here," I said. "A car approaching the house is going to make noise."

"In the middle of the night, it might not matter," Rich said. "If everyone in the house is asleep, there are no other people nearby to hear it or see it."

"Whoever did this chose the place well." I frowned. Whoever dumped the body here did it on purpose. It was a calculated decision, not an impulsive act. We were dealing with an intelligent adversary. I looked over the body. A small puncture mark showed on the girl's left arm right below the elbow. I pointed it out. "You think this is a needle hole?"

Rich crouched and scrutinized it. "Looks like it," he said.

"Drugs?"

"We'll need a tox screen," Cabrera said. "I don't want to speak for the ME, but it usually takes a couple days at least."

Rich echoed my thoughts when he said, "I hope this doesn't get worse before it gets better."

I appreciated the sentiment but couldn't share his optimism.

WE STOOD at our respective cars. The state's medical examiner and forensics team combed the scene. We could do nothing but stand and watch, and with the discovery of the most recent body ramping things up in the case, the tactic seemed poor. "We're heading back," Rich said. "You coming?"

I stared at the dead girl in the field. Could I save Ashleigh from the same fate? What about Brittany O'Connor? "No," I said after a few seconds. "I'm going to poke around up here some more."

"Why?"

"Norton said the county responded first." I shrugged. "Maybe they know something. Never hurts to ask."

"All right," he said. "Let's reconvene later. We'll probably have some more manpower on this now."

I agreed, and they left. My GPS directed me to the closest Frederick County sheriff's office. I parked amid a cluster of marked vehicles and walked inside. The deputy at the desk did not appear impressed with my PI license and directed me to wait for someone else. A few minutes later, I was summoned to the desk of a tall deputy who looked like he'd been chiseled from the mountains of western Maryland. He was taller than me, probably a few years older, and would soundly defeat me in an arm-wrestling match.

"Who's the victim?" he said when we both took our seats.

"I don't know," I said. "It was the girl found on the farm. The state's ME hasn't made an ID yet."

"Not sure how I can look it up, then."

"You have a database?" He nodded. "With more fields besides 'name?'" Another head bob. "You might try one of those."

He gave me a patient smile. I wondered how many big-city hotshots came out here to tell him how to do his job. "I'm saying we probably don't have a record of anything yet. Someone went to investigate and got chased away by the state." His was an uncharitable version of events, though not unexpected. And maybe not inaccurate. "Unless the deputy already wrote up some notes, there's nothing for me to find no matter what field I search under."

"Anything you know about where the girl was found, then?"

"You know whose farm it was?" he asked.

Didn't they keep records of these things? Were people simply dispatched to crime scenes willy-nilly in Frederick County? Maybe when your county only saw three murders a decade, you could afford to be a little looser with the record keeping. I recalled turning off the main drag onto the farmer's dirt road. "The mailbox said Donaldson," I told him.

He worked the keyboard for a minute. "No incidents reported there in the last ten years. Before then, we'd need to look through old paper records."

Most likely the farmer and his wife weren't serial killers. It also meant their farm probably hadn't been chosen to house a dead body for some malicious reason. "A girl is dead. Two more who look an awful lot like her are missing. I came here hoping you could tell me something."

"I wish I could," he said, spreading his meaty hands.

I thanked the deputy for his time out of politeness and made my way back to the door. In the parking lot, someone called after me. A uniformed woman jogged up behind me. "You're looking into the dead girl?"

"I'm trying to," I said.

"I might be able to tell you a little." She glanced back toward the building. "There's a Dunkin' Donuts not far from here. Meet me there in a few minutes."

I said I would.

CHAPTER 6

I ORDERED A COFFEE AND SLID ONTO A CHAIR ACROSS FROM Deputy Graiman. She was a redhead with short hair and freckles. If she wore something other than a uniform, I might have called her cute. Dressing as an agent of the system docked a point. She selected a small table in the corner away from prying eyes and eager ears. "I shouldn't be talking to you." She sipped her drink and scanned the room.

"Not the first time I've heard it."

"Just part of the job, or are you something of a scofflaw?"

"Definitely some of both," I said.

"How did you get caught up in this?"

"The parents of a missing girl in Baltimore hired me."

She frowned. "I heard something about other girls."

"Two more, both gone from Baltimore. The three look a lot alike. I don't think they'd pass for triplets, but if you saw pictures of the trio, you'd figure they were related."

"I didn't see the one on the farm," she said. "I talked to the deputy who responded."

"I heard he left when the state police showed up."

Graiman studied her cup for a few seconds before answering. "You work with them much?"

"Here and there."

"They like to say they're only coming to help. We're not a huge county, so they have resources we don't. They can turn things around a lot faster. If it comes to lab results, they're usually just lending a hand." She paused to drink some coffee, like she needed to steel herself for the screed to come. "If one shows up at your crime scene, though, you're probably fucked. Some asshole in a wide-brimmed hat strides up, and your case is over. They say they're not going to take over, and it happens anyway."

"Sounds like you've experienced it," I said.

"Yeah. Same for our deputy who answered the call . . . Franks. He's lost a couple cases that way. So when the trooper showed up and said they wanted to be involved, he left."

"What if they just wanted to lend a hand, though?"

"It doesn't work that way often."

"You told me you're not a huge county," I said. "Baltimore's a big city with a large police force. They've gone through some pretty serious issues the last few years. They kind of had to let the Justice Department come in and smack them around. They never lie down for the state, though."

"What are you saying?" Graiman took a long pull of what must have been warm java by now.

"Maybe your sheriff could push back a little harder. Defend the turf."

She shrugged. "Maybe. It's not happening overnight, though."

I drank some coffee. Its heat faded into a pleasing warmth. "What do you know about the farm?"

"It's nothing special. No incidents. The farmer's not a serial killer or anything."

Our nascent investigation figured as much, but I put in by way of conversation, "Maybe his wife is. We live in progressive times."

Graiman smiled. It was a pretty good one. "They're good people. Probably shaken up at walking out to find a dead girl in the field."

"No doubt." I slid a business card across the table. "In case the county gets involved again at some point. Keep me posted?"

"I will," she said.

I thanked Deputy Graiman for her time, tossed my cup in the trash, and walked back outside. Other than potential overreach by the state police, I didn't learn anything new. The clock still ticked for Brittany and Ashleigh, and I needed to devise some way of stopping it.

* * *

I SAT in the S4 outside Dunkin' Donuts and pondered my next move. Deputy Graiman failed to drop a revelation in my lap. It would have been nice of her. While I searched my memory for something to trigger an epiphany, Rich called. "I was deep in thought," I said when I answered.

"No loss, then."

"What's up?"

"We have an ID on the girl in the field."

"Wow," I said. "Quick turnaround."

"Norton and I went to the barracks in Frederick." I heard the captain say something in the background. "He told me it's Barrack B."

"Give him my thanks. I've been dying to know how the state designated its stations. By letter or by number was keeping me up at night."

"We're going to talk to the parents," Rich said. "You want to come?"

I didn't hear Norton say anything. They must have already done their familiar dance. Rich would want me involved, Norton would object, and my cousin came out ahead. Several months ago, he worked on a task force with Norton and got an offer to join the state police. I wondered if another would be forthcoming. How much longer could Rich say no? "Sure," I said. I hated talking to the parents of the dead, but anything I could learn about the case would be helpful.

"I'll text you the address," Rich said.

His message arrived a moment later, and I navigated to the destination. Frederick has long been one of my favorite cities. I love the mix of old and new, as if the town can't decide on an identity. The area we drove to featured exactly such a blend with old houses and a couple quaint bed and breakfasts on one street and much newer construction on the next. Only an alley separated the early twentieth century from modern times.

We parked along the curb among the homes built this decade. I would have preferred the old ones for their character. These were single-family units close together with garages at the bottom. I've seen them all over the state. They weren't special or unique. The three of us walked up to a house with tan siding and a dark green door. Rich and Norton stood side-by-side with me behind them.

A woman answered the door. Her face carried a hopeful expression at first, but it quickly faded when she saw the badges and heard Norton make the introductions. "Can we come in, ma'am?"

"This is about Trisha, isn't it?" She asked the question, but she knew. I saw it on her face, and I'm sure my more experienced colleagues did, too.

"I think we should talk inside," Norton said. He didn't insist. His tone was gentle. It wasn't his first rodeo. Technically, it wasn't mine, either, but I didn't need to be the bearer of bad news this time.

She invited us in and left to get her husband. The three of us sat on a sofa appearing as new as the house. Well-kept laminate floors stretched in every direction, yielding only to wood-looking vinyl in the kitchen. A minute later, a man joined the woman in a morose march to the living room. They both looked tired, the husband more so. He also appeared to be about ten years older than his wife, who looked to be in her mid-thirties. I wondered how long their daughter had been missing and how little of the time they slept.

Norton facilitated a new round of introductions. George and Melanie Lange sat before us on the loveseat facing our sofa, the latter wringing her hands over their daughter Trisha. "She's dead, isn't she?" George said. He dressed in sweats, and the general mess of them suggested he threw them on when Melanie summoned him. Bags under his eyes and wild stubble suggested he hadn't shaved or rested.

"I'm afraid so," Norton said. "I'm very sorry for your loss."

Melanie dissolved into tears. She leaned into George, who mechanically put an arm around his wife. He betrayed little emotion. Maybe he was trying to be strong for her. "What happened to Trisha?" George said after a few minutes of Melanie's sobs being the only sound in the house.

"I'm not sure knowing will—"

"Tell me." George looked at his wife, who nodded through her tears. "Tell us. We want to know."

"It's still early," Norton said. "We just found her body about an hour ago. She was shot once in the head."

Melanie wailed again. George gripped her tighter, which didn't help. "How long had she been gone?" Rich asked.

"Three days," George said. "We filed a report with the sheriff's office after the first day. Since then, it's been a whole lot of nothing."

"Do you think I could look at her room?" I said.

George frowned but eventually nodded. "Hell, I don't care. Upstairs, first door on the left."

"Thanks." I stood and walked upstairs to Trisha's room. It looked similar to Ashleigh's. No posters on the walls. A few bookshelves, a long dresser, a queen bed, and a small desk with a laptop sitting on it were the extent of the furniture. I perused the book collection first. Trisha loved young adult novels—everything ranging from the Harry Potter series to *The Hunger Games*, *The Maze Runner*, and similar titles. She'd amassed an impressive collection of volleyball trophies dating back nine years.

I didn't find anything incriminating or *verboten* in her dresser or desk. Looking under the mattress and bed yielded the same results. I flipped open the laptop. It lacked password protection and opened to the Windows home screen. So much for schools teaching basic computer security these days. I pulled a flash drive out of my pocket and started copying all of Trisha's data folders. Muted voices from the first level carried up here. As long as Rich and Norton kept the parents talking, no one would see what I'd been up to. George may not have cared if I came upstairs to look around, but his opinions on data privacy might have been vastly different.

A few minutes later, everything finished copying. I unplugged the flash drive, closed the laptop again, and walked back downstairs. Rich and Norton were wrapping things up. They both promised to keep the Langes in the loop. George and Melanie—who'd recovered the power of speech while I'd been away—thanked them.

We walked out. "Can I ride back with you?" Rich asked.

"Sure," I said.

"I'll let you know when we have more results," Norton said. He directed it to both of us, but I knew he meant Rich.

"I look forward to it," I said. He simply nodded and got in his state-issued car.

"He likes you," Rich said when Norton pulled away.

"He just doesn't want to involve me."

"He's something of a stickler for proper procedure."

"Let's not let it catch on," I said.

* * *

I WALKED into the precinct house with Rich. He wanted to check for any updates on the other girls' cases. A few minutes of searching and reading turned up nothing. Rich's lieutenant, a loudmouthed recent arrival named O'Malley, bellowed for him. He saw me sitting at the desk, stared for a few seconds, then disappeared back into his office. I chose to interpret his actions as feeling threatened by a younger, more handsome man who could communicate without yelling.

Several minutes later, Rich emerged. He sat heavily in his seat and took a deep breath. "We're focusing on Brittany O'Connor," he said.

"Something new in her case?"

"Lieutenant's decision."

I frowned. "Did he elaborate?"

"He mentioned it would be our most prudent use of resources," Rich said.

"She's been missing a little longer, but you said there's nothing new in either case."

"A day matters." Rich went back to looking at something on his screen.

"This stinks of bullshit," I said.

"What?"

"The whole thing. Prioritizing one girl over another. You know there's a third case which happens to be outside the city, but they have to be connected somehow. Three girls who look very much alike disappear, and one turns up dead? Do you need me to go in there and plead our case?"

"It won't help," Rich said.

"I think I know why he made the decision."

Rich rolled his eyes. "Really? Why?"

"Brittany's parents must be donors to something or someone important."

"Why would it matter?"

"Your system takes care of its own first and foremost. One girl's family can write a check, and the other one can't. It comes down to status over everything."

"You think O'Malley is making this decision over money?" Rich said.

"Maybe it wasn't his decision. Maybe someone above him gave him the edict. Either way, the result is the same."

Rich waved his hand. "It's all speculation."

"How much you want to bet?" I said.

"What?"

"A wager. You know I can figure out if Brittany's parents made the right donations." Rich's sour expression told me he was aware of this. "Want me to try?"

"No." He focused on his computer again.

"Because you know I'm correct." He didn't say anything. "I know it matters to you. You're far too upright to put money over justice."

Rich closed his eyes and sighed. "What are we supposed to do if you're right?"

I looked around the room. Mostly empty. Still, I kept my voice low out of courtesy for Rich's situation. "How about you march into O'Malley's office and tell him to go fuck himself?"

"Sure," Rich said with a snort. "Why not torpedo my career?"

"You'll have another offer from the Staties, anyway."

"I didn't expect the last one I got. I'm not anticipating another."

"We have two cases," I said. "Two missing girls. I got hired by the family who doesn't have a large bank account, so I guess I'll focus my efforts there." The corner of Rich's mouth turned down. I knew my theory—which I felt sure was fact and not supposition—bothered him, or I wouldn't have kept harping on it. "I'll look into the other one when I can, too. Maybe we can meet in the middle somewhere."

"Yeah," Rich said, adding a small nod.

I got up and made for the exit. O'Malley's door remained open. Never a fellow to turn down so clear an invitation, I peeked my head in without knocking. He glanced up at me and scowled. "Can I make a donation here?" I asked.

"What? Why?"

"It seems to buy investigative priority. Just wondering where the tithing office is."

"Why don't you get out of here?" O'Malley said. "I don't have to take your shit. Rich puts up with you because you're related."

"And because I'm right so often. Like now."

O'Malley's red brows pulled down. Along with his beard, they remained untouched by gray. The hair on his head was not so lucky. "Like I said . . . get out."

"Let's hope both girls get reunited with their families soon."

O'Malley didn't respond. I followed his advice and left.

CHAPTER 7

AT MY OFFICE, I PLUGGED THE FLASH DRIVE HOLDING Trisha Lange's data into a laptop. A virus scan came back clean. I examined the folders. She named everything clearly, at least. I checked documents first, found a bunch of papers and research for school, and dismissed it all.

Next, I combed through photos and videos, and there were plenty of both. Cell phone cameras were around when I was in high school, but the iPhone didn't hit the streets until my senior year. Mine was the last generation not to document every aspect of our lives in pictures. Trisha and others her age made up for our slack. I ballparked the photo count at eight thousand. It made me wonder where Trisha's phone went; others on there probably hadn't synced yet.

Maybe one of the faces in a picture was the person who killed her.

It was a sobering thought as I looked through snapshots with friends, stills from the beach, and other commemorative moments. Date tags told me Trisha's birthday was August 2nd, and she celebrated at Ocean City like a good Marylander should. Moving to the fall, she wore the number 82 on the basketball team. All the trophies I saw in her room were for volleyball, which was in season now. Trisha's teammates would soon be dealing with her untimely death.

In the videos folder, I discovered the VSCO girl craze made it to Frederick County. Nothing struck me as unusual in any of the clips. Just high school girls recording their days and trying to make them—and themselves—sound interesting. Something else my generation missed out on by a few years. I felt no poorer for the loss.

After a couple hours, I concluded Trisha Lange kept gigabytes of data, and they signified nothing. Much of it held value to her, but for someone looking into her disappearance and death, there were no smoking guns. There weren't even any charred sparklers burnt all the way to their bottoms. Someone took Trisha Lange, and presumably the same someone shot her in the head and left her body in a field. A reason existed. I simply didn't have it yet.

My office phone rang, snapping me from my reverie. When I picked it up, a deep voice said, "Drop it."

"What?"

"You heard me. Drop it."

"The phone?" I said. "How will we continue this scintillating conversation if I do?"

"You know what I mean." As usual, I only worked one case. However, it grew from beyond the disappearance of Ashleigh Swain. Two other girls and their families were now involved. While the three victims were similar, I couldn't presume the same person was responsible for the whole mess, even though I felt it likely. Whoever called and threatened me now could be involved in any of the disappearances.

"Why don't you come to my office and threaten me in person? You found my phone number, so you must know where I am."

"I do," the voice said. "This is your only warning. Drop your case."

"Go to hell," I said.

The line went dead. I set the receiver back onto the base. Someone didn't want me figuring anything out. Now, I only needed to figure out who my mystery caller was.

* * *

THE LANGES LIVED in a nice house, but they didn't strike me as people of extraordinary means. The Swains definitely weren't. Simple elimination left the O'Connors as candidates who could have been targeted through their daughter, and whoever did it called and encouraged me to back off. Why did the other two girls disappear, then? I couldn't find any friends in common, so it seemed unlikely they knew each other.

Brant and Cathy O'Connor had plenty of money. They lived in a penthouse in downtown Baltimore, and Brittany went to a private school. Both still worked, Brant in investment management and Cathy as the director of their foundation. They were probably acquainted with my parents. None of their wealth mattered at all when Brittany vanished, however.

Their foundation declared itself dedicated to improving and empowering Baltimore and was happy to leave those nebulous criteria as its goals. To this end, it made donations to the current mayor and to various police-related charities. I snagged a screenshot of their gifts to send to Rich later. He may have believed me when I questioned his captain's motives, and he should know the truth. And the fact I was right. Again.

Speak of the devil, and he shall call. "I just took a screen shot for you," I said to my favorite cousin.

"Want to interview the O'Connors?"

"No one did it yet?"

"A couple uniforms when it first happened," Rich said. "We know more now. Two other girls are gone under similar circumstances. Want to come along?"

"Sure."

"You at home?"

"The office."

"I'll pick you up in ten minutes," Rich said.

Exactly six hundred seconds later, his muscle car idled in front of my building. I climbed into the passenger's seat. Rich drove a late-model blue Camaro. I loved it for its throaty V8 but disliked the automatic transmission. Rich's knee injury in Afghanistan gave him a good excuse for the two-pedal setup, but I still took him to task over it occasionally. What are cousins for, after all?

"O'Malley send you out on this?" I asked when we were underway.

"He suggested it."

"Uh-huh."

"I think it's a good idea," Rich said.

"I think so, too. By the way, I was right about the O'Connors. They're donors to the mayor and several police charities."

Rich drummed his fingers on the steering wheel as we waited for a light to change. "I guess I shouldn't be surprised."

"It's OK to be disappointed, though. You could also tell your brilliant cousin he called it again."

Rich smirked. "I don't know if your intelligence or your cynicism was responsible."

"Mostly column A," I said, "but a little from B, too."

We drove into Federal Hill. It would have been an easier drive had I worked from what remained of my home office. A few luxury high-rises stood at the edge of the harbor, affording a great view in just about any direction and coming with a price tag to match. Living in the dinkiest unit would cost a pretty penny; I didn't want to think about how much it would take to buy a penthouse. Rich and I showed our badges to the first security guy, who directed us to visitor parking. The garage was for residents only; peasants left their cars behind the building. We hoofed it around to the front where another guard greeted us.

He tried to be serious and protective of his residents, but Rich reminded him which one of them was the actual cop and which one carried a badge made of tin. After being put in his place, the fellow phoned the penthouse and got the affirmative word. He put us in the elevator, swiped his card, and sent us on our way without a word of farewell.

"Nice job with the guard," I said.

"What a prick." Rich shook his head. "Some people get a fake badge, and the little bit of power it comes with goes right to their heads."

The bell dinged and the doors parted as we reached the top floor. The elevator opened into a hallway ending with a suite in each direction. The O'Connors lived in the north penthouse. Rich banged on the door with the pewter knocker. For the prices this place fetched, I was disappointed by anything less than gold.

A man and woman answered the door. He looked to be in his early forties and she in her mid-thirties. They were dressed like former models who snuck onto the pages of the Ralph Lauren catalog. Both had hair so perfectly colored—brown as dark as mine for Brant, and platinum blonde for Cathy. The only question would be who made the bottle? They invited us in, and Brant requested we remove our shoes. Can't let leather soles scuff the marble foyer or dig into the plush carpeting.

A moment later, we sat in the living room, whose vaulted ceiling extended into the second story of the suite. Stairs led up behind us. A fire crackled even though there was little need for heat. The O'Connors' furniture looked better than any I'd seen in years, and once I sank into the couch, I didn't want to get up again. Husband

and wife sat facing us in matching recliners, both with hands folded across their laps. "What can we do for you?" Brant said.

"We're looking into your daughter's disappearance," Rich said. "Since then, two other girls have also gone missing. Can you think of anyone who might have targeted Brittany?"

"No one."

"What about someone using her to get to you?"

Brant shook his head. "I don't think so, and it wouldn't explain the other two girls."

"Are those girls still missing?" Cathy asked.

"Yes," Rich said, and I silently gave him props for telling a convincing lie. Knowing the truth wouldn't help the O'Connors, and it would only serve to complicate our interview. "Did Brittany have a boyfriend?"

"Not currently," Cathy said. "She dated a boy in the fall and winter, but they split up a month or so ago."

"He wouldn't have anything to do with this," Brant added. "His parents are good people . . . clients of mine, in fact." Of course they were.

"Why do you think he's not involved?" I asked.

"He's not the type. A very quiet young man, and he comes from good stock."

I thought about comparing him to a bull but figured it wouldn't help. "What about new friends? Someone you didn't approve of?"

"We liked the young ladies in Brittany's circle," Brant said. I wondered how many of their parents were also in his company's contact list. "When you have a teenaged daughter, you expect not to like some of the people she hangs out with." They both offered small smiles. "Brittany's always chosen her friends well."

"None of them have heard anything from her either, correct?" Rich said.

"That's right."

"What about her phone or a computer?" I said.

"She had both with her."

I wondered if the BPD tried looking for the phone signal. They probably did. I figured it couldn't hurt to do it again, even if the battery were likely to be dead by now. "We've told the police everything we can think of," Cathy said. "We're really at a loss why Brittany isn't back home yet."

"These things can take time," Rich said. "Very few cases we get are easy."

"The longer she's gone, the worse her chances get, right?" Rich bobbed his head in the affirmative. "Easy or not, we expected your department to find her by this time."

"We've been in contact with the commissioner," Brant added. "The mayor, too. We've supported both in the past, but it may not continue."

"Donations don't buy quick resolutions," I said, and both husband and wife stared at me as if a second head grew from my neck.

"We're doing our best," Rich said. "We're working with the state police, as well. With our combined resources, I think our odds are better."

"I hope so, Detective," Brant said.

A few minutes later, Rich and I slipped back into our shoes and rode the elevator down. "I don't like them," my cousin told me.

"I didn't think you would. I figured you'd especially dislike how their donations correlated to their case's priority."

"Don't start."

"They're threatening not to support the mayor." Rich remained silent, so I carried his part of the conversation, too. "Vincent Davenport is a cinch to run. Maybe he's behind all this as a way to shake the public's confidence in the current administration."

Rich snorted. "Even you're not so cynical."

"No," I said after a moment, "I guess I'm not. He makes a convenient bogeyman, though."

"How about we find the real one instead?"

"Let's. But I reserve the right to say, 'I told you so' if Davenport ends up being the puppet master."

Rich's reply was uncharitable.

CHAPTER 8

I arrived home to find Gloria lounging on my couch. She would always be a welcome sight. I noted with interest the way her small shorts rode high on her thighs before she sat up and smiled at me. "Welcome home."

"Thanks," I said. I plopped down beside her, and we kissed. "It's been a heck of a couple days."

She slipped her arm around me and rubbed my shoulder. "Tell me about it." I gave her the details. Over the time we've known each other, Gloria has taken more interest in my cases, and she's proven herself a very useful sounding board on more than one occasion. Early on, I provided her the abridged versions of events. Now, I laid it all out there—the good, bad, and ugly. When I finished recounting the details of the missing girls and their families, Gloria wore a sharp frown. "You think Rich was told to visit the O'Connors because they're big donors?"

"I can't prove it, and I'm sure I'll never be able to. But yes, I think he's come around on the idea, too."

"I'm sure he's not happy about it," she said.

"He's not. Rich holds a strong sense of justice, and something like this suggests it's for sale. I'm sure it bothers him." I paused. "Do you know the O'Connors?"

Gloria shook her head. "My parents probably do."

"Mine, too," I said. "I might have to inquire about them."

After a few moments of enjoying the quiet, Gloria changed the subject. "You realize Vincent Davenport is running for mayor, right?" I nodded. Davenport gave Gloria her first big break as a fundraising coordinator and employed her to put on a few swanky events since. "How do you know?"

"Melinda gave me an advance warning," I said. "She's aware of the regard in which I hold her father."

Gloria grinned. She also knew my opinion of Vincent Davenport. We rarely discussed the man because of our differing views on him. "He's asked me to setup some dinners for him. A thousand dollars or more a plate, a bunch of hand shaking and photo ops . . . that kind."

"I'm sure you'll do great. You're much better than he deserves."

"I'm not sure I want to, though."

"Why?" I put my arm around Gloria. She leaned her head on my shoulder.

"I don't know," she said. "It just feels different. It's one thing to do something like this for a charity. It's what I've always done for him before. His name is selling the tickets, but someone else is benefitting. This time, he'd be benefitting."

"I'm sure he would argue the entire city will enjoy the perks," I said.

"Maybe. I don't understand why he wants to go all out. He's going to win. The primary's in less than two months, and I don't think either of the other candidates are going to do much against him."

"And it's a *fait accompli* from there. He'll roll in November."

Gloria nodded against my shoulder, which messed up her hair. "I haven't told him yes or no yet. I'm going to need to soon, though."

"I'm positive you'll do what you think is right," I said. I didn't mention my cynical thought about Davenport being responsible for the missing girls to sour the public on the current administration. My negative opinion of him didn't extend quite so far.

"You hungry?" Gloria asked.

"Definitely."

She stood. "Let's go out somewhere. I need a shower first, though."

"I think I'll join you," I said. "Purely in the interests of hygiene, of course."

"Of course." Gloria grinned. "Might be a late dinner, then."

"I'm OK with it."

"Me, too," she said.

* * *

THE NEXT MORNING, I set a pot of coffee to brew while Gloria remained asleep, then went outside for a run. A light drizzle fell, and a cool wind knocked the temperature down at least fifteen degrees from the prior morning. I felt a little underdressed, but pounding the pavement allowed me to warm up in a reasonable time. The weather deterred many of the joggers and dog walkers I normally see on my rounds, so my laps around Federal Hill Park were more quiet than usual.

When I returned home, Gloria sat at the kitchen table drinking coffee. She didn't attempt to make breakfast, for which I was thankful. Her lack of kitchen experience and talent extended to breakfast as well. I let her try to make a smoothie once. Cleaning liquid and bits of fruit off my floor, counters, and walls was not worth the experiment.

I showered, got dressed, and joined Gloria for some java. "What's for breakfast?" she said after a good-morning kiss.

"Probably something basic," I said. One of these days, when I wasn't trying to find missing girls and keep them from turning up dead, I needed to visit the grocery store. Today, I toasted two wheat bagels and made a simple yogurt parfait. Maybe I would ask Gloria to hit the market for me. Sharing the grocery responsibilities felt a little formal, but we were already more or less living together. She spent a couple nights a week in her own house but stayed with me the rest of the time. The arrangement worked for us.

After breakfast, I bade Gloria farewell and drove to the office. As I drew closer, I noticed an older SUV behind me. Its dingy blue color resembled my other car, a late-'eighties Chevy Caprice. I swung the S4 into the CareFirst Building parking lot and chose a spot near the end of the row. The other vehicle parked a few spaces closer to the building. Two guys who looked fresh from the gym stepped out and blocked my path. By this hour, most workers were already inside. No one noticed our simmering confrontation.

"You get the message?" the dark-haired one said as I approached.

"Did I miss biceps day?" I patted the muscle in my arm. "I'll need a few sessions to catch up to you two."

"He means the warning to drop what you're working on," the other said. He made up for his shaved head with a large reddish-brown beard. As someone who struggled to grow respectable facial hair, I felt a pang of jealousy.

"Mixed messages, guys," I said. "First, you want me to do biceps day, and then you tell me to drop it. You're confusing me, and I don't think our dynamic is supposed to work this way."

They both frowned in thought. If I squinted, I could probably see the smoke seeping out of the ears. "You give up the case?" the first one asked.

"If I say yes, can we all go about our day? I have a case to work on. Oops . . ."

They glowered at me and fanned out. Both were taller than me. They looked large and slow, but I didn't think I could dart between them. Not like I planned to. Someone had to send these two assholes to discourage me, and I meant to find out who. I assumed a defensive stance. Dark Hair stalked forward from my left.

When he lunged to try and wrap me up, I grabbed his arm and spun him into his advancing comrade. They collided, but neither went down. The whole thing served to make them madder. I didn't mind—angry fighters tend to be careless. True to form, the bearded one rushed me. I used his outstretched arm to flip him onto his back.

The other guy was on top of me before I could follow up. I turned a punch wide, then blocked a strong kick. Maybe this fellow knew what he was doing. My footwork steered me away from the goon on the asphalt, who rose to a seated position and shook the cobwebs loose. This wouldn't be *mano-y-mano* for much longer.

My dusky-maned foe fired off a few quick jabs and crosses. A lot of big guys use their arms to punch, thinking their bulging biceps will pack the power. This fellow knew real power came from driving his hips, and he did it every time. He dropped his guard on the crosses, however, and I stepped forward and elbowed him hard in the face while his hands were down. He staggered back and covered his mouth.

Redbeard waded in, throwing clumsy haymakers and hoping they would connect. He was the bulkier of the two, and he clearly expected his strength advantage to be enough. I blunted a couple of his punches before the energy expenditure took its toll. His breathing grew louder, and the wild swings slowed enough I could step to the side. After a huge left, I slipped next to him and kicked him in the back of the knee, taking his leg out.

I followed with a quick kick to the face to stun him. While he shook his head, I moved in front of him and gave him a hard boot square in the nose. It broke with a sound reminiscent of a firecracker, and the goon collapsed onto his back, moaning and covering his bleeding face. By now, the other recovered enough to stomp his way to me.

As before, I deflected his attacks while also steering us away from his partner. The bearded guy was probably down for the count, but I didn't want to presume. If he got back up, he'd be really pissed. We stood behind their SUV. Dark Hair's punches rained in like before, and he didn't correct the hole in his defense. I gave him a sharp jab in the solar plexus, causing him to gasp and take a step back.

While he was on his heels, I grabbed him by the hair and smashed his face into the rear window of their vehicle. The glass cracked, a couple trails of blood ran down it, and my opponent dropped to the parking lot. I kicked him in the face for good measure, and the moaning and thrashing stopped. So far, we hadn't attracted any attention, but I didn't want to count on my luck holding.

I searched his pockets, finding the keys for the Blazer. He didn't carry anything else of interest. I dragged him to his feet, opened the rear driver's side door, and shoved him in. The other supposed tough guy stirred, so I crouched beside him and walloped him in his already wounded face. The extra punch plus his head hitting the asphalt turned the lights out. I rummaged through his pockets and snagged what looked like a lawyer's business card.

The heavier man was harder to move, but I wrestled him to his feet and stuffed him into the passenger's seat. I used the hand cranks to roll both windows down about eight inches, locked the vehicle, and threw the keys into the grass beyond the lot.

As I walked toward the building, I looked at the business card I confiscated.

McLelland and Katzenberg, P.A.
Abraham McLelland, Senior Partner

I frowned. Gabriella's words played in my head. *McLelland and . . . something or other.* It was the same firm Tony Rizzo hired to clear the way for his park.

Why did these two idiots carry the card? What the hell did it mean?

* * *

WHEN I SAT behind my desk, I searched for updates on any of the missing or dead girls. Someone added a few administrative notes to the O'Connor and Swain case files, but I saw nothing of substance. The BPD held no information on Trisha Lange, and she didn't even merit a mention in the other two files. If I wanted information there, I'd probably need to get it from Norton. Maybe I could visit him, and he would be as careless as Rich with his computer.

I tried his cell and left a message when voicemail picked up after the sixth ring. The lawyer's business card bothered me. I researched the firm. It had operated in Baltimore for some ninety years and got handed down to what must now be the founders' grandchildren. A third partner, Siegel, separated from the others about fifteen years ago. Two generations of McLellands staffed the place, plus a part-time Katzenberg who reduced his schedule due to age.

The firm seemed reputable—at least as far as lawyers could stretch the word. I called Gabriella and asked her who represented her father in his quest for a park. "McLelland," she said. "The son. Why?"

"How old is he?"

"I don't know . . . a few years older than us. Mid-thirties, I guess. What's this about?"

"I was recently introduced to two gentlemen outside my office," I said. "They're the type who might work in collections for your father." And for Gabriella someday when she took over. "Guess which law office's business card I found on one of them?"

"Why would they hire a couple of goons?"

"Good question. A better one would be why they're trying to discourage me from working my current case."

"I don't know anything about it, C.T.," Gabriella said. "We've never worked with them before, and it's just for the land deal Dad wants to do."

"I guess I'll have to go to the source, then."

"Why do I get the feeling you'll wind up in trouble?"

"I'm just going to go there and ask some questions," I said.

"Uh-huh."

Gabriella knew me too well.

* * *

THE LAW OFFICES of McLelland and Katzenberg, P.A., sat downtown. They shared a twelve-story building with a bunch of other attorneys. It was within walking or cabbing distance— senior lawyers would not call an Uber—of the important court-houses. I left the S4 in a nearby garage and took the elevator to the ninth floor.

Inside, one middle-aged woman staffed the front. Two distinct workstations, each with its own monitor, perched atop the desk. She must have also checked in the four people who waited in chairs and leafed through the dreary magazine selec-tion. The effort seemed too large for one person. The phone rang a few times, she placed people on hold, transferred others, and flashed a tired smile when she'd dealt with all callers. "Can I help you?" The nameplate on her desk identified her as Elaine.

"I hope so," I said, showing her my ID. "I recently came into contact with two disreputable gentlemen. They tried to dissuade me from working an important case." Her eyes snapped to the ringing phone, but she didn't pick it up. "One of them had a business card for this office in his pocket."

"I can't imagine why." Elaine's frown showed genuine concern. Maybe the partners kept her in the dark about their shadier dealings. Her earnest features reminded me of my mother about fifteen years ago.

"The card belonged to Abraham McLelland," I said, lowering my voice. "I don't know why those two were so insistent, but I figured I would come and ask Mister McLelland directly."

"I'm afraid he's with a client," Elaine said.

"I'm afraid his meeting will be cut short."

"Sir, you can't just come in here, claim you got bullied by a couple of men with a business card, and expect to see the senior partner."

The phone rang again. Before Elaine could answer it, I reached over the counter and snatched the receiver. "McLelland and Katzenberg," I said, summoning my best professional voice. "If you don't like our rates, we'll send a couple guys to beat your ass."

"What?" came a confused voice from the phone.

"You heard me. Better pay up."

"Give me the phone back!" Elaine said. She got up and hurried around the desk and counter as fast as her heels would allow.

The person on the other end hung up. Fortune smiled on me, however, when another call came in right away. "McLelland and Katzenberg. Do we need to send the goon squad to find you, or will you pay your bill?"

I didn't even get a query; the caller simply hung up. "Sir, this is ridiculous," Elaine said in a scolding tone. Now, she really reminded me of my mother.

We'd attracted the attention of the waiting clients. "What's ridiculous," I said, playing to the tiny audience, "is this office sending two legbreakers to keep me from investigating a case of missing girls." The waiting patrons harrumphed and conferred with one another over this latest development.

"Do I need to call the police?" Elaine asked, crossing her arms.

"Go ahead. I took pictures of both guys. I'm sure the cops would love to know why Mister McLelland would hire known criminals." Two of the clients got up, scowled at Elaine—who didn't really deserve it—and stormed out. The cordless handset trilled in my grip. "What'll it be, Elaine?"

"Fine," she said. "I'll send you back in a minute. Just give me the phone."

I handed it back to her, then I sat and waited my turn.

CHAPTER 9

Elaine made me wait a couple more minutes, but I took her at her word. Sure enough, a red-faced older man who managed to look both confused and angry at the same time emerged from behind a door, didn't look at anyone, and slammed it behind him on his way out. I took this as my cue to stand. Elaine said, "Mister McLelland will see you now." She pointed to the door as if some other option would lead me to the promised land. "Through there, office on the left."

"Thanks," I said as I walked around her desk. She pursed her lips but didn't respond. Few people probably took her handset and answered the office phone in the worst possible way. It felt a little immature of me, but I needed to make a point, and it worked.

Abraham McLelland's office was open, so I walked in. He didn't look up. The senior partner sat behind a giant mahogany desk. His chair was the nicest in the room, but the two for guests were better than most places provided. Behind him, degrees in ornate frames decorated the wall. I noticed the J.D. I come across a lot of amateurs in my job, and I'm able to snow them most of the time. McLelland would not be an easy mark.

Thin wispy white hair prevented him from being completely

bald, and when he looked up at me, his bushy eyebrows pulled down into a frown. "What's the meaning of this?" He did not have a typical old man's voice. These pipes shouted down prosecutors and stood up to judges.

"I came here with the same question," I said.

"I just hurried a twenty-year client out of here."

"He'll be back. He only wanted to look put out for whomever was in the waiting room." Might as well be grammatically correct —I don't face off against many doctorates.

McLelland scrutinized me a long moment. "Elaine didn't tell me much about why you're here. She did say you caused quite a scene."

"How long have you practiced law?" I asked.

"Forty-five years," he said after blinking at my question.

"In your time, have you ever made a scene in a courtroom to get a desired outcome?"

The older man's jowly face cracked for a brief smile. "I might have done it once or twice. The thing is you can always get tossed in jail for contempt. There's a risk involved, or else lawyers might do it all the time."

"I'll tell you why I'm here," I said. "Three teenaged girls are missing across the state." I raised a hand to hold off McLelland's interjection. "Two of them are from Baltimore. The first is from Frederick County, and she's already dead. I'm working for the third girl's parents. This morning, two gentlemen with large arms and no necks came to dissuade me from investigating. They . . . were not successful. One of them carried your business card, and I doubt he's a client."

McLelland steepled his fingers and didn't say anything. I wondered how many times he made the same gesture in a courtroom. He was preparing to pounce on the closest thing to an opposing attorney—me. "Did you ask this man where he got the card?"

"No," I said. "I was too busy fighting him and his partner, then knocking both of them out. Call it a general lack of opportunity."

"I don't know why a man like the one you described would carry anything related to my office. I don't recall meeting or hiring anyone who fits the legbreaker description. Like I said, I've been doing this forty-five years. A lot of my cards are out there." He shrugged, hamming it up with his expressive face. "Who's to say how he got it?"

"I presume you have investigators?"

"Of course," he said. "But they look more like you than they do a pair of weightlifters." He spared a look at my casual attire. "I do make them wear suits, though."

Another reason to be in business for myself. I scanned the office, especially the shelves. Attorneys always have three tons of books handy, and McLelland was no exception. Between his desk and the bookcases, I was surprised his furniture didn't crash through the floor and crush some poor sap in the space below. "What kind of law do you practice?"

"The boring kind. TV makes it all look glamorous, but we're not all rock stars. I mostly do estate cases, buyouts . . . things like those."

"And your partners?"

"Katzenberg's part-time now. Hell, he's even older than me. He performs similar work. My son does corporate law."

"Maybe he gave the gentlemen in question one of your cards."

McLelland frowned anew. "I don't see how my son would be involved in some cases about missing girls. Besides, if he wanted to hand out cards, he could dip into his own stock."

Unless he wanted to implicate his old man, of course. It's not like he couldn't get into the office. Broaching such a scenario wouldn't help my cause, however. I already got the impression

McLelland was eager to be rid of me. I also didn't think he lied to me, which is a rare thing for a lawyer.

As if on cue, he said, "We done here? I have actual paying clients to get back to."

"Sure," I said as I stood. "Thanks for your time."

He didn't offer to shake hands. Neither did I.

* * *

I LEFT THE LAW FIRM—ELAINE declined to validate my parking, and I couldn't blame her—and returned to my office. Hoping for anything new in the case, I checked the BPD and came up empty. Either they didn't have anything, or no one bothered to put it on the network yet. I remembered Norton never called me back, so I tried him again and left another message.

Abraham McLelland gave me no reason to disbelieve him other than the fact he was a lawyer. He'd been practicing far longer than I'd been alive, kept an office in an expensive building, and worked mostly on estates and similar matters. There was zero chance a guy like the one I tangled with earlier would be a client. Maybe not zero. Everyone has parents, and they inevitably die. He wouldn't shop in the McLelland price tier, however. I thought the two goons sent after me today came from the corporate entity, yet I believed him when he professed his innocence.

A real conundrum.

My phone buzzing on the desk jerked me from my thoughts. When I picked up, Gabriella asked, "You want to have lunch with my dad and me?"

I looked at my watch. Almost twelve-thirty. No time like the present. "Sure," I said.

"Great. Half hour?"

"I'll be there," I said, and I hung up.

I spent twenty minutes looking for anything I could find on

Trisha Lange, Brittany O'Connor, or Ashleigh Swain. I checked their friends' social media feeds. Nothing struck me as relevant. Two girls were still missing. I wondered if I should blow off the lunch with Gabriella and Tony. Considering the frost between the old gangster and me recently, I figured it was in my best interests to keep the appointment.

I texted Rich, who said he didn't have anything new and hadn't heard from Norton. Lunch wouldn't cause me to miss anything. I grabbed my car keys and left.

* * *

I FOUND street parking in Little Italy and walked about a block to *Il Buon Cibo*. The maître d' smiled at me as I went past. He didn't even acknowledge me the last time I came here. Maybe this would be a sign of the thaw. As usual, Tony sat at his table near the fireplace. Bruno—Tony's *consigliere*—and a goon parked themselves nearby and made a point not to acknowledge me. Gabriella sat with her father. Both regarded me fondly as I approached.

The last time I saw Tony, he looked rough. I remembered him as hale, hearty, and a little overweight. If I ran a restaurant, I'd probably pack on the pounds, too. When I got the boot from Hong Kong about two and a half years ago, I was surprised at Tony's weight loss. He didn't seem unhealthy, but he'd definitely dropped some sixty pounds. Since then, he'd lost even more. In March, he looked thin and sickly. Now, two months later, his face was a little fuller, and he'd regained some color. Maybe his health problems were in the rearview. "Good to see you, C.T.," he said, and we shook hands as I dropped onto the chair.

"You, too, Tony," I said. "Gabriella."

"Thanks for coming." She always presented as picture perfect. I never met her mother, but Gabriella hardly resembled her father. She possessed a classic Italian complexion, hair the color of midnight, and enough beauty to turn heads. I might have dated her in our younger days if I hadn't worried about her father dismembering me.

"Thanks for inviting me."

No sooner did I speak the final syllable when a waiter appeared at the table. With a pair of Rizzos to impress, this fellow would need to stay on his toes. His hand showed a slight tremble as he held a pen above his small notepad. I knew the menu well enough to order from memory. Tony and his daughter both chose salads. I represented proud carnivores everywhere when I selected veal parmesan with meat sauce.

After the server left, father and daughter got down to business. "Gabriella told you about the park?" Tony said.

"She did."

"What do you think?"

"Honestly?" He nodded. "It seems like a legacy move . . . something a man does when he knows the clock is running out." Gabriella frowned at me across the table.

"You ain't getting rid of me so easy," Tony said. His voice sounded stronger than it did in March, also. "Legacy is a part of it, though. I know I can pass this restaurant to my daughter whenever I die." He reached out and grabbed Gabriella's hand.

"Dad," she said, giving his hand a squeeze.

"I could turn the other business interests over to her, too." His statement marked the first time I'd heard Tony broach the inevitable possibility. Before, I got the impression he didn't want Gabriella involved. I wondered what brought on his change of heart. "It's . . . uh . . . not something we could really talk about. The restaurant would be associated with her over time. You know my name. I want other people to know it, too."

The basic idea made sense. I still didn't get the significance of a park, but Tony's motives were his own. "Where are you looking?"

Before Tony could answer, the waiter dropped off our salads and freshened our drinks. When he walked away, Tony said, "Haven't narrowed it down yet. It'd be nice to get somewhere around here, but we'll see."

"Will it have a dedicated place for bocce?"

"Damn right," Tony said with a grin. "We have enough baseball diamonds. Let's play more bocce." The next game I played would be my first.

A minute later, our entrees arrived. Tony's salad looked to be entirely vegetarian. At least Gabriella chose blackened salmon for hers. It was part of the lighter, healthier fare Tony added to the menu about a year and half ago to keep up with the competition. The younger diners coming to Little Italy weren't interested in fettuccine alfredo anymore. He didn't seem happy about the change then, and I doubted his opinion changed in the intervening time. My veal was tender enough to cut with a fork, and the combined aromas of the meat, sauce, and cheese made my mouth water. Old-school Italian food was fine with me.

We ate in silence for a few minutes. Once we'd all consumed about half our meals, Tony dabbed at his mouth and set his napkin down. "Whenever this park thing happens," he said, "I'd like you and your parents to come to the dedication."

My parents had little contact with Tony since I got back to the States. About a year ago, Tony told me he helped them extract me from the Chinese prison I landed in during my stay in Hong Kong. The fact must have tipped my mother off as to the true nature of his job. Getting them to the ribbon-cutting at Tony's park may not prove easy. "I'll do my best to drag them along with me," I said.

After a few more bites of my delicious lunch, my phone

buzzed. I looked at the caller ID—Rich. I mouthed an apology to my hosts and stepped away to answer. "What's going on?"

"Another girl is dead."

I closed my eyes and blew out a deep breath. "Which one?"

"Brittany."

"Shit," I said.

"Yeah. You want to come down to the precinct?"

"I'm on my way," I said. I walked back to the table. "I have to go. Something came up in the case I'm working."

Gabriella gave me a quick hug. Tony frowned in concern while he shook my hand and told me to come back for another lunch sometime soon. I hustled outside to my car and tore off for the police station.

CHAPTER 10

RICH STOOD OUTSIDE AS I APPROACHED. "LET'S TAKE MY car," he said by way of greeting. The car in question was an unmarked Charger which would be an obvious police vehicle to anyone with two eyes and at least as many brain cells.

"Where are we headed?" I asked when he pulled out of the lot.

"To see the body. Patterson Park."

The ride wasn't very far or—thanks to the Charger's suspension needing work—very comfortable. Rich parked it along Linwood Avenue. We walked between two tennis courts, past some well-groomed trees, and went to the pool. The officers already on the scene had taped off much of the area. The pool itself was a large rectangle, Olympic sized, with a pavilion past it and a separate shallow play area for kids.

Rich and I ducked under the tape and neared the edge. It was May, so the pool was already full in anticipation of opening on Memorial Day. I smelled the chlorine as we stood and looked at the water. A girl's body floated face-down. Part of the back of her head was missing, but despite its condition, little blood tainted the water. After a round of photos, a couple forensics workers waded in to get her.

The medical examiner, a slender woman I'd never seen before, took over once Brittany's body lay atop a blanket on the concrete. Rich gave her a few minutes before we wandered to her. "Cause of death is obvious," she said, pointing to the damaged part of the head. "Definitely killed somewhere else."

"Anything to tell you where yet?" Rich asked.

The ME's ponytail wagged as she shook her head. "I'll have to get her back to the lab."

"How long has she been dead?"

"It's a guess because of the water. It's cooler than the air." She turned to us and frowned. "I'll be able to narrow it down more later, but my estimate is she was killed sometime this morning." She rolled the body onto its back. Thankfully, Brittany's eyes were closed. Seeing a pretty blonde girl lying dead in Patterson Park gave me flashbacks to working my late sister's case six months ago. I turned and stepped away.

Rich caught up to me a moment later. "Bad memories?"

"Yeah," I said. "I only saw photos of it, but the blonde hair, the location . . . "

"She's not Samantha."

"I know." I found my sister's killer, and the waste of flesh currently awaited trial. The pictures I saw of the thirteen-year-old crime scene did not want to leave my mind's eye, however.

"Want to talk to the parents?" Rich said.

"Not really, but I'll do just about anything to get away from here."

"Let's go." We walked between the tennis courts again and climbed back into the Charger.

* * *

WE PARKED in the same spot as last time but enjoyed a much easier interaction with a different security guard. He called the

O'Connors while Rich and I entered the elevator. When we exited at the penthouse level, Cathy O'Connor waited for us outside the door. Her eyes were red and puffy. Without makeup, she looked younger than the last time I saw her, and it struck me how all three mothers I'd met were barely older than me.

"The police called," she said before we could tell her anything. "They didn't say much. What's going on?"

"Missus O'Connor," Rich said, "I'm very sorry to tell you Brittany is dead."

She shook her head as if the sheer power of denial could undo the past and bring her daughter back. "You bastards couldn't find her." Her eyes welled as her head moved from side to side. "You couldn't find her, and now she's dead."

"I'm very sorry—"

"Screw your sorry!" She jabbed her finger into Rich's chest. "You didn't find my daughter." Before we could say anything, she opened the door. Brant moved aside to let Cathy stomp into the penthouse. He watched after her a moment, then joined us in the hallway.

"She's dead, isn't she?"

"She is," Rich said. "I'm very sorry for your loss."

Brant stared ahead for a few seconds. "Cathy was barely eighteen when she got pregnant. She was going to head off to college." He paused to collect himself. "Brittany changed those plans. It was something she managed to do a lot." He showed a fleeting smile. "They've basically been inseparable since Brittany was born. I don't know what we're going to do now."

"I hate to sound like I'm piling on, but we'll need someone to identify Brittany at some point."

"Can it wait until tomorrow?"

"I'm sure it can."

Brant's head bobbed in a fractional nod. "How did it happen?"

"Mister O'Connor," Rich said, "there are some things you're probably better off not knowing."

"She's my daughter," he said. "I want to know. I might never tell Cathy, but dammit, I need to know."

I fidgeted in the hallway. These conversations were always awkward, especially when people wanted to learn the details. Rich was right—there would be no benefit. "We're still piecing some things together," Rich said. "She . . . was found in Patterson Park."

"Someone killed her there?"

Rich frowned and avoided Brant's gaze. He clearly didn't want to answer any more questions. "We don't think so," I said, picking up the slack. "It's one of the things we're still working on."

"Do you think you'll know more tomorrow when we go to . . . the morgue?"

"We hope so, yes." If Rich wouldn't answer, I would speak for him and the department. They'd be devoting a bunch of resources to this now, anyway. An idea struck me. I figured it was a long shot, but I needed the information. "Did Brittany know anyone in Frederick County?"

Brant's face scrunched as he pondered this. Rich shot me a sour look. "I don't think so. Most of her friends are from around here. We've done a little traveling for sports, but it's usually to the south, not the west."

"Thanks for your time, Mister O'Connor," Rich said again, having recovered the power of speech after I posed a question he didn't like. "We're very sorry for your loss."

One corner of Brant's mouth nudged upward. It was the closest he could manage to a smile. Under the circumstances, I couldn't blame him. Rich and I got back into the elevator. "Why'd you ask him about the girl in Frederick County?" he said.

"Trisha Lange. Haven't you noticed all three girls have similar features?"

"Sure."

"What about their mothers?" I asked.

"I don't think they look much like each other."

"Their ages. All of them look younger than you."

We walked out of the elevator and back into the fancy lobby. "I'm thirty-seven," Rich said.

"I know. You'd be considered pretty young to have a child who's seventeen. Now subtract two or three years."

Rich's eyes flittered back and forth. "I can see their faces. You're right . . . they're all young. What do you think it means?"

"I don't know," I said. "You think the girls looking a lot alike is a coincidence?"

"No."

"How about the mothers all being thirty-five, tops?"

"No," Rich said again as we reached the Charger.

"Me, either," I said.

* * *

RICH ENCOURAGED me to walk into the precinct with him, so I did. No sooner did we sit at this desk than O'Malley stomped to us. He wore his sleeves rolled up to the elbows, and he had a pen tucked behind his ear. "What's going on with the dead girl?" He looked right at Rich, ignoring me.

"Found floating in the Patterson Park pool," Rich said. "She wasn't killed there. Forensics processed the scene, and the ME has the body."

"Where have you been?"

"Notifying the parents," Rich said.

O'Malley waved a hand. "Send a couple uniforms next time."

What an asshole. "How would you keep their sweet donor dollars coming in, then?" I said.

"What the hell are you doing here?"

"Pointing out the intersection of basic public relations and economics to a man who should already understand it."

"I told you I didn't have to put up with your shit," O'Malley said, leaning down and pointing at me to emphasize his words. "Get out of here, or I'll have you arrested."

"On what charge?"

"Obstruction of justice."

Before I could point out exactly how much justice I'd contributed to in my two-plus years on the job, a booming voice from behind us said, "He stays."

I knew who it was before turning around. Captain Leon Sharpe walked past Rich's desk and stood before us. Overhead lights reflected in his shaved black head. Sharpe was tall, broad, and looked like he bench-pressed motorcycles before eating a dozen eggs for breakfast. Among his better qualities was his generally favorable attitude toward yours truly.

O'Malley glared at me and then glanced at Sharpe. "Captain, I—"

"He stays," Sharpe repeated. "We need all hands on deck for this one. Brittany O'Connor was missing for about three days, and then she turns up dead. The same thing recently happened in Frederick County. Now, we see it in Baltimore." Sharpe gestured toward the whiteboard on the side wall. "Ashleigh Swain, gone almost two days now. If the timelines stay the same, we have a little more than twenty-four hours to find her."

"Captain, why don't we leave this to the real cops?" O'Malley said. "We're trained professionals." He cocked his head in my direction. "He's a loose cannon."

I couldn't object, so I didn't. Leon Sharpe took up my defense. "Loose cannons can still hit their mark. C.T. does good work. He consulted on a task force I put together late last year. I'm going to convene another one." Sharpe glanced at me. "I hope you'll work with us like before."

"Of course," I said.

O'Malley's face looked like he sucked on a lemon. He remained quiet, however. Sharpe already put him in his place mildly. If it happened again, it wouldn't be so pleasant. The lieutenant stalked back to his office. "He's kind of a prick," Sharpe said after the thwarted man left.

"Fire him, then," I said.

"Not so easy."

"Looks like you're going to have some help on the Swain case," Rich said.

"Good. I'll need it." I stood.

"Where are you headed?" Sharpe asked.

"Home. You have your task force, Leon. I'm going to put my own together."

* * *

I PULLED onto the concrete pad and parked beside Gloria's rocketlike coupe. When I walked into the house, I didn't see her on the first level. "I'm upstairs," she called down a moment later.

"I'll be working for a while," I said from the bottom of the steps.

"Everything all right?" Gloria emerged from the bedroom. She wore a tight T-shirt and the tiniest pair of shorts I'd ever seen. I felt my resolve waver.

"Honestly, no. It's pretty much gone to shit. Don't wait up." I offered her the best smile I could summon under the circumstances and then trudged to my home office.

It grew late, but I knew someone who never slept. I texted Rollins a few pictures, first of the two dead girls, and then the final one of Ashleigh Swain. I hoped she was still alive. If the pattern we'd seen so far held, she had a day. I didn't feel confident. My phone vibrated a moment later. "Who are they?" Rollins said.

"Three missing girls. The first two are dead. The third has about a day by our guess."

"You working with the cops?"

"Yes," I said. "They're putting a task force together. I figured I could do the same."

"Got anybody else yet?" he asked.

"You're my first call." I've worked with Rollins a few times after initially hiring him as a bodyguard during an especially nasty case. He was retired Army and very good at what he did. Somehow, he managed to do it without ever sleeping as far as I could tell. No matter the hour, he would answer his phone and be ready for anything.

"Who other than me do you plan to bring in?"

"Not sure yet," I said. "Why don't you come to my house and we can strategize?"

"Put some coffee on," he said and hung up. I walked into the kitchen and prepared a strong pot to brew as I texted the same photos to another acquaintance. My phone rang in short order. "What the hell?"Joey said.

Joey Trovato and I have been friends for years. Like me, he helped people through technology. Joey's specialty was in crafting new identities. If someone needed to disappear and could afford the fee, Joey was the best man to see. "I know we normally like to do lunch," I said, "but time is short. The first two girls got shot in the head, and the third might join them if we can't figure this out. She been to see you?" It was a long shot, but they occasionally connected.

"No," Joey said. "I wish I could help you here."

"Me, too. I'm going to try someone else, then. Thanks." I

hung up and shot the same three photos off to another person. My phone rang again a minute later. "For Christ's sake," Mouse said, "why are you showing me this stuff?"

"I need information." Mouse—who was short, shifty, and favored a monochromatic wardrobe which earned him his rodent nickname—was a man who heard things and sold what he knew to anyone who met the criteria of having the money and not being evil. Thankfully, I fit the bill on both counts. "The first two are dead, and the third girl's running out of time. Her name is Ashleigh Swain." I spelled it for him. Mouse groaned into the phone. "I need whatever you can find out on her as soon as you come up with something."

"How old is she?"

"Seventeen," I said.

"Fuck. All right . . . I'm on it. I'll let you know if I get something."

"Thanks." I ended the call. Fresh coffee wafted from the kitchen. I poured a cup and waited for Rollins.

CHAPTER 11

Rollins and I sat at my kitchen table. We'd strategized here before, and we did so again now. The other times, I felt like we knew more. We had more of a chance. Despair crept in. Joey was a bust. If Mouse didn't uncover anything, I wasn't sure where we would go. "We'll figure it out," Rollins said as if he sensed my apprehension.

"I hope so," I said. "I don't think I've ever felt so unsure of what my next move is."

"You said you looked at the girl's phone and tablet?"

I nodded. "Nothing of interest. If you want to see what's on them, feel free."

"I just think what's of interest might have changed in light of recent events," Rollins said.

"Fair point." We took our coffees to the office. Rollins and I took turns looking at the cloned phone and tablet data. I felt glad to have an ally who possessed more experience and insight than I could bring to bear. Despite being able to charge a premium for his services, Rollins pitched in on some of my more difficult cases and never asked for any money. He struck me as someone who didn't care much about it.

"These girls have any friends in common?" he asked.

"None."

"Not even on Facebook?"

"A few," I said, "but I don't think there's anything there. Social media has distorted the word 'friend' over time. We're talking about casual acquaintances. Looking at their profiles, you can see who's in the inner circle. None of those people are anywhere close."

"Still," he said, "it might be worth a look."

"Keep it in the back of your mind, then. If we strike out somewhere else, we can revisit it."

We finished perusing all the digital information we owned. "Doesn't look like much," Rollins said. "Damn. I was hoping something would've come to light."

Before I could concur, my phone buzzed. Mouse. "You have something?" I said.

"Maybe."

"I'll take a maybe at this point. What is it?"

"You know there's a fair number of titty bars in Baltimore, right?" he said.

"I've heard rumors."

"Well, there's one on Route Forty called The Wild West. Let's just say they don't always check the IDs of girls they put on stage."

"Someone saw Ashleigh there?"

"It's possible. A girl who looks like her, which could be someone else."

"Or we might've found her," I said. "We'll check it out. Thanks, Mouse."

"Thank me with the usual rate," he said and hung up.

"We got a lead?" Rollins asked.

"Want to go to a strip club?"

He chuckled. "Not really my scene."

"Want to beat up the owner if he turns out to be using under-aged girls?" I said.

"Now we're talking," Rollins said.

* * *

THE WILD WEST struck me as a place which began its corporate life as some sort of Texas-themed steakhouse. The exterior was brown, and a tall sign promising live nude girls hung out over Route 40. Whatever this place used to be, it retained a large neon ten-gallon hat above the marquee. Nothing but class.

The parking lot was only about one-third full on a weeknight. Rollins and I left our weapons in his pickup, got a quick patdown from the bouncer, and walked in. Loud music assaulted us right away. On a busier night, more bodies would soak up the sound waves. Tonight, we got maximum volume. A slender redhead gyrated onstage. She was both live and nude, so false advertising could not be counted among the establishment's sins. An elastic strap around her thigh held many one-dollar bills, and men crowded the rail for the chance to add another.

Rollins and I walked to the bar. A couple other girls strolled around dressed in bras and panties. To our right, a curtain led to what must have been the lap dancing area and private rooms. Even on a less busy night, I figured several men eagerly parted with their money. I noticed another security guy patrolling the floor. He wore the same black T-shirt and jeans as the doorman. "Another one in the corner," Rollins said. I struggled to hear him over the music. He was right—an additional guard sat in a padded chair near the stage and rail, keeping an eye on the drunks.

The brunette behind the bar looked too young to serve alcohol legally. She also wore lingerie, and it fit her well. When she leaned in to listen to an order, everyone at the bar caught an eyeful. After slinging a couple drinks, she made her way to us. "What'll it be?"

"Is your boss in?" I asked. I needed to shout to be heard, and her ear was about a foot from my face.

"You haven't even ordered anything yet."

Her spiel must have been part of talking to the man. No one will be seated, especially in the manager's office, without ponying up for overpriced booze. "Fine. You have an IPA?" She snorted. "All right. Whatever your haughtiest imported beer is, then." I made a drinking gesture to Rollins, who leaned in and told the girl what he wanted.

One beer, a pink drink, and a twenty-five-dollar hit to my wallet later, the bartender directed us to the curtain. "Go in and to the left. Boss' office is back there."

I thanked her, and we made our way through. Rollins went first. Behind the veil, the music got a little quieter. Stations for lap dances dotted both sides of a carpeted hallway, with doors at both ends. We followed directions and headed to the left. A large wooden door stared back at us. A camera looked down from above. We knocked. An intercom to the left of the door crackled to life. "What is it?" a man's voice called over the line.

I held my badge up the camera long enough for it to be seen for what it was but too quickly to tell it didn't belong to a cop. "We're looking for a girl. Heard she might be here."

"Lots of girls here."

"We'd like to talk about one of them. Open the door, please."

A soft buzzing came from the speaker. Rollins pushed into the room. It was a large office, probably fifteen feet square, with a massive desk toward the back. A pudgy balding man who looked and dressed exactly like the manager of a seedy bar should regarded us through squinted eyes. "Talk. I ain't got all night."

"Sure," I said. "You're really fending them off with a stick out there."

"You looking for a girl or not?" A patch of graying black chest hair stood out from his half-buttoned silk shirt.

I queued up a picture of Ashleigh and showed it to him. He reached for the phone, but I shook my head. There wasn't enough disinfectant in the state. "Seen her?"

"Looks young," he said.

"We heard age is just a number here."

"You heard wrong."

"Have you seen her or not?" Rollins asked, getting right in the guy's face. He leaned back in his chair to put some distance between them, but Rollins bent down and closed it again. "If not, you're wasting our time."

"You cops?" he said, glancing between Rollins and me.

"Private investigator."

The guy snorted. "I don't have to tell you shit, then."

"You're right," I admitted. "You don't. I think you'll find it's in your best interest, though." Rollins grabbed the man's greasy hair and yanked him out of the chair.

"Hey!"

"You may not have to talk to me. If you answer us honestly, we'll leave. If you bullshit us, we'll storm the stage and start chasing your guests off. My guess is when I flash my badge, a bunch of them will bolt for the door. And I think a few of your girls would be right behind them."

"I have security," he said with as much dignity as he could muster. It wasn't a lot.

"Do we look like the kinds of guys who are scared of the idiots out there?" I said.

Rollins kept a grip on the guy's shoulder and yanked his hair again. "You sure I can't get you a lap dance? Maybe a private room?"

"I'm gay," Rollins said.

"And I'm determined to find a missing girl," I added.

"All right, all right. Sure, we might be a little . . . uh . . . fast and loose with checking IDs from time to time. I ain't seen that girl, though. All the ones I got here are at least eighteen."

I didn't think he was lying, and I got the impression Rollins shared my opinion. Otherwise, he might have ripped the mane from the manager's head. "Great. Thanks." Rollins shoved the guy back into his seat.

"This was a waste of time," I said as we made our way toward the exit.

"We'll find something else," he said.

"We'd better."

* * *

AFTER WE GOT BACK to my house, I paid Mouse his usual rate via his preferred app. He found the intel, he'd never acted in bad faith in the past, and it wasn't his fault Ashleigh didn't turn up at the strip club. Before I could pour another cup of coffee, Rollins suggested I rest. "Even killers sleep," he said. "Take a few hours."

I wanted to argue with him, but I felt tired. I'd been all amped up to rescue Ashleigh from the shithole club and its sleazy manager only to discover she wasn't there. The adrenaline fade made my hands shake on the ride home, and now I felt like I'd pulled an all-nighter and been going non-stop. "Yeah," I said. "Probably a good call."

"I'm gonna head home and catch a few zees, too."

"You sleep?"

Rollins grinned. "As little as I can. Call me when you're up, and we'll reconvene." I said I would. When he left, the house sounded empty and quiet. Gloria would be sound asleep upstairs, and I didn't want to wake her. I kicked my shoes off, stretched out on the couch, and closed my eyes.

When I opened them, rays of early sunlight struggled to

make it through the blinds. I glanced at my phone—seven-thirty. It would mark the closest I'd been to seeing the sunrise in a while, and the least sleep I'd enjoyed in quite some time. No matter. Ashleigh Swain had it worse. If she were still alive. I called Rollins and asked him to stand by; he told me he would. Then I dumped out the old coffee from hours ago, made a fresh pot, and pondered my day.

It was still early, but people would be getting up and going to work. I called Melinda Davenport, whose just-awakened voice possessed a very appealing huskiness. "Rise and shine," I said.

"C.T., it's . . . not even eight," she mumbled.

"I have a missing girl and a ticking clock. I realize the hour, but I was hoping you could help."

"Sure. What do you need?" Her voice perked up. I ran down the three missing young blonde women, the gruesome way the first two died, and the very real timeline hanging over Ashleigh's head. Melinda asked about identifying details, and I gave her as much information as I knew. "We haven't taken in any girls in the last week or so," she said. "Reports come in from time to time, but I haven't seen any fitting your girl's description."

"Damn." Melinda ran the Nightlight Foundation, which provided a safe haven for girls and women trapped as sex workers. She was Vincent Davenport's daughter, and Daddy Dearest made a big deal about his little girl coming home after five years despite—in my unprovable opinion—knowing where she was and what she did. He funded the organization and enjoyed the good press; Melinda did the hard work. "I guess this is a good development overall, but I was hoping to catch a break."

"We're working on some job training now," she said. "T.J. is learning Office. She wants to be an executive assistant."

"Good for her," I said. T.J. certainly possessed the brains and determination.

"I'll let you know if I hear anything, though. Sometimes people come to us rather than go to the police."

I thanked her, and we hung up. Another swing and miss. My options dwindled. Yesterday, I'd considered going to Ashleigh's school. Talking to a teacher, counselor, or some of her other friends might give me a lead.

It felt like grasping at straws, but I didn't have anything else to hang onto.

* * *

Forty-five minutes later, I swung the S4 into a visitor's parking spot at Reginald F. Lewis High School. It was all brick and looked to be at least twice my age. I saw a few window air conditioner units bulging out from under the blinds. After getting buzzed in the front door, I spoke to a young secretary who thought my needing to talk to the principal was the funniest thing she'd heard in a while. Then I mentioned kidnapping and murder. The chuckles stopped.

The principal was a middle-aged black woman. The streak of gray in her dark hair lent her a more serious air than the twit working the desk outside her door. Her navy pantsuit matched her earrings. "We've been concerned about Ashleigh," she said after we exchanged introductions and bona fides.

"I'm hoping someone here can tell me something useful. A teacher, an adviser, one of her friends . . . I basically have no leads, and the clock is ticking."

"You said the first two girls were killed?"

"Yes."

"I'll take you to see Ashleigh's guidance counselor. Then we'll see who else we can find for you to talk to."

"Thank you," I said as we got up and marched out of her office.

The counselor beckoned me into her office after a quick chat with the principal. Ms. Ramirez was a Latina about my age. Two degrees hung on the wall, centered precisely between two bookshelves. They were straight, too. I appreciated the effort. Her pink dress hugged her body in several places, and it made me wonder how many boys came to see her solely to check her out. Her counterparts at my high school were all self-serious older men. "What would you like to know about Ashleigh?"

"It's all useful at this point," I said. "We're up against the clock now, and I don't know where to find her."

"All right." She typed a few things on her keyboard and then looked at the screen. "She hasn't been to see me in about a month. Not unusual. I see all my students once per quarter as a requirement. They can make additional appointments as they need them."

"Did Ashleigh need them?"

"A few times," Ramirez said.

"What did you talk about?"

She frowned. "I'm not sure I should—"

"If you hold something back, and she dies, I'll be sure to remind you of it. Constantly." She gaped at me. "You have a chance to help me help your student. Take it."

"OK," she said after a puzzled look came over her face. "Yes. Getting her back safely must be the priority." She scrolled through what must have been Ashleigh's file. I'd get it for myself if I needed to. Maybe my usual methods would have been better than coming here. "Ashleigh and her mother didn't always get along."

"I gathered this on my own," I said. "Anyone who's listened to Karen talk could tell you."

"Karen got pregnant when she was seventeen," Ramirez said. "My guess is she resented Ashleigh because she saw having a baby so young as something that derailed her life."

"It would certainly throw her world into upheaval." A thought popped into my head. "Do you know if her father is . . . well . . . her father?"

"It's never come up. They were married when Ashleigh was a toddler. I don't think she knows if he is or not."

"She knows," I said.

"Why do you say that?"

I remembered one of her blog posts. *I wish Jon could get through to her.* Jon—not Dad. "Because adults don't give kids enough credit."

Ramirez's frown told me she knew I counted her in with the adults. "Perhaps you're right."

"Anything else in there? A boy she was obsessed with? A stalker? A girl who hated her?"

"I'm afraid not," Ramirez said. "Ashleigh didn't need to see me very often. She had issues in eighth grade, and we talked about them, but here, she was a pretty well-adjusted kid."

One who knew her father wasn't her father. Did this lead her to try and uncover who was? "I don't like the mother very much," I said, "but I think she loves her daughter. Karen strikes me as a dead end."

"I wish I could tell you more," she said, turning her palms up.

"Me, too," I said, and I left the office. The principal took me to see a couple of Ashleigh's teachers. They couldn't tell me anything I didn't already know. A few of Ashleigh's friends chatted with me in the library. I held out the most hope for them —she struck me as much more likely to talk to someone her own age than a counselor or teacher.

None of the girls knew where Ashleigh could have gone. There was no stalker, no crush, no bitter ex, no vengeful former friend. They told me Ashleigh was nice and a good friend, but she also kept a lot to herself. She was a great listener and a poor sharer. I needed to read her blog again. Maybe I could ask

Gloria or Melinda to do it. They could pick up on something I missed.

I thanked the girls for their time, said good-bye to the principal, and walked back to my car. Coming here left me no closer to finding Ashleigh. The only thing I learned was the nugget about Jon, which I should have picked up on when I read her blog the first time.

The clock still ticked, and I was no closer to stopping it.

CHAPTER 12

In this job, my phone can ring at any time, and anyone could be on the other end of the connection. It's something I've learned to live with over the last two-plus years. All this said, I didn't want Vincent Davenport calling me at any time, let alone while I drove home during a vexing case. I declined. He tried again a minute later. I wondered if something happened to Melinda. He'd probably be the one to call me if it did. I picked up this time. "Mister Ferguson, you sound busy," he said when I answered.

"Good reason."

"I'll try to be brief, then. My daughter has told you I'm running for mayor, I presume?"

"You're not trying to get my vote, are you?" I said. I steered the S4 onto the ramp to I-83 South from the Baltimore Beltway.

"Would it matter if I were?"

"I turn in a blank ballot in every election. Voting for terrible candidates only encourages more of them to run."

"Am I in your category of terrible candidates?" he said. Davenport knew my opinion of him. Despite his reputation as *the* power broker in Baltimore, I'd never been afraid of him. He was an asshole who did his daughter wrong. I'd be nice to him in public, but it stopped there.

"I'm sure you didn't call me to ask a question you already know the answer to."

"No," Davenport said, "I didn't. Despite your opinion of me, I know you're a good friend to Melinda. I'm glad. She needs a strong support network. I also know you're good at your job." I wondered what he was trying to butter me up for, but I didn't say anything. Silence holds value in conversations. Let him fill his own gap. Which he did. "I was hoping to hire you. The campaign needs to be secure."

"You want me to work for you?" I said.

"For a few months, yes. Probably through the election in November."

"Do you think there's a universe out there in which I say yes?"

"I hope it's this one," he said. At least he took it in stride.

"I'm in the middle of a hell of a case," I said. "There's no way I have time to even think about this right now."

"And when you do?"

"I'm sure I'll still tell you no."

"Disappointing," he said, "but not unexpected. I have a filing deadline coming up if I want to get onto the ballot. Maybe I'll try you again once things have settled for both of us."

"I don't see my answer changing," I said.

"You can't fault a man for optimism."

"I hope you have a better campaign slogan," I told him.

Davenport chuckled. "Perhaps I'll ask you to join up for your copywriting skills. Good day, Mister Ferguson."

I clicked off the call. Vincent Davenport was a complication I didn't need.

* * *

I still used Google Alerts. Like the name suggests, they notify you when a particular event happens online. Toward the beginning of the case, I set alerts to get notified when any of a list of websites showed the name Ashleigh Swain. It was standard procedure, and it paid off now when my phone buzzed in my pocket.

Someone on Twitter made a post. *I think I saw that missing girl Ashleigh Swain. She was getting on a train to somewhere. Guess she don't wanna be found lol.* The user displayed no profile picture and had amassed a handful of followers. It could have been bunk. I looked at the picture. It must've been taken with an older cell phone. A blonde girl stood in front of the steps to an Amtrak car, looking about three-quarters into the camera. It could have been Ashleigh.

The poor resolution made enhancing the photo impossible. Despite what movies and TV like to show, zooming in on a digital picture only reduces the clarity as the image gets more pixelated. I focused on other details. The platform certainly looked like Baltimore's Penn Station, from which someone could hop on a train to just about anywhere. Because the girl in the image stood near the door, a number was visible.

The Amtrak 27 originated in Philadelphia, stopped in Baltimore, and terminated in Charlotte. Before I sped off for North Carolina, however, I needed to be sure this was Ashleigh. I used Google again, this time searching for documents with common Office file extensions under the Penn Station website. I combed through the results and found an equipment list. A file like this should never be available on the Internet, but here it was, and the problem was pervasive. This was a boon to people like me and a nightmare to those trying to keep networks and companies secure.

Once I knew who made the security camera system, I researched it. The company also provided a computer to manage the entire setup and store the recordings before uploading them to the cloud. Vendor-supplied PCs sound like a good idea, but they rarely turn out to be. They're often customized and can't be updated without breaking a delicate setting somewhere. Because of this, they tend to be excluded from normal patching and maintenance. Sometimes, the company will come in periodically and provide updates. Sometimes not.

Considering how easily I gained access to the computer, I went with the latter. Penn Station saw a lot of commuter traffic every day. Management installed cameras all over the place. Trying to find the right one by looking through the feeds would have taken forever. Instead, I found out which platform the 27 left from and located the camera pointed at it.

Using the time on the tweet to guide me, I rewound the footage and played it forward, looking for the mystery woman about to board. I fast-forwarded until I spied her almost walking through the door. This footage proved no better, and if anything, the resolution was worse. I needed another way to see if Ashleigh boarded the train.

She was tall and athletic. As such, she would stand even with the average man and several inches above most women. I rewound the footage, eventually tracking her movements via another nearby recorder. She passed one woman, then another, then a small group. Finally, she squeezed by two guys in suits. The girl on the tape didn't stand over anyone. She was no taller than any of the women she encountered and definitely shorter than both men. Unless everyone else in the shot happened to be professional basketball players, this wasn't Ashleigh Swain.

"Dammit," I said to the empty office. I made sure to cover my online tracks before logging off.

Ashleigh's clock still ticked.

* * *

I PONDERED my remaining options for finding Ashleigh when my phone rang. Rich. A cold feeling clenched my stomach. Did the clock run out? I answered the call and expected the worst. "I need you to meet me," Rich said, which did zero to alleviate my anxiety.

"What happened?"

"We had another girl disappear."

"Oh," I managed to say. It still constituted bad news, of course, only not the kind I'd been expecting. What did this mean for Ashleigh? Was she already dead?

"You want to know where?" Rich's question shook me from my morose musings.

"Yeah . . . sure."

"You know where Catholic High is?"

"I think I remember," I said. "If not, my GPS will. You there now?"

"Just got here," he said. "I'll look for you."

"I'm on my way." I grabbed my keys and dashed for the car. Catholic High is a private girls' school in Baltimore. Many of the parochial high schools in the city cater to a specific sex, so mixers and dances between institutions are common. In my time, I mingled with Catholic High girls, but more than a decade passed since I gave the place a second thought.

I got off of I-95 at Moravia Road and picked up Sinclair Lane. Soon, I drove past Archbishop Curley, a boys' high school. I remembered beating them in lacrosse four years running. My destination was only a few minutes and a couple turns away. I drove onto the lot and parked near the police cars. Red and blue flashing lights bathed the athletic fields. The uniform guarding the police tape lifted it for me, and I walked under. Rich jogged to me a moment later followed by Detective Paul King. "You two are working together again?" I said.

"I got to choose my partner," King said. "Seniority and all.

Your cousin's pretty good." King was tall and slender with a mop of sandy blond hair atop his head and a face which could never be rid of its pale five-o'clock shadow. His thrown-together sportcoat and pants stood out in comparison with Rich's pressed gray suit. Despite looking like he lived in a cardboard box, King was a heck of a cop, and he and Rich formed a potent duo.

"Did you change your status yet? It's not official until it's Facebook official."

King chortled. "Come on. I could pull better than this square." He jerked his thumb at Rich, whose sour expression conveyed what he thought of the conversation.

He was probably right. Time to get serious. "What happened?" I asked.

"Twelve girls got on the bus for a work study program," Rich said. "Eleven waited to get back on it."

"No one noticed their classmate vanished?" I said.

"They all work in different areas. It's common the girls won't see each other except on the rides to and from."

"They get breaks?"

"Yeah," King said. "They can come and go like any other employees, though. They don't have to eat in the cafeteria. We think this girl left campus, and someone grabbed her."

We walked farther inside the yellow plastic barrier. "Where do the girls go?" I asked.

"A nursing home on Belair Road," Rich said. "Busy street, plenty of choices for lunch. We have a team over there now interviewing the people in charge of the program."

"Our missing girl is Violet Graham," King added. "She's a junior. Seventeen. This is her first year in the work study program."

"Let me guess," I said. "She's blonde and pretty?"

"Right on both counts."

"This is definitely a pattern."

"We're not going to talk about it outside the task force," Rich said. "Sharpe is on his way now. After he gets here, we're going to meet the parents."

"I've had enough of it to last me for years," I said.

"Let's hope it stops with this case."

I hoped . . . for all the good I expected it to do.

* * *

Violet Graham lived with her mother in the White Marsh area of Baltimore County. Their townhouse sat a stone's throw from the mall and surrounding shops and restaurants. Leslie Graham worked as a nurse. Rich told me someone contacted her early on, and she would be waiting for us. The houses were single-car-garage models. Rich pulled the Charger into the short driveway, and we all got out.

Leslie Graham opened the door before we'd taken two steps. "What's going on?" she said from her small porch. "Do you know where Violet is?" She wore light blue RN scrubs and still had her ID badge clipped to her breast pocket. What struck me most about her was her age—she barely looked older than I did.

Four missing girls who bore some resemblance to each other. Four young mothers. The pattern held. I wish I knew what it meant. "We're still looking, Miss Graham," Rich said. We all showed our badges, and the four of us walked inside.

"My ex-husband is on his way over," Leslie said once we all sat around the carpeted living room. She blew out a deep breath. I got the impression his presence wouldn't help the situation. The house certainly looked lived in. It needed a maid or at least someone to ask if a bunch of things still brought joy. Marie Kondo could film an extended episode here.

"We'll try to be brief," Rich said. "Has Violet ever not been on the afternoon bus before?"

Leslie shook her head. "Never. She knows. We've talked about this." Her voice cracked, but she pushed on after a short pause. "She takes a lunch and eats in the cafeteria four days a week. On Fridays, she can go to lunch at a place nearby."

"You're a nurse," King said, showing how he earned his detective's badge. "Did Violet want to follow in your footsteps?"

"I guess." She ran a hand through her hair. "I'm a supervisor at a hospice facility. I drop Violet off every morning and pick her up after work every day. Sometimes, she has to get to school early or stay a little late, but we make it work. She's a good kid." Leslie's eyes welled, and she grabbed a nearby box of tissues.

"We have detectives talking to people at her work site, also," Rich said. "We'll find her."

"I heard about another girl who vanished recently," Leslie said. "A few days ago maybe? Have you found her yet?"

I wanted to tell her the truth but also didn't see how it would benefit her. Knowing Ashleigh was still missing would simply make her worry more. "It's still an open investigation," King said. Before the inevitable follow-up, he added, "We don't believe the cases are related."

The front door opened, and heavy footsteps stomped into the house. "What the hell is going on?" a man roared as he walked into the living room. Rich, King, and I all stood. Leslie didn't turn to acknowledge the new arrival. He stood about six feet tall, was overweight, and his ruddy face suggested he'd already made the better part of a six-pack vanish.

"You're Violet's father?" Rich asked.

"Of course I am. Ed Graham." He turned to Leslie. "You insisted she live with you, and now look what's happened!"

"Don't you pin this on me," Leslie said.

"Shut up, both of you," King shouted. "I don't give a damn if you're on good terms or not. You want to yell at each other on your own time, be my guest. You're on our time, now." He pointed at Ed Graham. "If you can't be civil and cooperate, we'll march you out of here. You understand me?" Graham frowned and offered a sheepish nod, like a student who got scolded for something he regularly did. "Good. Violet is missing. You both know. We're very early in the investigation, and we're trying to learn as much as possible."

"We'd like to ask you both some questions," Rich said. "We can do it separately. It might be easier for everyone." Rich and Ed Graham adjourned to the downstairs family room. Leslie told me I could look at Violet's bedroom upstairs while she talked to King. I opened the door and took in the scene.

This was much neater than the living room. I went through the bookshelves and desk and found nothing of interest. Violet didn't leave a phone or tablet behind, so I had no device to clone and peruse later—for whatever good the other ones did. I looked in her nightstand drawers, finding a hardback copy of Shakespeare's collected tragedies. The tome felt odd in my hand. I rapped on the cover, and it sounded hollow.

The first hundred pages or so were legit. Beyond them, they'd been cut away to reveal a hidden cubby. Inside was a box of a dozen condoms. Torn cardboard on one side told me the box had been opened, and I counted five remaining when I looked. A secret boyfriend? It was already different than the other similar cases. I snapped a photo of the secret stash, put the book back where I found it, and discovered nothing else of note.

Downstairs, the interviews concluded. Rich walked out with Ed Graham, who groused the whole time and continued blaming his ex-wife for something beyond her control. Once the jackass drove away, we bid Leslie farewell and climbed back into the Charger. "She has a boyfriend," I said once we left the driveway.

"You find a love letter?" King said.

"A box of condoms . . . pretty well hidden. Five out of twelve remained."

"The mom didn't say anything about a boyfriend."

"She'd be the first of the girls to have a current paramour, I think," I said.

"It might not mean anything," Rich said. "High school relationships often don't."

"I know. You noticed the mom is young, right? Four for four so far."

"You think it's important?"

"It has to be," I said. "Four seventeen-year-old blonde girls go missing. They don't live near one another. They don't go to the same school. We can't even find any friends in common. But they all have mothers who would've gotten pregnant somewhere between sixteen and eighteen."

"Those are really specific criteria," King said. "What the hell would it all mean?"

"I don't know," I said, "but now two girls' lives depend on us figuring it out."

CHAPTER 13

THE TASK FORCE MACHINE HUMMED AT THE PRECINCT. RICH and King, sitting at back-to-back desks, worked on the latest disappearance. I kept plugging away at Ashleigh Swain's. A couple other detectives dug into Brittany O'Connor. Casey Norton and Deputy Graiman from Frederick County joined us and plumbed the depths of the Trisha Lange case.

Leon Sharpe directed the whole thing. He was a curious choice to lead the operation. Despite being a captain, Sharpe was an old-school cop who always said he favored kicking in doors and busting heads to banging away at keyboards. This style of policing fell out of favor in Baltimore after Freddie Gray's death and the subsequent smackdown the Department of Justice levied. Despite changes, Sharpe remained in charge of the Violent Crimes Enforcement Division and appeared to suffer little professional blowback even as new commissioners came and went.

He sat on the edge of the desk where I worked. "What do you think?"

"Desperate for an outsider's perspective?" I said.

"I'm desperate to figure out who's kidnapping and murdering these girls."

"I think there's something we're not seeing."

"Such as?" Sharpe asked.

"The girls have the obvious things in common. They're all seventeen, white, blonde, and pretty. I'm sure the media is running those into the ground."

"They are," Sharpe said with a weary sigh. "Our PR folks are going to be getting overtime at this rate."

"There's another factor, though--the mothers are all young." Sharpe cocked his eyebrows, so I elaborated. "Meaning they're all about thirty-five. We always hear about career people having kids later and later. These women all got pregnant when they were seventeen or eighteen."

"Before they had careers."

"Sure," I said, "but it's unusual. How many girls give birth by the time they're eighteen? How many have blonde babies? How many of those babies grow up to be murdered at seventeen? The intersection of those three sets must be very tiny."

"You find anything the mothers have in common yet?" Sharpe asked.

"Past the obvious, no."

"Keep at it."

"I am." I glanced at the clock mounted on the wall. "I wonder how long Ashleigh has. I feel like I should be . . . I don't know . . . doing more."

"Listen to me," the captain said, leaning closer and lowering his voice. "We can't act without knowledge. Right now, we just don't know enough to roll out on a rescue mission. I know the clock is ticking. We probably have less than a day at this point. It sucks. You're not used to operating under a hard deadline." I nodded at the sentiment. "You can't let it distract you. Going off half-cocked doesn't help anyone, least of all the girl we're all trying to save."

"Was this a pep talk?"

Sharpe shrugged. "Did it work?"

"For now," I said.

"I'll take it." He clapped me on the shoulder, which felt like someone whacked me with a heavy paddle. What if investigating the mothers was a rabbit hole? I couldn't let the time constraint dominate my thoughts, but we all operated under the presumption these cases were related on some level. Which meant Violet Graham could provide a vital clue to finding Ashleigh. She was the only girl who had a current boyfriend. Three seconds on Facebook told me who he was, and determining where he lived didn't take much longer.

I headed for the car.

* * *

Justin Moore attended Loyola Blakefield, a private Catholic boys' high school. While he could have chosen a better institution, at least he possessed the good sense to play lacrosse. He and his parents also lived in White Marsh about a mile from Violet and Leslie. Sneaking off together to put their condoms to good use must have been easy.

I curbed the S4 in front of a single-family house. Like so many modern neighborhoods, all the homes looked alike on some level. There were only a few different designs to go around, and the only other choices were color options and a one or two-car garage. Welcome to suburbia, where everyone has escaped the character of the city for the county's cookie cutters.

A dog barked when I knocked. It was a deep, loud woof probably audible a few houses away. A man came to the door a moment later, opening it with his left arm while using his right and his body to block the dog. "Can I help you?"

I showed him my badge and ID. "I need to talk to your son."

"What's this about?" The guy was middle-aged, though his

brown hair looked untouched by gray. His paunch made his Polo fit in a way Ralph never intended.

"It's about your son and Violet Graham," I said.

"What about Violet?" The dog whimpered now, probably wanting to see who was at the door.

"She's missing."

His face dropped. "Justin didn't do it."

"I'm not accusing him of it," I said. "Two other girls disappeared, too. They died, and their cases are similar to Violet's. Maybe Justin knows something."

"I don't think he does." The man pushed the door.

I blocked it with my foot. "I'll be the judge of his knowledge when I talk to him. You can either let me in now, or I'll have the cops drag you and your son out of here for questioning." I glanced to the left and right. "What will the HOA think of you then?"

He glowered a moment but relented, opening the door. "Fine. I'll get Justin." He pointed a finger at me. "If I don't like your questions, I'm calling our attorney."

I held up my steady fingers. "Look at me tremble." He muttered a curse and walked away. A boxer stared at me with its brown eyes and wagged its nub of a tail. I offered my hand, and the dog sniffed it for a moment before deciding I was all right and licking it. I patted its head and waited for Justin.

He walked into the living room a minute later followed by his father and a woman I presumed to be his mother. I joined them. We all sat on the run-of-the-mill furniture and introduced ourselves. The parents who eyed me warily were Glenn and Heather, the latter breaking the streak of young mothers. To my surprise, Justin spoke first. "Violet's gone?"

I nodded. "Unfortunately, yes." Heather turned away and bit her bottom lip; Glenn remained stone-faced. "How long have you been dating?"

"Six months or so. We met at a Halloween party and went on our first date a week later."

"Were you together a lot?" I asked.

Justin frowned. "Not as much as we would've liked. Between her job and my lacrosse schedule, we didn't have as much time."

"Her job during the school day?"

"No, she works at a restaurant not far from here. Just a couple nights a week, but it makes it hard for us to see each other, y'know?"

"Did she mention anyone new hanging around or talking to her?"

"No," he said. Glenn continued frowning. I wondered if it served as his default expression. Resting Asshole Face. "Is she in trouble?"

"I think anyone who disappears is in trouble," I said. "We think someone took her. A couple other girls who look like Violet also got kidnapped recently."

"What happened to them?"

Why didn't Justin's parents prepare him for this part of the conversation? "They died," I said.

"Oh, Jesus." Justin buried his head in his hands.

"You've upset him," Glenn said.

"These are upsetting times."

"Maybe you should leave."

"Maybe you should fuck off."

Before Glenn could try to play the lawyer card again, Justin interceded. "It's fine, Dad. If I can help, I want to." Glenn grumbled to himself and resumed his eternal scowl.

"Good," I said. "What about someone new at the restaurant?"

"No." Justin shrugged. "Violet was nice, y'know? She got along with people."

I rattled off the names of the other missing or dead girls. "Any of those ring a bell?"

"I wish I could say yes, but they don't."

I pulled a business card from my wallet and held it toward Justin. When Glenn grabbed for it, I pulled it back, stared him down until he relented, and handed the card to his son. "If you think of anything, let me know. Day or night. We think the cases are related, but we're still not sure how."

"I will," he said.

Glenn walked me to the door. I expected a snide remark, and he didn't disappoint. "You should bring the police next time." He gave me a satisfied smirk. All the time he sat in silence on the couch, and a dig at my lack of official status was the best he could come up with? I try not to engage in battles of wits with unarmed people, but sometimes, they push my buttons.

"If you give me cause to come back," I said, "I'll bring an ambulance, too."

His smirk disappeared. I walked back to my car.

* * *

When I drove down the alley and swung the S4 onto the parking pad, I noticed an unfamiliar car parked a little farther along. It sat on a patch of grass, and squeezing past it with even a compact would prove a challenge. Two large men got out of the Toyota sedan as I stepped onto the concrete. I dashed off a quick text to Gloria, whose coupe I parked next to. *Stay inside. Goons out here.*

"Nice cars," one of them said. He was the taller of the two, with short blond hair. The other sported a black mohawk which looked ridiculous on anyone out of middle school.

"They're OK," I said. "My Aston Martin is in the shop." I shrugged. "British sports cars, right?" They exchanged confused glances before fixing me with the same. "OK, you got me. I'd never own an English car."

"You were told to back off," the blond said. Perhaps he served as the duo's spokesman. They inched closer. I didn't see the tell-tale signs of a gun bulging from under a shirt anywhere, though they could have pistols in their rear waistbands. I wore mine holstered at my left hip, and I knew they noticed it. I quickly used my elbow to verify it was strapped in place in case one of them made a grab for it.

"Ever since I left college, I'm a slow learner. What was I supposed to leave alone?"

"We ain't here to tell you again," the one with the silly hair said. "We're here to make you stop."

I scanned up and down the alley. "Are more of you coming? Maybe we should wait until they get here."

"Just us, asshole," the blond guy said.

"Guys, I have to tell you . . . I don't think you're going to succeed here today."

Mohawk approached, sizing me up. I assumed a defensive stance. He made a show of talking to his friend. "This one thinks he knows what he's doing." His leg stiffened as he drew his fist back for the world's most obvious punch.

Before he could swing at me, I kicked him in his front kneecap. It bent in a way the joint is not designed to, and he dropped to the concrete with a shriek, clutching his leg. I walked on it as I stepped over him, and he screamed anew. The blond one's eyes flickered between me and his fallen comrade. "Spoiler alert," I said. "I definitely know what I'm doing."

He waded in to test my confidence. At least he took a proper stance when throwing a punch. I blocked a few, then stepped aside when he tried to grab me. I moved to the right, putting him between me and the fellow still on the ground. My foe fired off a few jabs and crosses. When I blunted the last one, he grabbed my arm. I headbutted him between the eyes.

It hurt me a little, but it staggered Blondie back a couple

steps. He looked woozy on his feet, so I capitalized. I fired off a quick side kick into his stomach, bent him in half with a stronger front kick, then elbowed him twice in the side of the head. He fell and didn't move.

The first one still clutched his wounded knee. He glowered up at me through narrowed eyes as I approached. "Want to tell me who sent you?" I said.

He spat at me, so I hit him with a short, quick jab which bounced his head off the alley and turned his lights off. With both goons out cold, I searched their pockets but found nothing of interest. Lot of it going around this case.

I heard a siren getting closer. Gloria had texted during the scrum. *Be careful. I'm calling the cops.* I turned and saw her peeking from the kitchen window. I waved and blew her a kiss. She reciprocated.

Then I leaned against the rear of the S4 and waited for the cops.

CHAPTER 14

Two officers I'd never met before arrived. They took my statement, verified my license, and still eyed me skeptically. It took Gloria corroborating my version of events for them to believe me. The two goons—one revived by smelling salts and the other with a dislocated kneecap—got to ride in a pair of ambulances. Once all the emergency vehicles pulled away, I walked inside my house.

Gloria wrapped me in a tight hug. "I always worry for you."

I patted her back. "Most of the guys they send are just big oafs."

"What if it's more than two next time? Or one of them has a gun?"

"I'll handle it," I said. "If it happens here, I'll make sure you're safe inside the house."

Gloria nodded. A smile spread over her lips. "It was kind of hot watching you take it to those two jerks."

"Thanks." I flexed and patted my bicep.

"The girl still missing?"

"Yeah," I said, "and I'm running out of ideas."

"You'll think of something," Gloria said as she rubbed my shoulders. "You always do."

Her hands working their magic definitely brought some thoughts to mind, but they wouldn't help the case. I thanked Gloria for her confidence in me and went down the hall to my home office. The first welcoming committee came from the law firm of McLelland and Katzenberg . . . or at least carried the senior partner's business card. Abraham McLelland told me he didn't know anything about it, and he seemed sincere. This most recent duo went card-free. Maybe old Abraham didn't send the goon squad either time.

Or maybe their tradecraft improved after the first incident. I didn't have a lot of options, and I hated to tread ground I'd already stomped over, but I needed to find something somewhere. The firm had earned a positive reputation—not to mention favorable reviews on Google, Yelp, and other sites—over the years. Abraham McLelland served on the boards of a couple different local charities, donated some of his time to people who couldn't afford a lawyer, and seemed like a good egg all around.

I thought about the mothers of the missing or dead girls. The fact they entered the maternal ranks so young must be significant. I might be able to look past two as a weird coincidence, but a quartet formed a pattern. Cross-referencing the women with McLelland and Katzenberg yielded no results.

Over time, more old case files and court records become available online. I dug into Honest Abe and his merry band of lawyers. They appeared in the news often, in legal journals almost as frequently, and in digital case records more than I would have thought for a small firm doing boring work. Estate resolution and corporate buyouts were enough to put me to sleep. I skimmed their cases to see if anything interesting cropped up.

After a few minutes, I stopped scrolling and sat up. This could mean nothing for the case, but it jumped out at me all the same.

Davenport. Vincent v. Sullivan, Keith. D&S Bakery

Dissolution.

"Hello," I said, continuing my habit of talking to my empty offices. So long as they never answered me, I was good. While I'd barely glanced at the other cases, the buyout required my attention. Thankfully, the summary spared me from reading eighty-odd pages guaranteed to be the cure for insomnia.

Eighteen years ago, Vincent Davenport bought his partner Keith Sullivan out of the company. Sullivan wanted a lot, Davenport offered a fair rate, and the two settled closer to the latter's figure. The business would continue to be called D&S for the sake of branding, but Sullivan and his family relinquished all claims to future revenues, profit sharing, etc. They received a lump sum and went away quietly.

I checked news archives for the time this would have happened. Nary a peep got reported. Mentions of the buyout came up in an oh-by-the-way manner in articles about Davenport or the company. Going back a few years, I surmised Sullivan had been the silent partner. A big pile of money ensured he remained so.

Maybe Davenport could tell me something. It bothered him I had his personal cell, so of course, it was the number I used to text him. *Did anything unusual lead to your buyout of Keith Sullivan?*

He replied a moment later. *It's an old case, Mr. Ferguson. What does it matter now?*

It might be important to a missing girl.

Framing it as important to someone other than me increased my odds of getting an actual answer, or so I hoped. A minute later, I had an answer. *The relationship soured. Buying him out and continuing alone was the best course of action.*

One question remained. *He didn't do anything unusual to cause the split?*

The answer came quickly as a single word. *No.*

I didn't trust Vincent Davenport. It well could have been a

routine business deal between partners who had a falling out. Or despite what he said over our brief text exchange, it could have been something more sinister. I took a stab at finding out which.

* * *

MELINDA ANSWERED RIGHT AWAY. "Hi, C.T. Did my father talk to you?"

It took me a second, but I remembered the non-text conversation. It felt like a month ago with everything happening since. "He did. It's not why I'm calling you, though. Do you have a couple minutes?"

"Of course."

"Thanks," I said. "This was a while ago, so you would've been young. Do you remember when your father bought out the Sullivan part of the business?"

She blew a deep breath into the line. "I guess I was . . . six or seven at the time?"

"Sounds about right."

"I don't remember much of it while it was happening. Dad didn't really involve me or Mom in the business." She paused. "Keith Sullivan had a daughter, though. She was a few years older than me. Her name was . . . Shauna. We used to be friends back then. I haven't seen her since the company split. Wow."

"Sorry," I said.

"It's fine. I haven't thought about her for a long time is all."

"As you got older, did your father talk to you about the business more?"

"Sure," Melinda said.

I expected her to elaborate there. Maybe the part of the stroll down memory lane where we ran into a childhood friend distracted her. "Did he mention the buyout?"

"Some. Probably when I was in high school, especially once

the business classes started. Dad always thought I could learn more from him than from the teacher."

"As much as I dislike your father," I said, "he was probably right."

"Yeah," Melinda said with a chuckle. "He'd skip things like the English or math homework, but he always wanted to know what we were learning in business class. Sometimes, dinner turned into him telling me what I really ought to know about a particular topic."

Having been exposed to brief instances of Davenport pontificating, I didn't envy Melinda. "I hate to keep harping on the Sullivan thing, but it's an anomaly."

"It's all right," she said. "Dad always loved the quote about victors getting the spoils." People who won a lot generally liked it. "One of his big things was showing strength in business. 'If you're soft, people will walk through you like mud,' he would say. He never said why he wanted to buy out Sullivan so much. I asked him. He'd just tell me it was time, the partnership ran its course . . . stuff like that. Sullivan apparently wanted a ton of money to walk away. Dad offered something more reasonable. He said it was the market rate. I know they settled for close to his figure."

"Do you remember what it was?" I asked.

"Not exactly. I remember him telling me the market would support thirty-five million. Sullivan wanted about twice that, I think."

For half a bakery, even a regional powerhouse like D&S, thirty-five million struck me as an eye-watering price. The legal overview I read said the actual sum was above Davenport's offer but close to it. Melinda confirmed this. Call it forty million. It was a hell of a lot of money to have available to buy out a partner, especially if—like Vincent Davenport insisted—nothing unusual happened to spur the transaction. "It's a lot of money either way," I said.

"What made you interested in this?" Melinda asked. "It was a long time ago."

"It was a tangent to the case I'm working on. The same lawyer who helped your father with it just cropped up again, and not in a favorable light."

"Do you think it's related?"

"I don't know," I said. "I'm getting desperate. Something about the lawyer bugs me, though."

"I'm sure you'll figure it out," she said, and I could picture the smile her voice conveyed.

"I appreciate your confidence." I wished I could share it.

* * *

A FEW MINUTES LATER, my phone vibrated on the desk. I looked at the number and bit off a silent curse. One of my least favorite aspects of the job—a list which gains entries on a monthly basis—was the client update. It would be especially hellish here. The combination of a missing girl and a ticking clock until someone shot her in the head was not something I wanted to go into with a parent. "Hi, Jon."

"Have you found Ashleigh?"

At least he got right to the point. "Not yet. I'm working on it."

"We're getting concerned," he said. "Karen keeps checking the Internet and watching the news." His voice cracked. "She's in a panic. I'm trying to be strong, but I don't know how long I can keep it up."

"I know it's tough," I said. "I'm even working with the police on this one."

"One of the things we liked about you was your habit of not working with the police. They haven't been helpful in any of these cases."

I wondered how much of this conversation came from Jon

and how much Karen pressured him into. "It's all hands on deck," I said. "We're all working hard to find Ashleigh."

"Please keep us updated," Jon said. His voice lacked strength. It sounded like he'd resigned himself to the worst. "Let us know if we can help."

"There's one thing I've been wondering. You're not Ashleigh's father, are you?"

"Legally, I am."

"You know how I meant it," I said.

Jon inhaled and exhaled a long, slow breath. He remained quiet a few seconds after. "I'm not sure why it matters, but no. When I met Karen, Ashleigh was an infant."

"Have you told her?"

"I wanted to," he said. "Karen didn't. I deferred to her."

"I think Ashleigh knew," I told him.

"Do you think it's important?"

"I'm not sure," I admitted. "When you don't have a lot to go on, it's hard to say something doesn't matter. So far, all the mothers of the missing girls are young. They would've gotten pregnant at seventeen or eighteen."

"Why would someone care how old they were?"

"I don't know, but it can't be a coincidence. Has Karen . . . mentioned the father?"

"No," Jon said. "She doesn't talk about it. Never really has. Not to me, at least."

Who would she have talked to, then? I could probably figure it out and track the person down, but would doing this get me closer to finding Ashleigh? "All right," I said. "Thank you. I'll keep you in the loop if I know something."

"Please do," he said and hung up.

I set my phone back on the desk. The next time I talked to Jon and Karen, I wanted to tell them I'd found their daughter. Now I needed to make it happen.

CHAPTER 15

THE D&S BREAKUP NAGGED AT ME. TIMELINE-WISE, IT lined up with when the mothers of the missing or dead girls would have gotten pregnant. This could be a coincidence—business owners squabble for a great many reasons, and the yawn-inducing machinations of corporate life rarely interested me.

When you don't have much to go on, however, you follow any possible trail you can. I drove back to the office of McLelland and Katzenberg. Elaine frowned when I walked into the empty waiting area. She snatched the handset off the receiver and held it close. "You're not going to do that again," she said, sounding like a teacher admonishing me for some classroom slight. It was a voice I heard often during my school years.

"It was a means to an end," I said. "I would like to talk to Mister McLelland again, though. It's important. I'm not exaggerating when I say it might be a matter of life and death."

She eyed me suspiciously and put the handset in her pocket. "Wait here." She knocked on the big man's door, disappeared inside, and closed it behind her. I did what she asked. Causing a scene got me what I wanted the first time, but I wouldn't do it again. Elaine didn't deserve it, and I didn't want to get pegged as predictable.

The door opened, and she emerged. "He said he'll talk to you if you pick up lunch."

"What?"

"I have an order for Lenny's Deli. It's on—"

"I know where it is. What am I, Uber Eats?"

Elaine shrugged. "You're a man who wants another unscheduled meeting with the senior partner, and you acted like a child to get the first one." She gave me an insincere smile.

I couldn't really argue with anything she said. Elaine included her lunch choice on the list, as well. "Fine." If this was what it took, I would do it.

* * *

ELAINE GLANCED at her watch and regarded me with wide eyes when I returned a short while later. "I drive fast," I said. The speeds at which I tore through Baltimore streets went well beyond any accepted definition of fast, but I wasn't about to cop to it in a law office. I dropped a paper bag on Elaine's desk and inclined my head toward the rear of the suite. "He ready for me?"

"He told me to send you in when you got back."

I walked into McLelland's office without knocking. He frowned at me, probably for my breach in protocol, and went back to whatever papers he was reading. A moment later, he said, "Delivery boys shouldn't come in without knocking."

"They also shouldn't tell you you're going to be wearing your lunch if your tone doesn't improve." I shrugged when he looked up. "Then again, I'm neither a boy nor one who delivers."

McLellan stared at me. I stared back. We did this for a few seconds before he chuckled and looked away. "Anyone ever tell you you're a bit of a prick?"

"Sure," I said. "Though they usually don't try to spare my feelings by saying 'a bit.'"

He pushed the papers he'd been reviewing away. "No problems finding Lenny's?"

"I used to live in Fells point." I set McLelland's brown bag and can of Dr. Brown's cream soda on his desk. "I walked there a couple times."

"Bit of an adventurous walk."

"The triple-X theater really classes up the journey," I said.

"It's still there?" McLelland unwrapped his sandwich. Pastrami on pumpernickel with deli mustard, plus a pickle and potato chips. I'd never acquired the taste for pastrami, so I stuck with turkey on rye.

"Can we get down to business?" I asked. McLelland nodded around a bite of his food. "About eighteen years ago, you negotiated Keith Sullivan's exit from D&S Bakery."

McLelland's brows knitted. "You're here about something I did almost two decades ago? Elaine told me you said this was life and death. No one died when the bakery's co-founder went away, Mister Ferguson."

"I don't trust Vincent Davenport," I said.

"You're wise not to."

"Four young women went missing. Two are dead. They're all blonde and seventeen, and all their mothers aren't much older than I am. The D&S split roughly aligns with when they would've gotten pregnant."

"Not much to go on."

"I'm not asking for your legal opinion. I'm trying to save the other two girls, one of whom is running out of time based on how long the first two survived before they got shot. The timing here is a big coincidence, and it might end up being nothing. I need to know before I close it off as a possibility, though. What can you tell me about the corporate breakup?"

The lawyer chomped on more of his sandwich before answering. "Davenport and Sullivan fell out," he said after wiping a dribble of mustard from his chin. "I'd never been involved with the company before, but everyone said they got along pretty well. College friends, I think. You ever hear you shouldn't go into business with your friends?" I nodded, though McLelland continued as if monologuing for the jury. "Turns out it's true. Something caused a rift between them, and Davenport bought out Sullivan to get rid of him."

"Sullivan took the money, though," I said. "He could have dug in and held a harder line."

"He knew the writing was on the wall."

"I did a little research on this settlement. Turns out he took a lot less than he initially sought."

"Yeah." McLelland ate some of his pickle before elaborating. I wanted to hurry him along—he wasn't the one on a time constraint, after all—but I needed his cooperating, so I stuck it out. "I represented Davenport as I'm sure you know. He made a fair offer. Sullivan wanted the sun and moon. A pile of money, ongoing profit sharing, licensing revenue in perpetuity . . . you name it, he asked for it."

"Why did he take a much worse offer, then?" I said.

"We weren't budging. Both of them wanted to be rid of the other. I couldn't say which man disliked the other more by this point, but there was a lot of enmity between them. I think he wanted to put it all behind him. Besides, it was a good offer. More than half what the company was worth at the time."

"What did Davenport do to cause the split?"

"Why do you think it was him?" McLelland said.

"He's an asshole," I said. "I'm sure he's always been one. Did he knock up a girl Sullivan knew?"

"If he had, I couldn't tell you." McLelland tore open the bag of chips, and a couple of them spilled onto his desk in the process. He picked them up and crunched on them. "As far as I know, he didn't. Davenport's wife wouldn't have stood for such shit. They eventually divorced, but the genesis of it wasn't him screwing the help."

I felt a little disappointed. I wanted Davenport to be the villain here. It might get me to Ashleigh faster. A happy side effect would be the complete derailment of his mayoral bid. I didn't like any of the other declared and likely candidates, but they all enjoyed the advantage of not being Vincent Davenport. Call me a single-issue non-voter. "You think the timing is coincidental to my current investigation, then."

McLelland nodded. "I can't see how it connects. Sorry. I know you want a breakthrough, and I'd like to help." He shrugged. "There's nothing here, though."

I spent a couple minutes wolfing down the rest of my lunch, thanked McLelland for his time, and walked out of his office. The door swung closed behind me. Elaine wasn't at her desk. It was the middle of the afternoon, and the boss was still working, so she probably didn't leave early. Maybe she took a break. I glanced down the hall. McLelland's son's office was right there. He did similar work.

I knocked on his office door as quietly as I could. No response. I tried again. Same. Elaine still wasn't back. I pulled an old credit card out of my wallet and bypassed the cheap lock in about three seconds.

No harm in looking around.

THE YOUNGER MCLELLAND's office was setup as a mirror of his father's. It felt a little smaller standing in it. The junior partner got the junior office. I made sure the door closed quietly behind me, then crept to the desk. I didn't know what I was looking for yet, but hoped something would spark an epiphany.

McLelland kept the surface of the desk neat and uncluttered.

A laptop sat closed in the center. A wire cup held pens, and a stapler and paper clip dispenser flanked it. This was the most boring office I'd ever been in. Behind the laptop, a pretty woman smiled in a dark brown wooden picture frame. She wore her wavy blonde hair short, and she managed to look serious even while smiling. A Post-It hung from the left side of the frame.

You're the best, Abe! Love you!

~S.S.

For extra flair, the exclamation points ended with little hearts. I moved on to the drawers. The one on the left was crammed full of files. There must have been over a hundred. The tabs lined up for easy reading. I scanned the names but didn't see any I recognized. The file drawer on the right side was locked. I hadn't brought my lock picks. Shimming it with the credit card didn't grant me access.

I moved on to the bookshelves. McLelland displayed his law degrees and state bar association membership. Like me, he attended Loyola College. Judging by a few photos on the shelves, he must have been a few years ahead of me. The books were giant law tomes more useful as bludgeoning weapons than anything else. Considering the volume of online resources, lawyers must have displayed these books for show. They probably looked impressive to most clients.

If the firm possessed anything relevant to Ashleigh or my case, it must have been in the locked drawer. I contemplated other ways to gain access when I heard a voice approaching. "Are you in there, Abe?" Elaine. I ducked behind the desk. She knocked on the door. "Abe?" She rapped again. "Guess not." Soft footsteps trailed away.

I couldn't count on her not coming in for long. If an important piece of mail came, she might walk in and drop it on the laptop for maximum visibility. Going out through the front door would be difficult. If Elaine saw me coming from the wrong end of the hallway, she'd know something was up. Considering my earlier stunt, I didn't think she'd merely smile and wave me along.

I looked around the room. Beside the smaller bookshelf was another door. Suites in professional buildings often had one entrance but multiple exits. If I understood the geometry of the room, this door should open into the main corridor of the floor. I'd be outside the esteemed offices of McLelland and Katzenberg.

Exactly when I thought all was quiet on the Elaine front, I heard her voice from the outer area. "I'll leave it on his desk." The jig would be up if she came in. I called the firm's main number, hoping she'd stop to answer the phone. She did.

"Elaine, this is C.T. Ferguson," I said when she finished her secretarial spiel.

"What do you want now, Mister Ferguson?"

I eased the door open and peeked. Main hallway. The elevators were to my left. I slipped out. "I just wanted to apologize for making a scene earlier." I gripped the knob and let the door close an inch at a time.

"That's nice of you. Anything else?"

"Nope," I said. "Have a good day." I hung up and hoofed it for the elevator.

CHAPTER 16

THE LOCKED FILE DRAWER BOTHERED ME. MAYBE IT shouldn't, but I wasn't awash in investigative leads at the moment. What could Abe—who used the nickname professionally to differentiate himself from his father—McLelland stash in there? Confidential case records and the like were a certainty but which cases? And did he send the goons who twice tried to get me to back off?

I eschewed returning to the precinct for working out of my office. Rich and King didn't need me for the police side of things, and I preferred to do my job in my own way without a slew of questions. I rode the elevator up, checked for miscreants, and sat at my desk after finding none. First, I wanted to know the kind of work Abe did. A lawyer who tried to give himself a cool, hip nickname should bring some interesting matters to the docket.

Not so much, it turned out. Abe dealt more with corporate dealings like the D&S buyout his father negotiated almost two decades ago. The elder McLelland now focused more on estate resolution. I skimmed Abe's last three years of cases and found nothing other than the need for caffeine. How people could perform this drudgery day in and day out was a mystery I would never solve.

Perhaps his personal life spilled over into the job or vice versa. With so many people on social media, having a distinct name helps people like me with searches. I perused Abe's LinkedIn profile, saw way too many lawyers for my liking, and closed the tab. He didn't tweet, and his Instagram profile languished with nary an upload since he created it. Facebook was his platform of choice.

Most posts were generic status updates. Like most other people on the platform, Abe posted cat memes and occasionally complained about politics. His Sunday updates painted him as a Ravens fan, which almost mitigated the fact he was a lawyer. Scrolling down, I came to a bunch of photos, including several of Abe with the woman in the picture frame from his desk. They dressed up and went out a lot.

I was about to keep scrolling when I saw her name appear as being tagged in the post.

Shauna Sullivan.

THE S.S. at the bottom of the Post-It made sense now. I probably should have seen it before. Eighteen years ago, Abraham McLelland negotiated the breakup of D&S Bakery. Today, his son dated the daughter of the man who took Vincent Davenport's money. It may not have crossed any ethical lines—I was certainly not the person to make an accusation here—but it was definitely interesting.

Shauna Sullivan, daughter of Keith, now worked as a biotech executive. She'd started her own company, sold it to a larger one, continued her work there, and then left to form another new venture. Several articles hailed her as a brilliant young mind in the field of Parkinson's Disease research. She ran a lab which conducted cutting-edge research and may soon be ready for a clinical trial.

I looked through the photos again. She and Abe attended a lot of fancy events, he in a tuxedo and she in a gown. I called Melinda again. "You told me about Shauna Sullivan recently," I said when she answered.

"Yeah, but I haven't seen her in years."

"You keep tabs on her?"

"Not really."

"Does your father?"

"If he does," she said, "he wouldn't admit it. He's tried to erase any mention of Sullivan from the company's history books. I doubt he's thought about Shauna in eighteen years. Why?"

"She's apparently dating the son of your father's old lawyer," I said. "While there's probably nothing against it, it strikes me as a little fishy."

"Huh." Melinda fell silent for a few seconds. "I guess it is. I don't know. Sorry . . . I wish I could tell you more, but when Dad fell out with the Sullivans, he fell out hard."

"Shauna have any siblings?"

"She didn't when I knew her," Melinda said.

"OK. Thanks, Melinda." We hung up. I called Gloria next.

"I was just thinking about you," she told me.

"Do I want to know in what context?"

"Probably not in the middle of a case."

I smiled. "Best to save it for later. I want to run a name by you . . . see if you know her. Shauna Sullivan."

"Sure," Gloria said. "I wouldn't say we're friends or anything, but we definitely know each other."

Now we were getting somewhere. "How are you acquainted?"

"She's a fundraiser. I think her full-time job has something to do with medical research. She gets really involved in the events she and her company put on. I've been to a few of them."

"What's your impression of her?" I asked.

"Smart," Gloria said. "Driven. I get the feeling it's personal for her, but I've never asked."

This was an avenue to investigate. "Ever meet her boyfriend?"

"Once, I think. I can't say he made much of an impression. Why?"

"No reason," I said. "Their names came up in the case. I'm probably grasping at straws, but this is interesting, and I don't have any other leads to pursue."

"You'll find that girl," Gloria said, and I could hear the conviction in her voice. "I know you will."

"I wish I believed it half as much as you do."

"Don't get down on yourself. You still have time."

"I hope so," I said. "Right now I'm trying to figure out if Shuana and her man are involved somehow. Thanks for the information."

"Glad to help," Gloria said. "Love you."

"Love you, too." I put the phone back on the desk. Gloria mentioned Shuana's work might have been personal. It didn't take long to confirm her suspicion. Keith Sullivan had been in poor health for a few years. He'd contracted Parkinson's some time ago, but it was far from his only malady. A bout with lung cancer, a heart attack, and a car accident had combined to leave the man in a bad way. No one had seen him in public for over a year. He was still alive as far as I could tell but managed to disappear from public life.

This explained his daughter's drive. She'd probably be too late to help her father, but maybe she could eventually cure someone else's. I admired her spirit and her sense of charity even while I wondered how she factored into the case. I called

Sullivan BioGenesis and was told I could not get on Miss Sullivan's calendar anytime soon. No, she wasn't in the office. No, her return time wasn't known. Yes, I was annoying for asking questions. The receptionist implied the latter rather than stated it, but I picked up on it loud and clear.

I poked around on the company's website. Among their laurels, they'd won an award for cybersecurity best practices. Normally, I would take this as a challenge and try to breach them anyway. I didn't know if Ashleigh Swain could wait, however. Instead, I texted Gloria to see if she could get me in to see Shauna as soon as possible. She told me she'd try.

I've never been good at waiting, and the looming unknown deadline filled me with nervous energy. When Gloria didn't confirm an appointment after a few minutes, I paced around the office. After several more moments of silence, I headed for the door. Maybe Rich and King could use me after all.

On my way into the precinct, I passed Captain Casey Norton leaving. He looked even unfriendlier than usual. "What's going on?" I said.

"I'm off the task force for now," he told me.

"What? Why?"

"Three of the four girls are from Baltimore."

"And the fourth one isn't," I said even though he didn't need the reminder. "Besides, I can't imagine the BPD wouldn't want the state's resources and help."

"It's not them," he said. "We all answer to somebody, and there's a major who wants me on the Frederick girl. I'll still be tangentially working on the same thing."

I frowned. Politics ruined everything, especially kidnapping and homicide investigations. "You'll keep us in the loop?" I asked.

"Us?" He smirked. "You're official now?"

"Stick around. I'll help you add a few more commendations to your trophy wall."

"I'd need a trophy wall first," he said. "But if I'm ever running short on awards, I'll be sure to call you." He chuckled as he walked to his car. I headed into the precinct to find neither Rich nor King anywhere.

"They're both out," a uniformed officer told me as she passed me.

"Thanks," I said. I went searching for Leon Sharpe, finding him in an office around the corner. "New digs?"

He looked up from his paperwork. "Temporary. Keeps me closer to the action."

"You send Rich and King out?"

"Yep," he said. "They're working the Graham disappearance."

I frowned. "Why is her case the priority?"

"If they're all related like we think, focusing on one doesn't make a ton of sense." He held up a hand to cut off my objection. It worked for now. "I know the Swain girl's on the clock. You still at a dead end there?"

"More or less," I said. "Nothing I try to connect sticks."

"We all have cases like this."

"Not me."

Sharpe flashed a patient smile. "You've done the task force bit before with the pedo ring. I'm sure you can find something to do."

His comment planted an idea in my mind. It might be the last thing I had time to do for Ashleigh. "I'm sure I can," I said.

CHAPTER 17

THE PEDO RING SHARPE REFERRED TO CAME UP DURING A case where a troubled young girl fell in with a disreputable pimp. They're all of poor repute, but this fellow especially earned the label—he employed underage girls, and he paid them in drugs to keep them coming back. It made me wonder if Ashleigh fell in with someone like this, even involuntarily.

On an earlier case, I made the acquaintance of a pimp with the street name Romeo. He possessed some actual principles, making him a rarity in his profession. I sent him a text asking about anyone who might have an operation running which would reel in girls like Ashleigh. He replied right away. *Crazy John's, 15 minutes.*

I entered the restaurant at the appointed time. Crazy John's was known for fried chicken, a variety of games, and violence between the patrons. Not always in this order. Every time I drove by, I wondered how it hadn't been forced to close. It stayed open and did a good business many nights. I saw Romeo and his enforcer Tank sitting at a table, so I dropped onto a chair opposite them. "Gentlemen," I said.

They both nodded. Romeo was a light-complected black

man, probably in his mid-thirties. He always dressed well, and tonight was no exception: powder blue jeans, a red Polo, and a red Lacoste windbreaker. He and the prostitutes in his stable consistently wore red and blue as his homage to surviving life in both major Baltimore gangs during his teen years. Tank was aptly named, standing almost a head taller than me and probably outweighing me by a hundred pounds or more. He looked like he could snap me in two over his knee and do bicep curls with each half of my corpse. The first time I met him, it nearly happened.

"Why you only call me when you need something?" Romeo said.

"Want to go to an Orioles game next week?"

"Naw."

"All right," I said. "Let's keep our current arrangement."

"You wondering about anyone trying to sweep up young girls?" he said.

"More or less." I took out my phone to show him Ashleigh's picture, but he held up his hand.

"Me and Tank gotta eat first. You buying."

I was surprised he didn't mention it sooner. "What am I getting?"

"Whatever. We're hungry, and you know Tank can put some food away."

If the thought didn't disgust me, I'd love to see an eating contest between Tank and my longtime friend Joey Trovato, so long as I didn't pick up the check. I went to the counter, made selections to feed a family of six, and returned to the table. "What are we getting?" Romeo asked.

"You'll just have to be surprised when it comes," I said. A young waitress set a pitcher of iced tea and three glasses on the table. I poured a round for the three of us.

"You were about to show me something?"

"Yes." I pulled my phone again and displayed Ashleigh's picture. "She's been missing . . . close to three days now. I can't find anything about where she might have gone. She's seventeen."

"You're looking for someone who don't check IDs, then," Romeo said.

"Kind of like the last guy you put me on to. There's a catch with this, though. She's the third of four girls to disappear. They're all blond, pretty, and the same age. The first two are dead." Romeo and Tank frowned in unison. "I don't know how long I have on this one, but we need to presume time is short."

"Damn," Tank said. "You got a serial killer on your hands."

"Don't mention it too loud," I said. "The FBI will be waiting at the door for us."

"Most underage girls are caught up in some trafficking thing," Romeo said. "You got Russians or some shit there. Not hard-working entrepreneurs like me."

"You said 'most.'"

"Yeah." Romeo nodded. "Only asshole I know might take 'em underage is Scatter."

I rolled my eyes. "At least your street name is a good one."

"He got the name because he always has a scatter gun under his coat," Romeo said. "Be careful."

"I will. Where can I find him?"

"Harbor East," Tank chimed in.

"Really?" I asked.

"Sure," Romeo said. "Lots of rich white folks, plenty of hotels. Even some no-tell motels a few minutes away by Uber."

"I can't very well question this guy in the middle of Whole Foods."

Another waitress came and set our food out. I ordered an entire fried chicken and a large cheese pizza. Tank plucked a breast off the plate and grabbed two slices right away. I took a single piece of pizza. Romeo looked at the spread. "No vegetables?"

"Forgot," I said. "They didn't display the FDA food pyramid on the wall."

Romeo took both drumsticks and two slices. "Scatter's bound to be working by now. We're past hotel check-in time."

"You two probably need to get back to work, then."

"Yeah. You leave first. I can't be seen outside with a cracker like you."

I smiled for the first time all day. "Thanks for the tip."

"Good luck," Romeo said with a nod.

"It would be a refreshing change."

* * *

Harbor East was not a big area. Its southern end consisted of the Harbor East Marina, and it only ran two blocks north of there. I couldn't draw down on a pimp in the middle of a weekday afternoon. Maybe I'd get lucky and corner him in the discount wine section of Bin 604. Or I could whack him with a large organic carrot in Whole Foods and hope everyone nearby was too interested in their AirPods to notice.

I parked in the fancy market's not-fancy garage and hit the streets, walking down Central Avenue, the eastern end of the neighborhood. On the way over, I'd used my phone to connect to the BPD. Scatter—real name Raymond Brown—was a tall, slender black man with a long face, dreadlocks, and a scar on his right cheek.

I lucked out and found him eating in the Gordon Biersch Brewery around the corner on Lancaster. A gentleman of large size, no neck, and obvious skill set shared the table with him. Two chairs remained open. Never one to refuse such a clear invitation, I walked in and sat down with them. Scatter's eyes threatened to pop out of his head. His goon glared at me. Neither made a move, however. Sitting in a restaurant two-thirds full had its advantages. "It's fine," I said. "You didn't need to wait for me. I was late." I wasn't hungry, especially not after the slice of pizza I ate a few minutes ago. Still, the aroma of cooking burgers made my mouth water.

"Who the fuck are you?" Scatter said.

"A man with a question."

"We don't like questions," the enforcer said. He was white, about my height, and he wore his T-shirt a couple sizes too small to show off the fact he bench pressed four days a week.

"I imagine you don't," I said. "You're probably not very good at answering them."

The guy glowered at me some more. I somehow managed to avoid turning into jelly. Scatter said, "I don't know you, man. You want to talk, make an appointment. I got an opening next Thursday from one to one-oh-five." The boss and his henchman enjoyed a good chuckle at the alleged zinger.

I unrolled the unused napkin in front of me and took out the silverware. "There's a missing girl," I said. "Someone told me she might end up with a piece of shit like you." Now hatred burned in both their eyes. "She's seventeen. I hear you're not big on doing the HR paperwork."

"Why would I talk to you?" Scatter said.

I grabbed the fork and held it like I was ready to stab something with it. "Because if you don't, I'm going to stick this in your leg." Sitting to my right, Scatter wore shorts, leaving half his thighs exposed. "If the situation gets worse from there, I have a gun." I glanced at the enforcer. "I'll shoot you first." I returned my gaze to Scatter. "I'm going to show you a picture, and you're going to answer honestly."

He smirked. "And if I lie?"

"Then I stick the fork in your eye . . . Raymond."

Using his real name earned me another baleful stare. I picked up my phone in my other hand and showed him Ashleigh's photo. "She's seventeen. Missing about three days now. Three other girls who look like her also disappeared. Two are dead."

"I don't kill no girls," Scatter said.

"Me, either," added the muscle.

"Good," I said. "Standards are important. What about this girl in particular? Have you seen her?" I set the phone down between them and studied both for reactions.

Scatter and his enforcer scrutinized the picture. The latter shook his head first. "I ain't seen her," the pimp said, "and it's the truth." He met my gaze, this time without hatred, and I believed him.

My visit had been something of a long shot, so I shouldn't have felt disappointed it didn't pan out. Not ending up in the stable of someone like Scatter counted as a win for Ashleigh. If she were still alive. I needed to believe she was. Something would break my way soon. "All right," I said. I set the fork down and put my phone back in my pocket. "Thanks for your time."

"Would you really stick a fork in my leg?" Scatter said.

I snatched a French fry off his plate and ate it while staring at him. "And your eye. Don't forget the eye." I stood. "Enjoy your meal, guys."

They didn't say anything as I left.

* * *

I GOT BACK to my office, spiked my car keys atop the desk, and sat heavily in my chair. Every lead I thought I found turned into nothing. Ashleigh was in the wind, Jon and Karen were worried sick, the task force generated nothing, and the clock kept ticking. The first two girls each lasted a little more than three days by the medical examiners' best guesses. I've always been able to find people easily. Digital trails are everywhere. Not so for Ashleigh Swain. Any trail I found—online or off—led to another dead-end.

My phone buzzed, and my computer threw an alert. Someone opened my exterior office door. I drew my .45 and held it at the ready. The camera showed two large men leading a woman inside. They reached the inner door. A man pushed it opened. I leveled the gun at him. "Jesus," he muttered and backed away.

"The first four assholes couldn't discourage me," I said. "You won't, either."

"I think you have us confused with someone else," a woman's voice called back. "I'm Shauna Sullivan." When I didn't answer right away, she continued. "Gloria told me you were looking for me."

"You always travel with a pair of ogres?"

"They're not so bad. Can we come in?"

I set the pistol on the desk but didn't put it away. "Sure." The three of them entered. Shauna looked exactly like her photos. She was pretty, stood about five-five, and her short hair lent her the professional appearance venture capitalists favored. The pantsuit helped, too. Her two bodyguards—or whatever they were—both stood near the door. They were tall and muscular but a little paunchy, built like starting linemen in the NFL.

"A girl can't be too careful," she said with a smile. It was a pretty good one, even if it couldn't hold a candle to Gloria's. Hers weakened my knees and strengthened my resolve at the same time. Shauna's was only pretty good.

"Does Big Pharma have a contract on your life?" I said.

Her smile faded. "I know you're joking, but my work potentially threatens billions of dollars in research, development, and treatment options. When you're big in biotech research, you take a few precautions."

I was sure she wasn't alone in this respect. Some people liked traveling with bodyguards because it made them seem important, both to themselves and others they encountered. Broaching this possibility would not take the conversation down a productive road, however. "Thanks for coming by," I said instead, hoping for a friendly tone. I didn't feel especially chummy at the moment. "I'm glad Gloria could reach you."

"She said you're looking into some missing girls, and my father's buyout came up?"

"Indirectly. I'm investigating four missing girls. They're all the same age. Two are dead. The third one will soon join them if I don't figure something out soon. A pair of goons tried to dissuade me yesterday, and one of them carried Abraham McLelland's business card."

"That led you to the D&S case?"

"I'm sure you know the firm doesn't deal with riveting stuff." She reluctantly nodded. "I looked through their old cases, and it jumped out at me. I know Mister Davenport. I'm not a fan."

Shauna snorted. "Me, either . . . the prick. My father helped him build that goddamn company, and he made a lowball offer to get rid of him."

"Why did they split, anyway?"

"Dad never really told me," she said. "I was in eighth grade when it happened. All he said was they had a falling out, and it couldn't be repaired."

"He wanted a lot more money, didn't he?" I asked.

"Yes. Davenport's offer was insulting. I knew it then, and I'd never even taken a business class."

"Why accept it, then?"

"Dad told me he wanted it to be done," she said. "A long legal fight didn't help anyone. If it dragged on for months, he might've gotten a couple million more, but then he would've owed a bunch more in legal fees." She shrugged. "I don't think I would've made the same decision."

"Me, either," I said. "Can I get you anything to drink? I feel like I'm being rude."

"Water's fine. Thanks." I retrieved us each a bottle from the mini fridge. Shauna twisted the lid off and took a sip. "If you connected me through a business card, I'm sure you also know about my father."

I nodded. "I'm sorry. I'm sure his health problems aren't easy for anyone."

"He loaned me money to start my first company." Shauna smiled at the memory. "I paid him back sooner than we'd agreed on . . . with interest." I had no idea what to say, so I downed a little water and stayed quiet. "Now he's getting his affairs in order." She blew out a short breath and shook her head. "I'm helping as much as I can."

"It sounds like you don't know why two bruisers would be carrying McLelland's business card," I said.

"No idea," she confirmed. "It said Abraham, not Abe?"

"Yes. I know it's the father, not the son." The son, of course, enjoyed easy access to his father's office, and who would notice one business card going missing?

"I don't know if they even retain investigators. I don't know what they would need with the men you described."

"Maybe Big Pharma's going after them, too."

"Maybe," Shauna said with a grin.

"Can I show you the missing girl's picture?" I said. "Maybe you've seen her somewhere."

"I guess it's possible. Sure." I queued up the photo and slid my phone across the desk. Shauna squinted at it. The gesture made it difficult to read her face. "Can't say I have. We've had some interns who resemble her but no one current."

"All right. Thanks for coming by. Good tradecraft getting up here, too. Most people take the elevator, and it gives them away."

"My idea," one of the bodyguards said, pointing at his chest. "We got off on the floor below and took the stairs up."

Shauna grabbed her water bottle and walked to the door with her beefy escorts. "Good luck finding the girl," she said. She didn't show much of a smile this time. The three of them left.

I'd swung and missed again.

CHAPTER 18

I PONDERED MY DWINDLING OPTIONS. THE COMBINATION OF a countdown, the unknown time remaining on it, and the utter lack of usable leads meant this case stymied me like no other. Three other girls vanished, too. We worked under the presumption all their cases were related. I pulled them up and barely started hunting for common factors when my phone buzzed. I glared at it for interrupting me and then sighed when I saw it was Jon calling back.

"Any leads?" he said when I picked up.

"Nothing I can use."

"We're very concerned, Mister Ferguson."

"So am I," I said.

"Her time is running out," Karen yelled. Her throat sounded raw. She'd injected frustration, anger, and loss into her shout. I sympathized.

"I know it is," I said. "I'm chasing down everything I can. None of it has panned out so far, but I'm still working on—"

"Work harder, dammit! My daughter's going to die." She kept talking, but I couldn't understand what she said past the tears.

"You can hear how desperate we are," Jon said a few seconds later.

"I understand," I said. "I'm doing everything I can."

"You sure seem to answer the phone a lot!" Karen said.

"Would you rather I not?"

"I'd rather you find Ashleigh." She trailed off into sobs again.

"Jon," I said, "keep the phone away from her, or I'm hanging up."

"She's distraught," he said as if I couldn't tell.

"I told you I get it. The more I have to pick up the phone to hear about it, though, the less time I have to find her."

Jon was quiet for a few seconds, and when he came back on the line, his voice was barely above a whisper. "Do you think she's still alive?"

"Honestly, I don't know. I hope so, and I'm operating under the presumption she is. I've chased down a few leads today alone, been threatened more than once . . . someone doesn't want me snooping around. The issue is I don't know who."

"Thanks for your persistence," he said. "I hope you find her."

"Me, too," I said, and I hung up before Karen snatched the phone back and shrieked in my ear some more.

THE ADVANTAGE to two monitors is all the square inches of display space. Three of the four girls disappeared from Baltimore. The first vanished from Frederick County, but thanks to the task force, the BPD maintained a copy of the case file on their network. I looked at all four—two each on both my screens.

Trisha Lange. Brittany O'Connor. Ashleigh Swain. Violet Graham. Besides being seventeen, blonde, pretty, and born to young mothers, they must have shared other common factors. Early in the process, we learned they shared a scant few acquaintances but no actual friends. I made a note of these people's names in case I needed to reach out. Anything they could tell me would add up to more than I had at the moment.

All four girls worked, either part-time jobs or in programs at their schools. Their employers weren't connected, however, and I couldn't run anything down there. The coworkers and supervisors I could easily identify didn't turn up anywhere else. Nothing at their schools linked them, and I'd just ruled out employment, too.

This wasn't helping.

My phone buzzed with a text. Rich. *Any luck?* It made me let out a bitter laugh.

I texted back. *Yeah. All bad. I keep eliminating common factors rather than finding them.*

He replied quickly. *Hitting the streets again usually works for me.*

I set my phone down. The files still stared back at me. The answer lay in here somewhere. I simply needed to unlock it. Maybe the clothes they were wearing when abducted would tell me something. I quickly learned this was another dead end. Brittany wore her private school uniform, and the other three girls were dressed in normal clothes from all different companies.

Their parents attended different churches. Belonged to different social clubs and organizations. I couldn't find a single factor connecting two of these girls to each other, let alone all four. I glanced back at my phone. Rich's text remained on display. *Hitting the streets again usually works for me.* "Hell, nothing else is working," I muttered to my empty office.

I'd investigated the first three crime scenes but never visited the fourth. Violet Graham worked in a nursing home through a program at Catholic High. Somehow, someone snatched her from the facility in the middle of the day without anyone noticing. I grabbed my keys and headed there to ask how it could happen.

* * *

GRACEFUL MEADOWS NURSING Home was a four-story brick building at least the size of most high schools. I parked the S4 in a visitor's spot and walked in through the front door. The young woman at the desk didn't know anything about what happened, but she offered to get the head of security for me while I waited. I plopped down in a chair.

Brochures on the table advertised the benefits of the place. I wondered how many of them went into the cost. Caring for aged relatives proved too difficult for many folks, but farming it out to places like Graceful Meadows consumed people's life savings. I leafed through one brochure. It touted the many features of the facility but never once hinted at cost. Perhaps no one asked; they simply signed over their relative and their checkbook at the same time.

A minute later, a burly man strode to me. "You the detective?" he said in a voice suggesting he'd recently smoked three packs of cigarettes at the same time. He was at least my height but probably twice my age, and the years took a toll on a once-muscular frame. Still, I imagined this fellow could subdue an orderly stealing syringes from the supply cabinets. His shaved head gleamed in the fluorescent light overhead.

"I am." I stood, and we shook hands. Now I got the strong whiff of tobacco. I struggled not to cough.

"Name's Curran. Come to my office, and we can talk." I followed no-first-name Curran down the hall, around a corner, and into a small office. Degrees on the wall showed his first name to be Cornelius, and I knew why he introduced himself only by his surname. Having been inflicted with a family name myself, I empathized. "You got ID?" I showed him my badge and credentials. "Private, huh?"

"Yes. I'm working with a police task force on the disappearances of four girls, one of whom worked here through her school."

He gave me a curt nod. "Violet Graham. I already talked to the cops about her."

"Good. Then you won't mind repeating it all to me."

"What if I would?"

"What if I cram one of those bowling trophies down your throat?"

He smirked. "You think you could?"

"Yeah," I said, "I do. More importantly, I think you do, too. So why don't we dispense with the macho bullshit, and you help me find two missing girls?"

"Two?"

"Yeah. Violet's the latest. Another girl's been gone longer, and I don't know how much time she has."

Curran frowned. "What do you mean?"

"Violet is the fourth girl to be taken," I said. "They all look sort of alike. The first two were both shot in the back of the head." None of the degrees, plaques, or trophies on Curran's wall or shelf suggested he'd served in the military or been a cop. If he had, he could've been hardened against my casual description of murder. The police would have withheld this information, but I needed the reaction and the cooperation. Color drained from his face, starting at his crown and whitening its way down.

"Jesus Christ." Curran wiped a napkin across his forehead. He grabbed a coffee cup, and his hand shook as he set it down in front of himself. "I need a drink." He produced a bottle of Evan Williams bourbon from one of his desk drawers. "You want any?"

"I'm tempted, but no, thanks."

Curran poured himself a generous measure of bourbon and drained about half in a single gulp. I'd never cared for whiskey straight; Curran's agape mouth and watering eyes showed off the reason. My father tried to tell me Scotch was great for sipping. I found the best use of it was pouring it down the drain. "What do you want to know?"

"Everything you told the police," I said. "And I'm on the clock, so liquor up on your own time."

Curran set the bottle down and nodded. "Sure. Violet's a really nice girl. Great worker. She—"

"I don't want the HR report," I broke in. "I care about where she worked, who might've had access to it, and how someone took her out of here in the middle of the day without drawing attention."

"I wish I could give you some good answers." Curran took a small sip from the mug. "Violet's been on a rotation of various jobs. Currently, she's in the kitchen."

"Why is this important?"

"No cameras in the kitchen. We keep them where staff will interact with patients and residents. It's for everyone's protection. We don't keep any eyes on food prep, though. It's not worth it."

"What about in the cafeteria?" I said. "Would a camera in there see any of the kitchen workers?"

He shook his head. "No. We do monitor the cafeteria, but the view doesn't extend anywhere else."

I rubbed the bridge of my nose. The incompetence rampant in this case would give me a migraine before the day was out. "I heard she got off the bus from school this morning." Curran's head bobbed in confirmation. "At some point during the day, she disappeared because she wasn't there for the return trip. You can't see into the prep area, so it's reasonable to presume someone took her from there."

"Sounds likely," Curran said.

"Tell me about the area. How would I pull this off if I were a kidnapper?"

"It's big . . . probably triple the size of most restaurant kitchens." He presumed I could use this as a frame of reference, so I gave a nod in the interests of him continuing. "The way in is through a locked door. Key card required. There's a back door out of the building. We accept deliveries there."

"Did you get any around the time she would've disappeared?"

"No," he said.

Most restaurants received kitchen deliveries at the rear. This struck me as common knowledge. It seemed logical to extend this to places like Graceful Meadows. Someone could drive a van behind the building and grab Violet without attracting much attention. "You have a camera out back?"

"There's one behind there. It doesn't point at the exit, but it's within scope."

"The cops ask for the footage?" I said.

"Yeah. Told them to request it. We access the important feeds here. The rest get stored in the cloud. I don't understand how all this shit works."

I did—and I felt the head of security should, too—but I didn't know if I could afford the time to get the footage. Cloud providers had upped their security game the last several years. The BPD could have it by now, anyway. "All right. I'll presume she got snatched out the back door. Would she have a reason to leave through there?"

"Smoking?" Curran said. "Maybe tossing some trash bags."

This introduced the possibility someone cased the back door and waited for Violet to emerge. She was basically an intern, so garbage detail would fall to her. We needed the footage. "Thanks for your time," I said.

"We're done?"

"I need the video," I said. "I hope the cops have it by now."

I left Curran's office. He poured some more whiskey into his mug as I walked out. I sympathized.

* * *

RICH CALLED while I drove away from the nursing home. "I just visited Graceful Meadows," I told him. "The security guy there, Curran, is supposed to be getting you some footage."

"He did," Rich said. His voice sounded unusually monotonous and lifeless. "The tech people are working to clean it up now. We hope to have it back soon."

"Everything all right? You sound somber . . . even for you."

"No," he said, "I have bad news."

My stomach clenched in dread. I gripped the steering wheel hard enough to turn my knuckles white. "Don't tell me."

"Sorry. Ashleigh's dead. It just came in."

I jerked the wheel to the right and pulled into a parking lot, drawing a few horns of protest along the way. "Maybe it isn't her. We've had four girls—"

"We're pretty sure it's her," Rich said.

The clock ran out. I wondered if all the leads I chased down today even deserved the status. Did I simply waste time and try to keep myself busy on a difficult case while someone we didn't know shot Ashleigh in the head? What would happen to poor Violet Graham? Our task force was oh-for-three so far, and now the timer ticked again. How many more girls would disappear and die because we couldn't figure this out?

Because *I* couldn't figure it out.

"You there?" Rich asked.

"Yes," I said with a sigh. "Where am I meeting you?"

"Clifton Park."

"The golf course?"

"Yeah. King and I are on our way now."

"I'll meet you there," I said.

I sat in the parking lot and stared ahead. Jon and Karen were distraught before. They would be devastated now. They'd blame me for not finding Ashleigh, and I couldn't tell them they were wrong. I pounded the wheel a few times and let loose a string of curses profane enough to make a sailor blush.

Then I put the S4 in gear and headed back the way I came.

CHAPTER 19

CLIFTON PARK GOLF COURSE SPRAWLS OFF HARFORD ROAD in Baltimore. It's been there forever. I remember my grandfather talking about playing its links, and he even roped my father into it a few times. Despite their influence, I never acquired a taste for golf. It always struck me as a bit of an elitist sport, and I filled the bill nicely by playing lacrosse for years.

I turned onto St. Lo Drive from Harford, then veered left into Indian Head Drive toward the clubhouse. Parking was past the building itself, and navigating the area proved complicated with the many police vehicles stopped along narrow roadways. I eventually made it to a spot, ducked in under the tape, and walked with a uniform to where Rich and King surveyed the scene. A crime scene photographer snapped pictures.

A blonde girl's body lay face-down in the grass. Whoever dumped her here stashed her among a bunch of trees in the opposite direction from the first tee. Clever. Foot traffic in here would be minimal. The dead girl wore khaki shorts and a black T-shirt. Her feet were bare. Blood crusted her hair where someone shot her in the back of the head. I turned away and took a deep breath. If I thought I had any right to do it, I might've offered a prayer.

"This is your girl," King said with all the tact and grace of a charging rhino. "ME's initial guess is she's been dead a few hours. Body probably got dumped here not long ago."

"Who found it?"

"Groundskeeper." King pointed to where a weathered old white man talked to Rich and a couple of other detectives. "He says he saw something in the trees. I guess he knows this place better than anyone."

"I guess," I said.

"You seem pretty glum," King said, demonstrating his powers of understatement.

"I couldn't find anything. There's always something out there, and I kept coming up empty." I shook my head. "And now she's dead."

"You did what you could. Shit happens. You can't control it."

I walked past King to get a closer look at the body. A medical examiner turned her over, and the face definitely belonged to Ashleigh Swain. My faint hope the corpse belonged to another girl flew out the window. Her eyes remained open, of course, and I wondered what the last thing they saw was. Did she know the person who killed her? Did she wait for a rescue and eventually lose hope? "I'm sorry," I whispered. "I wasn't good enough."

"What?" Rich said as he walked to me.

"Nothing."

"King fill you in?" I bobbed my head once. "Scene's pretty new, so we're still learning what we can. No one saw anything, of course, and there's no camera pointing over here."

"There must be potential witnesses," I said. "How many ways in and out of here are there?"

"Four," Rich said. "The other end of St. Lo Drive hits Sinclair Lane. Indian Head takes you to Belair Road. And you can get in from Erdman Avenue, though it's a lot less direct."

"The Harford Road entrance has to be the best way in."

"Probably. It's the closest to where the body is."

"If this happened a few hours ago," I said. "it was midday. Plenty of visibility. You need a vehicle which can transport a body easily . . . two guys struggling to get it out of a Corolla's trunk doesn't work."

"I get where you're going. We're probably looking for some sort of van or SUV."

I walked behind Ashleigh's body and looked toward the clubhouse. Only slivers of it were visible past the trees. "The line of sight to here is bad. Even someone going out on the course may not see anything . . . especially considering they would tee off in the opposite direction."

"Yeah," Rich said. "Whoever did this chose the spot well. As long as no one pulled in behind them, they could have been completely unseen."

"Gentlemen," a familiar voice came from our left. Doctor Gary Hunt from the medical examiner's office waited for us. He was of average height and build, barely into middle age, and kept his brown hair neat. "I have a few preliminary things to share."

"Let's hear them," Rich said.

"Cause of death is definitely the gunshot to the back of the head. No exit wound as with the other girl. I'll get the bullet to forensics as soon as I can. No other signs of mistreatment or assault. She does have a needle hole in her left arm."

"So did Trisha Lange," I said.

"We'll have to see if the O'Connor girl did, too," King added.

"She did," Hunt told us. "I don't know anything more about it at the moment. We'll need to do a tox screen to see if drugs were involved, of course."

"Anything else, Doc?" Rich asked him. Hunt shook his head. "All right . . . thanks. We'll look for your full report later."

"Time to talk to the family," King said. He looked at me. "You coming?"

"I need to," I said. "They hired me. I should be there when they learn the worst. I'll follow you."

We left the crime scene in the capable hands of the remaining detectives and officers and left for the Swain's house. I dreaded this conversation, but I was required to be there for it. If I were going to trumpet my successes, I needed to own my failures, too.

* * *

I KILLED the engine and let out a deep breath. We were parked on Fleetwood Avenue, Rich and King directly ahead of me near Jon and Karen Swain's house. My cousin and his partner exited their car and waited for me. I got out and walked to the front door with them. Rich knocked. He stood in the front, which made sense. He was the best of us at delivering this type of news. Speaking to grieving parents struck me as a skill not in King's wheelhouse.

Jon came to the door. The faint hope in his eyes died when he looked at us. He knew. Parents always know in these situations. Rich asked if we could come in, and Jon said yes. We entered and waited in the living room while he fetched Karen from upstairs. They descended together, their steps heavy and their shoulders slumped. Karen's eyes already leaked tears.

"Mister and Missus Swain," Rich said, "I'm sorry to have to tell you this, but Ashleigh is dead."

Karen wailed, shouting negations into the sky as if one of them would undo what happened. Jon embraced her, but she was disconsolate. I remembered how I felt when at age sixteen I heard my sister died. I didn't think then what my parents must have been going through—especially since I learned last year Samantha was murdered—but I could see it now. No grief compared to the loss of a child. Life simply wasn't supposed to work in such a way. Children buried their parents, not the other way around. This was life's cruelest perversion.

After a few minutes, we all steered ourselves to furniture. The Swains sat on the couch, Rich and I shared a loveseat, and King occupied a recliner. "How did it happen?" Jon asked. He wiped at his eyes. Maybe he'd been putting on a strong front for his wife, but I was impressed with how composed he'd been since hearing the news.

"We don't need to—" King began.

"Tell us," Jon insisted.

"All right. She was shot once in the back of the head." Karen cried anew at hearing the grisly fact. Jon sat with his arms around her and patted her back. It didn't help. It couldn't help.

"Was she . . . uh . . . "

"There were no signs of any form of assault," Rich said. "We just came from the scene, and we'll have more details later. I hate to mention this part, but the medical examiner will need someone to verify the body is Ashleigh's."

"We will," Jon said. "Where was she found?"

"Clifton Park Golf Course," Rich said. "Is it significant to your family at all?"

Jon shook his head. A tear rolled down his cheek, and his voice cracked when he answered. "I don't think we've ever been."

"We don't want to take up any more of your time." Rich stood, and King and I followed suit. "We're very sorry for your loss."

"Thank you." Jon stood to walk us out.

"She's dead!' Karen yelled. She got up and stared at me. I couldn't meet her eyes. "You told us you'd get her back, and she's dead." I'm rarely speechless, but I had nothing to say in my own defense. My silence must have emboldened her, because she drew her hand back and slapped me hard across the face. It stung, and the force of the blow turned my head.

"Karen," Jon said. His tone managed to be both stern and sympathetic at the same time.

"You let her down," Karen said, tears streaming down her cheeks. "You let us down. You're a failure! A fucking failure!"

Jon grabbed her by the elbow and herded her toward the back of the house. We used the quiet to leave. Rich and King walked out first. "Don't take it too hard," Rich said. "She's reacting in the moment."

"Yeah," I said, and I trudged past them to my car. Rich and King pulled away. I stared ahead. Ashleigh was dead, and Karen was right—I'd let them all down. I thought I could find her because I always uncovered where people hid. This time, I couldn't do it, and a seventeen-year-old girl with the world ahead of her paid the price for it.

Karen cursed me for a failure. I certainly felt like one.

CHAPTER 20

I drove home. The darkness outside matched my mood. I parked on the pad behind my house and walked in the back door. Gloria padded out of the living room to greet me. Her beautiful cheery face faded into a look of concern as she saw me. "What's wrong?"

The only answer I could muster was a shake of my head. I got a bottle of whiskey from my kitchen cabinets, poured a generous amount into a glass, and filled the rest with ice and soda. I took a long drink and only stopped when the alcohol made my throat burn. It felt like a mild penance for my failure. Before I could repeat the process, Gloria grabbed my wrist. A little bit of liquid sloshed out of the glass and splashed onto the countertop. "What's going on?"

"She's dead," I said.

"What?" A look of dawning horror spread over Gloria's features. "You mean Ashleigh?"

"Of course I mean Ashleigh." Her hand fell away from my arm, and I capitalized by downing the rest of the drink.

"What are you going to do now?" Gloria asked.

"This," I said, pointing to the bourbon and soda bottles.

"You're going to stand there and drink?"

"I figure I'll sit down at some point. Either voluntarily or not." I refilled the glass with the same mixture as before. "To failure," I said as I raised it before taking a long draught. My throat felt like I'd just downed a mug of lava, and stars swam in front of my eyes.

Gloria opened the fridge and set a bottle of water down beside my ingredients. "At least drink some water, too."

"You think I'm worried about a hangover?"

"I think you will be tomorrow when you wake up and realize you need to get back to work." Gloria stood with her arms crossed, staring at me.

I smirked. "Is this tough love?"

"It's love," she said. "I know you feel awful now, but you won't later, and you'll want to get back on the horse."

I downed some more whiskey and soda. "I'm not sure how well I could sit on a horse right now." The kitchen began to make minor movements as if tilting on a very shallow axis.

Gloria took the glass from my hand and set it on the counter. She wrapped me in a tight hug. "It's all right," she whispered into my ear. "You did what you could."

"It wasn't enough," I said as I embraced her. "Nothing I did made a difference."

"You can try again tomorrow." Her hand rubbed my back between my shoulder blades.

"The task force can try again. I'm done. They don't need me."

"Don't decide anything tonight," she said. "You're upset and already half-drunk. Think about it in the morning." Gloria gave me a final squeeze and held herself at arm's length. "I'm going to bed. I think you need some time to process everything. Don't be too hard on yourself."

"I won't," I said. "I might even drink some water."

"I love you," she said, and she pulled me in for a kiss. "Whether you catch the bad guys or not."

"I love you, too."

She squeezed my hand and left the kitchen. Her footfalls trailed upstairs a few seconds later. I looked at my half-full glass. "Fifty percent doesn't cut it," I said, adding equal parts booze and soda to top it off again. "Sometimes, a hundred percent doesn't, either." I took a long pull and set it back down. The kitchen moved a little more now. I eyed the water bottle as it appeared to sway on the counter. "What the hell?" I twisted the lid off and drained half of it in a single drink. It didn't improve the room titling, but it did feel good going down. I guzzled the rest and grabbed another bottle from the fridge.

Then I refilled my whiskey and soda and carried both drinks to the couch. Might as well sit down on my own while I still could.

* * *

"RISE AND SHINE," I heard, and it shook off the top layers of sleep.

Then light flooded the room. I put my arm over my eyes. "What the hell?"

"Get up," Rich said.

"Piss off." I turned away from the glare and realized I lay on the couch. I must've fallen asleep on it the night before. An empty water bottle sat next to a glass with a couple fingers of melted-ice water in it. "How'd you get in here, anyway?"

"I have a key."

"Note to self . . . change the locks."

"How would your ghost protocol work, then? He said. I groaned. Rich insisted. "Come on. Time to get moving." I sat up. The light was still too intense, so I reached back and adjusted the blinds. "You hung over?"

"I don't think so," I said. "Gloria insisted I drink some water. I think I drained two bottles."

"She has enough sense for both of you."

"What time is it, anyway?"

"Almost eight."

"For fuck's sake," I said. "Why are you bellowing at me so early?"

"It's a new day," Rich said, dropping into a recliner. "Your time to wallow in self-pity is over."

"I wasn't *wallowing* in self-pity. I was indulging in it."

"Whatever. Go get a shower and wake up. I'll make coffee and breakfast."

"You?"

Rich spread his hands. "I've lived alone for years. You think I can't cook?"

"Fine," I said. I braced myself on the arm of the couch and slowly made it to my feet. The living room stood still, which was an improvement over the previous night. I'd never been in an earthquake, but it must have been similar to staring at the furniture while drunk. "Make sure the coffee's strong."

"Yes, sir," Rich said in his best British accent, which wasn't very good. "Very good, sir."

I dragged myself upstairs. Gloria lay sleeping, one shapely leg sticking out from under the sheet. She didn't let me wallow last night. Left to my own devices, I would have. She made sure I kept the big picture in mind. "Sometimes, I feel I don't deserve you," I whispered. She remained asleep.

I ran the water hot and got into the shower.

* * *

TWENTY MINUTES LATER, after inhaling a bunch of hot steam and scrubbing the whiskey out of my pores, I got dressed. Gloria remained asleep in the exact same pose as when I walked into the bedroom. I put my clothes on quietly and padded downstairs.

Rich sat at the kitchen table drinking a cup of coffee. I poured myself one before I surveyed the breakfast spread.

While I'd been upstairs, Rich cooked turkey bacon, made toast, chopped strawberries, and fried half a dozen eggs. "If you didn't get here so early, I'd suggest you come by more often."

"Don't get used to it," my cousin said, grinning over the top of his mug.

I speared two eggs, a couple strips of bacon, one piece of toast, and enough strawberries to fill the rest of my plate. Rich's held only crumbs. "Started without me, I see."

"I didn't know how long you'd need to wash the cheap liquor out of your pores."

"The fine people of Lynchburg, Tennessee, would disagree with your assessment of their chief export."

"Whatever," Rich said. He leaned forward, and I knew the conversation would now shift to business mode. "We still have work to do."

I shook my head. "*You* have work to do."

"You're a part of this task force, too."

"Can my official resignation wait until after breakfast?" I said. "These are good eggs."

"You can't quit now," Rich said.

"Sure I can. The people who hired me need to identify their daughter's body and plan her funeral. You can't fail any more spectacularly than I did. Your task force doesn't need me."

Rich rolled his eyes, but rather than engaging in the back-and-forth, he poured himself more coffee. I wolfed down an egg during his absence. Leaving two for Gloria would be difficult. When my cousin came back, he picked up the conversation as if he'd never left. "All hands on deck, remember?"

"My comment stands," I said.

Rich stared at me for a few seconds. "Did your lacrosse teams win a title every year?"

"No, but no one died if we didn't get a trophy."

"Welcome to failing in this job," Rich said. "Sometimes, you'll do everything right, and you still won't solve the case, and someone still dies. It sucks. It isn't fair, and it makes you feel like shit. I know. But you have to dust yourself off and get back on the horse." He paused. I remained silent. "Don't do it for me. Don't even do it for yourself. Do it for Violet. Do it for the next girl, because there *will* be one if we don't get to the bottom of this. It'd be nice to have your help with it."

I finished the other egg and ate some strawberries. "I'll think about it."

"Don't think too long," Rich said. He polished off his coffee, set the mug on the table, and stood. "I'll see you in the squadroom."

"Aren't we optimistic?" I said.

"It beats the alternative," Rich said. He walked out and closed the front door quietly as he left. Optimism did beat the alternative. I wished I could summon some.

I DRANK a second cup of coffee, then brewed another pot. Gloria should be waking up soon. The smell of my cooking usually roused her from her slumber. Perhaps I was a better chef than Rich. Maybe the java aromas wafting upstairs would get her moving. I eyed the remaining two eggs, remembered my self-restraint, and instead ate a piece of toast.

Like clockwork, Gloria's feet hit the hardwood floor next to the bed. A few minutes later, she came downstairs. She wore a T-shirt which barely reached her waist and shorts not appropriate for leaving the house. This was a bigger test of my resolve. If she sashayed to me and sat on my lap, I wouldn't think about the case again until noon. Instead, she paused at my seat long enough to kiss me good morning and poured herself a mug of coffee.

"Feeling better this morning?" Gloria said as she sat next to me at the table. She took in the remains of the breakfast spread, which consisted of the two eggs I'd reserved for her, a couple strips of turkey bacon, two pieces of toast, and a handful of berries. "Rich made a nice feast."

"He's all right," I said. "Thanks for putting up with me last night. I'm sure I wasn't much fun to deal with."

"You weren't." Gloria smiled. "You're going to have bad days. We all do. I hope you don't run for the bourbon every time it happens, though."

"This was the worst I've felt on a case. Every lead I thought I had turned out to be nothing, and Ashleigh died, anyway." Anger rose in me as I thought about it. I hoped we didn't dwell on it.

Gloria picked up the last plate and added the remaining food to it. "I should probably heat the eggs." She shrugged. Gloria almost never cooked, and her kitchen incompetence would summon the fire department one of these days. I tried to let her do as little as possible. Thirty seconds with the microwave was probably okay. She cut an egg, took a bite, and remained in her chair. "What are you going to do now?"

"I don't know," I said.

"I heard Rich giving you the pep talk earlier. Did it work?"

Now, it was my turn to shrug. "I'm sure the people who hired me are done with me. The task force doesn't need me hanging around." I didn't say anything. Neither did Gloria. She cut more of her egg, ate it, and watched me. She knew I couldn't resist the pull of the case, and she was waiting me out, letting me come to the conclusion on my own. How did I get such a smart girlfriend? "I think I'll take a fresh look at everything. Good place to start . . . see if I'm going to stay involved."

"Don't let me keep you, then." Gloria smiled again and

sipped her coffee. I grinned in spite of myself and took my mug down the hall to my home office. Driving somewhere else to work would feel too official. I didn't know what I'd be doing yet. Much easier to sort matters with a short jaunt of fifteen steps.

I started with Ashleigh. The details of the case didn't matter right now. I failed, and I didn't need to examine my shortcomings the morning after trying to drown them in a glass of whiskey and soda. We all felt the disappearances were related somehow. Logic meant the girls were related in some way, too. It needed to be a non-obvious factor. Plenty of pretty blonde seventeen-year-old girls across the state of Maryland were perfectly safe this morning. Why these four?

While I can get into a great many records illegally, being a private investigator allows me to access them legitimately. I stuck with the legal means for now. Ashleigh was born on March third seventeen years and two months ago. Birth records showed she entered the world at St. Joseph's Hospital. Her birth certificate was interesting, however—both Ashleigh and Karen were listed only as Jane Doe. No father's name appeared.

Karen had been young when Ashleigh was born. Maybe she didn't want the father to know she'd been pregnant. Or maybe her family wouldn't let her get an abortion. Seventeen years ago, getting pregnant at seventeen or eighteen was a bigger stigma than it would be today. I checked Violet Graham next.

She was also born on March third, though a few hours after Ashleigh. St. Joseph's saw to her birth as well. I pulled up the birth certificate and did a double take. Exactly like on Ashleigh's, both mother and newborn were listed only as Jane Doe, and no father had been recorded.

It couldn't be a coincidence. I also dug into Trisha Lange and Brittany O'Connor. Their birth records were the same. All four came into the world anonymously to mothers noted only as Jane

Doe and unlisted fathers. So far, they had been abducted in birth order starting on the first of March. What the hell did this mean?

I called Rich. "Back to work?" he said.

"I found something. I'm not sure what to make of it, though."

"What do you mean?"

"These girls are definitely connected," I said. "I finally know how. Now, we just have to figure out what to do."

CHAPTER 21

Before I drove to the precinct, I called St. Joseph's Hospital. After navigating an insipid automated system and being redirected a few times, I finally reached someone whose name I didn't catch. Whoever she was, she didn't want to transfer me right away. In a pleasant voice, the lady established she worked in administration for the labor and delivery unit. I introduced myself as a PI working with the police. "I don't think I've ever spoken to a private investigator before."

"It's all right," I said. "I try to avoid it, too."

She was silent for a second before continuing. Not everyone possesses a sense of humor. "What can I help you with today, Mister . . . Ferguson, was it?"

"Yes. I'm wondering about some babies born in your hospital a little over seventeen years ago. Their birth certificates were . . . unusual. I'd like to know how widespread the practice was."

"Tell me what you mean."

"The mothers were all young," I said. "Seventeen or eighteen. On the birth certificates, no fathers' names were recorded, and the mothers and their babies were all listed as Jane Does."

"Yes," she said. "We still do this today, though probably not as often."

"When would you do it?"

"The mother can request it. If she's eighteen, that is. Otherwise, her parents can request it. Sometimes, they decide to do it out of shame. Other times, it's to protect themselves and their children."

"From the fathers, I presume?"

"Yes," she said. "If a father is listed, he gets certain rights. It's possible these young women don't want those men around."

"You're talking about cases of sexual assault?" I said.

"Sometimes. Not always. When were the babies born?"

"Early March."

"That's probably when we do this the most," she said. She offered no further explanation. Clearly, I should have known the information sooner.

"Why?" I asked when no reason was forthcoming.

"What happens nine months before early March?" she said in a patient tone, like a teacher steering me to an answer right in front of me.

"If my calendar math is right, it would be the first part of June. Graduations, I guess."

"Yes. That and proms, both for juniors and seniors. Girls wind up pregnant after a night of partying and dancing, and they don't always feel good about it."

"And as a Catholic hospital," I said, "there are certain services you don't perform."

"Right," she said. "If a girl comes here, she's having the baby. We can take some steps to protect her, though."

"How do these anonymous birth certificates pass muster later? I can't imagine you could apply for a passport as Jane Doe."

"They can be reconciled. We maintain a paper system in cases like this, so it's never exposed on the Internet. Usually, these Jane Does come in with their parents as teenagers and resolve it all."

"Do you know if other hospitals do this, too?" I asked.

"Sure," she said. "I can't tell you about their system. They may not do it the same way we do."

I wondered how many babies were born as John or Jane Doe in late winter and early spring. The birth certificate wouldn't be foolproof, however. Someone could notice a young woman is pregnant or see her with a baby sometimes after the birth. The families would need to take extra steps. I would need to look into whether they had. "I think this will help us a lot," I said. "Thanks for your time."

"Glad to be of assistance," she said.

We hung up, and I did a little more digging. I would have a nice bit of information to take to the task force.

POLICE DEPARTMENTS LOVE PAPERWORK. One could make an uncharitable argument and posit it's what they're best at. The BPD was no exception. Understanding their love of dead trees, I took printouts of the information I'd gathered with me. Rich and King were not in the squadroom but in Leon Sharpe's proper office upstairs. One-stop shopping. I knocked, and Sharpe waved me in.

Despite his rank, Sharpe did not have a large office. Two people could fit, but three became tight, never mind the lack of a third guest chair. "We're strategizing," the captain said.

"Hang on," I said. "I think I left my buzzword bingo card in my pocket. Can you talk about synergy while I look for it?"

Rich inclined his head toward the printouts while Sharpe rolled his eyes. "What do you have?"

"An action plan to mitigate our synergistic deficiencies."

"What the hell do you mean?"

"I'm not sure, really," I admitted. "It just sounds like something to help you win buzzword bingo." I tossed the papers onto Sharpe's desk. "I started from the beginning. Birth. We kept presuming these cases were related somehow, but we only looked at the abductions and the obvious factors." Rich passed sets of sheets to King and Sharpe. They studied them, and I knew they saw the important parts when their eyes went wide.

"They were born within a couple days of each other," King said. "All in the same hospital."

"All anonymously," Sharpe added. "How often does this happen?"

"According to the woman I spoke to at the hospital, more than you might think. It's not common, but early March is a popular time."

"Why?"

"A fair number of babies get made on prom and graduation nights," I said. "If you were a teenaged girl, you might not want to see the guy you went to the dance with for the rest of your life." I gestured to the papers. "So you become a Jane Doe."

"People still see you, though," Rich said. "You'd have to become a hermit or move."

"Check the last page. All four young women had their learner's permits at the time, so the DMV knew who they were. They all filed change of address paperwork before their daughters were born."

Rich's brows creased as he looked at the data on his lap. "Four girls, all born in the same place and around the same time. All to unidentified mothers. Someone knows who they are."

"Maybe," King said. "It's also possible whoever's doing this is looking for someone."

"I'm with you," I told King. "I think we're dealing with a killer who's hunting for a specific girl."

"Why?" Sharpe said.

"I don't know yet."

"How does he know he hasn't found the right one?"

"Maybe he has," I said. "Trisha could have been the first. The rest could be him covering his tracks and trying to get us to spin our wheels."

"I don't think so," Rich said. He flipped through all the pages again. "This is a lot of trouble to go through for a false flag operation. How did you find the birth records?"

"I searched the state database for each of the girls."

"Could you look around by other criteria?" Rich asked.

I shrugged. "I didn't try, but I don't see why not. It's a database, after all."

"You think someone looked for girls born around a certain time?" Sharpe said.

"I do," Rich confirmed. "Maybe he even suspected they'd be Jane Does."

"Whoever it is knows how hospitals do this, then." I started to say something else but stopped. Knowledge of hospitals . . . each of the three girls' bodies had some kind of injection hole. "What about the needle mark we've seen on each girl?"

"Nothing on Trisha's tox screen," King said. "We haven't gotten the other ones back yet."

"You think it's someone who works for a hospital?" Sharpe asked.

"It's a reasonable guess," I said. "We know four girls were abducted, but we've heard nothing about a struggle. Maybe they were all injected with a sedative and just carried away."

Rich shook his head. "Not in the arm. If you're going to stick someone before you grab them, you'd do it in the neck. We haven't seen anything there."

When you're big in biotech research, you take a few precautions. Shauna Sullivan's words from my office came back to me now. "What if those weren't injection sites?"

"What would they be, then?" Sharpe asked.

"Maybe someone drew the girls' blood."

Rich's head bobbed, slowly at first, then with a little more speed. "I like it. If you're looking for someone specific, DNA testing doesn't lie."

"You can't kidnap a girl and send her blood to Ancestry, though," King said. "Even ignoring the illegality, you'd never get the results in time."

"What if you could test it yourself?"

Sharpe leaned forward in his chair. "You have someone in mind, C.T.?"

"Maybe," I said. "She's a biotech executive of some sort. Her company could certainly turn a DNA test around quickly."

"What's her motive?"

"No idea."

Sharpe looked at each of us in turn. "Find one."

CHAPTER 22

If Shauna Sullivan—or whoever the killer was— could access birth records, they could find any girls who fit the pattern they wanted. I'd only searched for the four I knew about. How many more would there be? The database was kludgy, but I entered the parameters I wanted while only complaining a little about the design. I sought girls born within a few days either side of March 4 seventeen years ago, listed as Jane Doe, born to another Jane Doe, and with no father's name recorded.

After a second or two of crunching, I saw seven results. "Shit," I said. "There are more."

"What?" Rich wheeled his chair to where I sat. "Violet isn't the last one?"

"If they find whatever they're looking for, I suppose she could be. If not, there are two more on the list." One remained in Maryland while the other lived out of state. I pointed to the top of the screen. "Plus one who came before Trisha."

Rich frowned. "There was no case before hers."

"You searched the entire state?"

"I don't think so," he said. "Norton didn't mention another before Trisha. I guess he was unaware, too."

"Must be a remote county, then."

"I'll look." Rich read the name under his breath, scooted back to his own desk, and keyed it in. "She lives in Cumberland."

"It satisfies the remote requirement." Situated in Allegany County, Cumberland sat about two and a half hours west of Baltimore. "The sheriff's office take a report?"

"Yeah," Rich said. "Three days before Trisha went missing. The timeline fits, too." He worked the keyboard a little more. "She looks enough like the rest."

I craned my neck to see his monitor. The girl on the screen could have fit in nicely with the other four. She wore her long blonde hair straight, and her bright green eyes leapt off the monitor. "Someone needs to talk to the parents," I said.

"We also have the other two to worry about," Rich said. "The timeline seems to be about three days, but we can't presume it won't accelerate at some point." He stood. "Wait here. I'm going to talk to Norton. We'll probably need his help on this one."

Rich walked away to make the call. I double-checked my query of the state's database. No more results popped up. None of this told us why these girls were selected, of course. If they were DNA tested, what story were their double helixes supposed to tell? Rich strode back and interrupted my thoughts. "Let's roll," he said. "Norton's going to work on the one out of state. You and I are going to Cumberland."

* * *

WHILE WE WERE en route in an unmarked BPD car, Rich mentioned an Allegany County deputy would meet us at the parents' house. "I don't see the point," I said.

"The deputy being there helps allay jurisdictional concerns."

I waved a hand at his comment. "The only people who care about jurisdiction are the ones being investigated. The parents will be happy someone's paying attention. I mean I don't see the point of this trip."

"Why not?" Rich asked.

"Either the sheriff's office sat on it, or they reported it, and no one thought it mattered. Either way, I think we're going to run into a dead-end here."

"It could be useful. This was the first abduction. By now, whoever the killer is has done four of them and has learned and refined the process. The first one might have been sloppy."

"How long ago did it happen?" I said. "I'm fine with chasing down a lead. I just think this isn't going to go anywhere."

Rich changed lanes to get around a slow pickup truck. The V8 in the police-issued Charger lacked some of the snarl of Rich's Camaro. "If nothing else, it's closure for the family."

"How? 'Hi, we think your daughter's dead because two other girls are. We don't have a body, though. Have a nice day!' Doesn't sound like closure to me."

"You're just a ray of fucking sunshine today," Rich said.

"Jack Daniel's really brings out my optimism," I said.

We rode most of the remaining miles in silence. Rich and I made a similar excursion before almost two years ago. We drove to Garrett County—the only one in Maryland west of our current destination—to look into the suspicious suicide of one of Rich's old army buddies. Like on this trip, our conversation turned sour at some point, and we both felt it was easier to not try and resume it. Rich and I have made strides in our relationship since my return from Hong Kong, but we'd always been a distant sort of close, and it manifested in moments like these.

Cumberland used to be a bustling town. Industry left over time, however, and the population shrank along with it. Today, the area was among the poorest in the country. I'd enjoyed my few trips to the area, however. The residents were always pleasant, and downtown Cumberland enjoyed a quaint, charming feel.

Brick buildings lined both sides of Baltimore Street as we drove through.

On the other side of the downtown district, Rich steered the car onto a side road, and we parked in front of a small two-story house. A sheriff's office car sat across the street, and a middle-aged deputy exited as we got out of the Charger. "Welcome to Cumberland," he said with a hint of a southern accent. His name tag identified him as Dunn.

"Thanks," Rich said, and we all shook hands. "You catch the case?"

"No. Deputy Gray investigated when the parents reported their daughter missing. They're frustrated, though, so now I'm handling it."

"Any new developments?" I asked.

Dunn shook his head. "Wish I could say yes. This has been cold from the start. No parent wants to hear it, though."

We approached the house and entered when a man and woman answered the door. Ken and Emily Wells reported their daughter Patti missing almost two weeks ago. Emily's eyes were puffy, but for the most part, they looked angry and frustrated. Both leaned forward on their loveseat when they talked to us. "Our younger daughter Jenny is upstairs," Ken said. "We're trying not to let her get her hopes up again." He looked to be in his early forties with wisps of silver appearing in his dark hair. He knew his way around the gym, and these factors plus his rigid posture made me wonder if he was former military. Emily was an attractive blonde and young like the other moms.

"We're looking into other disappearances we think are related," Rich said. "Can you tell us what happened?"

Ken rolled his eyes. He was about to object when Emily held up a hand. "Patti volunteered at the local pharmacy," she said. "She delivers prescriptions. They can't afford to pay anyone to do it, and she needs the service hours for graduation. She usually rides her bike to work and then walks to wherever she has to make a delivery."

"Where's the pharmacy?"

"Just off the main drag downtown. She went out on a delivery and didn't come back." Emily's voice cracked. Ken squeezed her hand, and she took a deep breath before continuing. "The pharmacist called us and said she hadn't returned. He thought maybe she came home early."

"We talked to the last people she delivered medicine to," Dunn added. "Old couple. They saw her walk away and don't know anything else."

"This is a pretty small city," I said. "Wouldn't an outsider or a strange vehicle get noticed?"

"Not really," Dunn said. "We still get a good bit of tourism here. There'd been a music festival the weekend before . . . Spring Country. Emily went missing on a Monday."

"What about Emily's phone?" Rich asked before I could.

"They found it behind the pharmacy," Ken said.

"Prints?"

"Only hers."

"We did all this work already," Dunn said, sounding a little defensive.

"Four other girls have disappeared since," I said. Dunn might've known, but the wide-eyed looks I got from Ken and Emily told me it was news to them. "The first three are dead. We're trying to figure out who did it before another family has to bury a child."

"At least they have a body to bury." Ken glared at Dunn, who couldn't meet the angry father's eyes. Emily turned away and cried quietly.

"Did Patti have a computer or tablet in her room?" I asked.

Emily wiped her eyes. "She had a Chromebook, but I don't

think she used it much. She did a lot on her phone. Plus, there are computers at her school."

I doubted I'd uncover much, so I let it go. "The state police are involved, too," Rich said. "We're treating all the cases as related. You'll know if we find anything."

Ken nodded and avoided looking at Deputy Dunn. "Closure would be nice."

We left, and Dunn didn't have a lot to say before climbing back into his car.

* * *

ON THE DRIVE back down I-68, we called Norton. He told us he'd talked to the Georgia State Police and apprised them of the situation. They would handle it from there. I wondered what it all meant, but Norton didn't have a lot of answers. "It's up to them," he said. "I hope they'd recommend protective custody, but I can't control their processes." The answer made sense, even if it felt unsatisfying.

Once we picked up I-70 and passed Frederick, Rich called the parents of the next local girl on the list. Nancy Meyers lived with her father Allen, and her mother no longer lived with them. Allen sounded frosty at the lack of information over the phone, but he told us we could stop by. They lived in Linthicum not far from BWI Airport. "You think the threat of a plane falling out of the sky holds down property values?" I asked Rich.

He shot me a puzzled look. "I have no idea."

"I don't think I'd want to live where the chance of a seven-thirty-seven crashing into my backyard was much above zero."

"I'm sure you and Allen can have a nice real estate chat," Rich said. "He sounds so warm and friendly."

"Let's hope he's cooperative."

Later, we arrived in a townhouse community in Linthicum.

All were two stories above street level and differentiated only by window style and the colors of the shutters and doors. With no garages or driveways, we found a spot on the curb about three houses down. Rich knocked on the door. A man of about forty who looked like he'd been sucking a lemon since high school answered the door. We both showed our badges, and he let us in.

Allen Meyers sat with his daughter on a shopworn couch. It matched the rest of the furniture and the house, which needed a thorough cleaning above all else. Nancy, like the other girls, was pretty and wore her blonde hair long. She must have inherited her looks from her mother. I hoped she got her personality from mom's side of the punnet square, too. "What's this all about?" he asked in a gruff voice.

"Before we get into all of it, I want to ask about your mother," I said to Nancy.

"She's out of the picture," Allen said.

"I wasn't talking to you."

"This is my house, and—"

"She went crazy," Nancy said. "It was a few years ago. I still see her on occasion, but she lives in Pennsylvania now."

"Happy?" Allen said.

"How old is she?" I asked, ignoring him.

"Thirty-five," Nancy said.

"What the hell is all this about?" Allen pounded the arm of the couch. "You can't barge into a man's house and interrogate his daughter."

"Seems more productive than jawing with you," I pointed out.

Rich held up his hand as Allen started to object. "The point is we're working on a case involving five other girls so far." He inclined his head toward Nancy. "They all look a lot like you, and their mothers are all young."

"What do you mean . . . five young girls so far?" Allen said.

For the first time, he sounded like a rational human being and concerned father. "Is Nancy in danger?"

"Yes," I said. Rich shot me a quick glare. I maintained our wordless sniping with a small shrug of my left shoulder.

"What happened to them?"

"Four are dead," Rich said. Allen's expression never changed, but Nancy's eyes widened, and she clutched a throw pillow to her chest. "The fifth is still missing. We're working with a task force, but we don't have much yet."

No one said anything for a few seconds. Allen broke the silence first. "What do you recommend?"

"Protective custody," Rich said. "You'd go to a safe house until we catch whoever's responsible."

"How long?" Nancy asked.

"There's no way to know. Hopefully no more than a few days."

"What about school?"

"I'm sure you could make up the work," Rich said.

Allen shook his head. "No. We're not doing protective custody."

"Mister Meyers, this is a serious matter. Four girls are dead. If we had them all stand with Nancy, most people couldn't pick her out of the lineup. They got kidnapped, and about three days later, someone shot them in the head."

"And you got no leads?"

"We're working on it," Rich said.

"Fancy way of saying you got nothing."

"Dad . . . maybe they're right," Nancy said.

"No. I'll keep an eye on you. I got guns. No one's taking my daughter."

"You can't stay with her all the time," I said. "There's no pattern to how the girls disappeared."

"I said no," Allen insisted. "We don't want your protective custody."

Further attempts at persuasion proved futile. We left a couple minutes later. Nancy looked disappointed when Allen slammed the door in our faces. Our message resonated with her but failed to make a dent in her stubborn father. "You can't force it on them," Rich said when we drove away.

"I know. It's frustrating."

"We'd better solve this quickly. If our kidnappers don't want to drive to Georgia, Nancy only has a day or two."

"Can we ask Anne Arundel County to check on them?" I said.

"Sure. It'll be up to them. If they have the manpower, if they want in on the task force . . . welcome to police department politics."

"Maybe I'll try talking to Nancy separately."

"What good would it do?" Rich said.

"Politics weigh your system down," I said. "This is why people come to me."

"You have some fancy tech to keep her safe?"

"As a matter of fact, I think I do."

* * *

RICH and I chatted about my idea. We'd been too late to try it on Ashleigh Swain or Violet Graham, but time remained to protect Nancy Meyers . . . so long as we could bypass her father, who paired his idiocy with a pronounced stubborn streak. As usual, Rich professed uncertainly, despite my string of success in these matters. "It would be better to put all this to bed," he said.

"Sure," I concurred. "If we can't, though, we should use it as a fallback."

We crossed into Baltimore. "I want to stop at the precinct and check in with the task force," Rich said.

"If only we carried devices in our pockets to allow us to talk to them remotely." He shot me a sidelong glance. "Someone should invent the mobile phone."

"I prefer doing some things in person. Sharpe does, too. I guess we're old school."

"OK, Boomer," I said.

"You know I'm technically a millennial like you," Rich said.

"From the grayer and more dour end of the spectrum."

"Still . . . same generation."

"No doubt a source of great personal shame," I said.

Rich glanced in the rearview and frowned. "We all carry our own burdens."

I heard the high-pitched whine of a motorcycle engine behind us. Rich's eyes flicked from the road to the driver's side mirror to the one centered in the windshield. "I think we've picked up a tail," he said. Rich flipped the red-and-blue lights on and gunned the engine. The few cars ahead of us moved to the side. I turned in my seat and looked behind us. A second motor-cycle joined the first. Both were crotch rockets driven by helmeted men in T-shirts and shorts.

The one closer to us pulled a pistol. "Get low," I said as I slumped in my seat. Rich did the same. Gunshots boomed from behind us. The rear window exploded, showering the passenger compartment with broken glass. My pulse raced like the Charg-er's engine. Rich got onto the radio and reported the situation, requesting immediate backup and a helicopter. I drew my 9 MM.

"Put the goddamn gun away," Rich barked. "We're not getting into a shootout."

"You abide by your BPD regulations," I said. "I'll try to make sure we get out of this alive."

Traffic grew heavier ahead of us. We'd be easier targets, to say nothing of the risk of bullets hitting innocent people nearby. Rich swung a hard right. As a Camaro owner, he was used to the behavior of rear-wheel-drive cars, and the back end stepping out didn't faze him. "I'm going to try and get us away from so many other people," he said as if I didn't understand what he was doing. "This doesn't mean you can start shooting."

"Yeah, yeah." I used the passenger's mirror to monitor the motorcycles. Both took the turn and accelerated behind us. "Here they come again." Both riders brandished pistols now. One zoomed up on the left. Rich steered the Charger in his direction, and the rider backed off before running into a parked car. It didn't look bad enough to count him out. "Where's the backup?"

"A few minutes away," he said. I heard chatter over the police radio, but it rarely made sense to me. It was the audio equivalent of a doctor's handwriting. Rich took a sudden right, then a left to get onto the Jones Falls Expressway, which was the fancy name for I-83 within the city limits. The move would eliminate parked cars and bystanders.

"Good call," I said. Other cars pulled over on either side as we sped along the highway. Both bikes remained in pursuit. The downside of being on the open road was the lack of things to ram a bike into. With so many fewer buildings, vehicles, and people around, however, shooting back became a more realistic option. One of the bikes veered to our right and zoomed toward my side. Rich fed the engine more gas, but the bike was quicker. The rider fired a few shots which blasted into the rear of the car.

"You all right?" Rich asked.

"So far." I took a deep breath to try and control my spiking heartbeat. With my lungs empty, I leaned out the window and shot at the driver. He backed off and veered behind us again.

"Goddammit, put the gun away," Rich said.

"It's open on the right," I said. "I'm not going to hit anyone."

The other bike approached on the left. Rich jerked the wheel toward it, and the rider eased off the throttle. At the same time, the other sped up on my side. I leaned out and squeezed off three shots. One hit the bike somewhere, which spewed smoke into the air. The motorcycle lost speed. "I hit the bike," I said. In the mirror, I watched it limp onto the exit ramp for 28th Street. "I think we're down to one."

"I see a couple marked cars coming up behind us," Rich said. He weaved between lanes to keep the rider off-balance. The guy kept his gun out but didn't attempt a shot. Sirens approached from the rear. Rich eased off the throttle to allow them a chance to catch up. "Don't shoot now."

I kept the nine in my lap. The rider maneuvered to Rich's side and fired a couple shots. One shredded the air between Rich and me to blow a hole in the windshield. My heart raced anew, and I felt my throat go dry.

The BPD cars in pursuit closed the gap. The rider must have noticed because he slowed, veered hard to the right, and took the ramp for Falls Road. "Both gone," Rich said. He got back on the radio and reported where the bikes got off, requesting the helicopter to pursue them. One of the marked cars took the Falls Road exit, also.

Rich pulled the Charger to the side of the road. Two other police cars braked hard behind him. "You're all right?" he asked.

"I might need to find a cardiologist later," I said, "but I'm good. You?"

He nodded. "Yeah. I think we've pissed some people off."

"Just means we're on the right track." Now we only needed to decipher the aggrieved party.

CHAPTER 23

WE WENT OVER WHAT HAPPENED WITH THE OFFICERS AT the scene. It took a few minutes for my hands to stop shaking from the adrenaline of the chase. The uniforms peppered us—me more than my cousin—with questions but deferred to Rich when his answers supported mine. We left out the part about me firing back. The cars which broke off to pursue the motorcycles reported finding only a damaged bike so far.

At the precinct, Rich and I plopped into Leon Sharpe's guest chairs. King joined us a moment later and stood leaning on the door he closed behind himself. "Everybody all right?" the captain asked as an opener.

"We're OK," Rich said, looking to me for confirmation. I provided it with a head bob. "I don't think the glass got us when the windows blew out."

"So far, we haven't caught either guy on the bikes. Any idea who they were?"

"No," I said, "but we must be getting close to figuring this out."

Sharpe steepled his fingers. "You're presuming whoever's behind the kidnappings went after you today."

"Kidnappings and murders. Of course I'm presuming it. Who else would it be?"

"I'm sure Rich is working other cases."

"Sure," my cousin said. "King and I have a few on the board. But Captain, I can't think of one where we'd get chased by two guys on bikes."

"I'm with Rich," King added.

I spread my hands. "There you go. Either the Red Cross has gotten really aggressive asking for blood, or our mastermind sent these two assholes after us. They aren't the first who tried to derail our investigation."

"Fine," Sharpe said. "I admit it's likely. The issue is we're no closer to figuring out who it is. You still think it's the Sullivan woman?"

Rich nodded. "She's the best fit. We don't know her personal finances, but she runs a successful biomedical company. We can presume she has the means."

"Have you found a motive yet?"

Rich offered no answer, so I picked up his slack. "Not yet. I keep coming back to her father getting bought out by Vincent Davenport years ago."

Sharpe's brows pulled down as he pondered it. "You think an old business buyout is causing girls to get killed today?"

"People have been murdered for less, Leon."

"We have to find the connection, then. You think you can give your notes to Rich?"

"Sure, but why?"

"You got shot at tonight," Sharpe said as if I needed the reminder. "I like you, but you're a civilian. Go home and get some rest. Come back tomorrow, and we'll see where we stand."

"What? You're sending me home?"

"It's been a rough day. You don't get shot at all the time, and—"

"To be fair," I said, "neither does anyone else in this room."

"He's got you there, Captain," King said from the door.

Sharpe closed his eyes and sucked in a deep breath. "Go home, and we'll see you tomorrow. Leave Rich what you know about the buyout."

"Fine," I said. "Whatever." I got up, sat at the BPD laptop I'd been using, and fired off an email to Rich with what I knew and suspected about the D&S buyout. When I finished, I prompted him to check his email. "I guess I'll go home and serve detention."

"You get in trouble a lot in high school?" Rich asked.

I shrugged. "Not really. When I did, though, at least it was for stuff I understood . . . not bullshit like this."

Rich didn't have anything to say. Neither did I, so I left.

I DROVE HOME, parked next to Gloria's coupe, and trudged inside. The first thing I did after tossing my keys down was fetch a pair of beers from the fridge—an IPA for me and some white wheat monstrosity for Gloria. She smiled as I entered the living room, but it faded when she saw my face. I set the brews on the coffee table and sagged onto the sofa beside her. "I'm starting to realize why so many people in my job develop drinking problems."

Gloria patted my knee. "You're stronger than that."

I picked up the IPA and took a long pull. "Here's to weakness."

"Rough day?" Gloria kept her hand on my knee.

"Maybe the roughest so far." I felt more despondent after Ashleigh's murder, but general weariness hit me harder tonight. Maybe this was the aftermath of the adrenaline wearing off. Gloria didn't prompt me, but I recounted the adventure Rich and I experienced driving through the city and up the JFX.

She fortified herself with some beer before replying. "I'm sure it was terrifying." Her grip on my leg tightened. "I get so worried about you on cases like this. You're burning the candle at both ends, and I think it's taking a toll."

"I'm in my prime," I said in protest even though I felt the toll Gloria mentioned.

"You look run down," she said.

"You should see the other guys." I wished someone caught them.

"I'm serious." Gloria took her hand from my leg and put her arm around me. I rested my head on her shoulder. Her body felt warm. "You need to take it easy every once in a while."

"I'm fine like this."

"I'm sure you are," Gloria said. "I know you won't, but maybe your present case is one best left to the professionals."

"It's in their hands tonight," I said. "Leon Sharpe sent me home."

"He's a smart man."

"He has his moments."

We sat quietly on the couch. Gloria stroked my head, and my eyelids grew heavy. "You falling asleep on me?" she said.

"Not trying to."

She tilted her head down and kissed me. "Think you can stay awake a while longer?"

"I suddenly feel much more awake," I said.

Gloria led me upstairs. She nearly ripped all my clothes off and threw me onto the bed. Afterward, we lay close together, my arm draped atop her. After a few days of wallowing in frustration and death, I felt connected to life again. I pulled Gloria closer, and she nuzzled into me. Tomorrow, I would be renewed for whatever we needed to do to bring down Shauna Sullivan or whoever the guilty party was.

Tonight, however, I slept in contentment next to Gloria.

* * *

I WOKE UP BEFORE EIGHT. No texts or calls came in overnight. I operated under the presumption no news was good news. Despite the early hour, I didn't think there was time for a full run, so I went downstairs and did some pushups, crunches, and jumping jacks. With the blood flowing—and coffee brewing—I showered, dressed, and walked downstairs ready to tackle malfeasance in all its forms.

While I ate a quick breakfast of yogurt and fruit, I texted Rich and inquired about any new developments. He didn't answer. Maybe Leon Sharpe sent him home, too. Rich was even more prone to burn the candle at both ends than me, a holdover from his army days. My next message went to Nancy Meyers. *I think you're much more concerned than your dad is. Can you ditch him for a while? I can help you keep yourself safe.*

She texted back right away. *I'm interested, but I don't want protective custody.*

I have a middle ground option. When are you free?

I'll ditch Spanish. Meet me at my house in a half-hour?

I told her I would need about an hour, and she agreed. I gathered a few supplies together, took them to the car, and drove to her townhouse. Despite my being a few minutes early, Nancy was already there. "Come on in," she said, looking up and down her street before closing the door behind us. "What do you have in mind?"

"Your dad can't watch you twenty-four-seven," I said. "No one can. If you don't want to go into protective custody, I understand." I held up the small duffel bag. "I think I have a solution."

"OK," she said, eyeing the bag warily.

"You wear any jewelry?"

"Um . . . sometimes." I pulled a necklace out of the bag.

Nancy stared at it. It was a thumb-sized amber brooch hanging from a slender gold chain. "How's that going to help?"

"By itself, it won't," I said. "This isn't an ordinary necklace, though. The gem isn't real. I can put a GPS tracker, miniature camera, and transmitter in it."

"What good will that do?"

I figured she'd make the connection herself. "The police and I are working to catch whoever's been kidnapping the girls."

"And murdering them," she added, staring at the floor.

I'd hoped not to go down this particular road, but here we were. How did people talk to teenagers every day? "Yes. In the event we don't catch them soon, you could be in danger. This will let us know where you are."

"Won't they just kill me?" Nancy asked.

"How much do you want to know?"

"All of it . . . I guess."

"OK," I said. "After getting abducted, the girls are alive for about three days."

"Why?"

"We're still figuring it out." I dug in the bag and extracted a tiny camera from its protective case. Mounting it into the brooch took time, patience, and tools. Once it was in place, I connected the transmitter to it. The tracker had already been built in. The whole thing got power via a cleverly-hidden micro USB port. I showed Nancy and told her she should charge it overnight. Once I finished setting up the brooch, she slipped it over her head. The chain was a good length for her, though the amber clashed with her current outfit. "You don't think people will question you wearing it?"

"I guess not," she said. "Maybe I can hide it under my shirt most of the time."

"You could, but the camera won't capture anything if it's blocked by fabric."

Nancy frowned at this latest wrinkle. "I'll think it over," she said.

"Good. Let me know if you need anything."

"I will."

I left and headed toward the precinct. With any luck, we would wrap this up before Nancy needed to use the necklace.

* * *

RICH AND KING sat at their desks when I arrived. King looked up from his computer and spread his hands. "No coffee?"

"No breakthroughs?" I asked.

He grunted and went back to his work. "Nothing new has happened," Rich said.

"Did my notes lead you to an epiphany?"

"Did you expect them to?"

"I thought the writing was clear and concise," I said. "Maybe even inspiring in places. It's some of my best work."

Rich rolled his eyes. "It was a perfectly adequate summation. No epiphanies resulted."

"Let's take a stab at it now, then." The station I'd been using was occupied this morning, so I sat at the desk next to King. "Have you seen anything to make you lean toward or away from Shauna Sullivan?"

"No," King said. "She's still our best suspect by default. We don't really have anyone else. The lack of connections between these girls makes it hard."

"There's a connection on some level," I said. "We just haven't found it yet. Whatever it is, let's presume it's important to Shauna Sullivan."

"All right," King said. "Let's ignore the fact they all look similar and focus on age first. They're all young and all born within about two days of each other."

"Their mothers are all young, too," Rich added. "Thirty-five or so today, so they got pregnant at seventeen or eighteen."

"Based on when the girls were born, it would be prom and graduation season," King said.

"End of the school year," I said, "or close to it."

Rich kicked his feet up onto his desk and leaned back in thought. "What else happens at the end of the school year? Programs end. I would think we had a teacher or staffer who was a predator, but the mothers didn't go to the same school. They didn't have any instructors or coaches in common."

"Who else could have been a predator?"

"Administrators?" King asked. "Were they in the same school system?"

"No," I said. "All in Maryland, but they were split between Baltimore and the county."

King smirked. "Could you get into the records?"

"Probably."

"Can we not do it from here?" Rich said in protest.

"Don't worry," I told him. "If anyone stumbles onto us, I'll just say I was you." He crossed his arms. "If I sound self-righteous enough, they'll believe it."

Rich sighed. "Can you do it without getting caught?"

"Have we met?"

"Go for it," King said. "You still have the guest login?"

"Yeah." I entered the credentials and surveyed my tools. The BPD's computer didn't offer me a ton of resources. The good news was the city school system, thanks to federated identities, was inclined to trust a police PC. Like any trust relationship in technology, it could be exploited. I soon gained administrative access on the computer I used. From there, finding the public school system's computers didn't take long.

I knew nothing of how those records were organized or where they might be stored. Fingerprinting the network highlighted all the servers for me. King stood and watched over my shoulder. The only barrier remaining was authentication. While the BPD credentials let me poke around and explore, I couldn't access anything without some form of school system account. "You all follow the same general IT policies?" I asked my detective partners.

"Fuck if I know," King said.

"I think a lot of things are standardized across the city," Rich said. "It's some new initiative."

If so, it could be helpful. Service accounts as their name suggests are created to allow specific operating system functions to run with defined permissions. They're not usually meant for user login, but many enterprises don't forbid the option. I looked at the BPD's file server and noted the nomenclature in use. If the city were standardizing much of its IT operations, this would carry over. I entered the same name on the school system's file server and tried the password I used when I elevated my privileges.

It worked.

"I'm in," I said. King clapped his hands once. Rich maintained a neutral expression. I knew he didn't approve of my methods, but I also knew he wanted to solve this case. It took me a couple minutes to find records by graduation year, then by school. "We're probably catching a break . . . these are digitized."

"We could use one," Rich said.

I pulled up Emily Wells and Melanie Lange, the mothers of the two girls born first. Both received good grades in school. They played sports, participated in clubs and other extracurriculars, and Melanie made the National Honor Society. They shared no common factors, however, until I scrolled down to work study programs.

Both interned at D&S Bakery.

"Hmm," I said, drawing interest from Rich and King. I

ignored their questions and looked at the files for the rest of the mothers. All of them spent time as interns at D&S. Keith Sullivan got bought out under mysterious circumstances seventeen years ago. "Son of a bitch."

"What?" Rich said, leaning in. I pointed to the entry they all shared. He and King looked at each other. "We've been looking at Shauna Sullivan, but the real factor was her father."

"You think he was screwing the interns?" King said.

"It makes sense. He got a big check to walk away from the company, and no one's ever offered a real explanation why."

"How does this tie into all these girls, though?"

"Shauna's looking for her father's illegitimate daughter," Rich said.

I nodded. "With the birth certificates having so little information, they couldn't find the girl the normal route. The old man must have figured she would've been born around a certain time. Maybe he even knew the hospital. There's your candidate pool."

Rich frowned at the screen. "Why now, though?"

"I hear Keith Sullivan's in poor health," I said.

"So they're finding and eliminating an heir?" King asked.

"It's a good theory for now."

"They're killing the girl either way. If she's not the heir, they shoot her. If she were, they'd probably do the same."

"They haven't found her yet, though," Rich said. "They're still looking."

"We need to find Violet," I said. "Whether or not she's Keith Sullivan's daughter, they're going to kill her soon."

CHAPTER 24

LIKE HE ALWAYS DID, ROLLINS ANSWERED MY CALL AS IF HE maintained a constant vigil by the phone. "I've been following the news."

"You're one up on me." I leaned back in the BPD-issued chair I used. The one in my office was much better. "How did the Orioles do last night?"

"You know what I mean," he said.

"Yeah. It's pretty much gone to shit. We have one girl on the clock, another one out of state, and a local one whose father is a piece of work." When Rollins asked what I meant, I realized he missed the bit about figuring out the birth certificates and trying to find whoever was next.

"Good work," he said.

"Thanks. We're working on finding the most recent abductee. The task force rides again."

"You think you'll get to her in time?"

I drew in a long breath. "I hope so. Our track record isn't good. Maybe this one will be different." After spending some quality time with Gloria, optimism pushed away the negativity in my worldview. The sun hadn't set on Violet yet, and the task force worked to make sure it didn't. Practicality tugged at me, however. "Just in case, I'm concerned about the next girl. If we fail here, we have to presume there's going to be one."

"And you're figuring they can't get to the one who's out of state?"

"Either can't get to or will come back to," I said. "It's inefficient to divert the resources down there now."

"Spoken like someone who's planned some operations," Rollins said.

"Sure. I play a mean *Call of Duty*."

He chuckled. "You want me to look in on the local girl?"

"Yes. I'll text you the address. Her name is Nancy, and her father doesn't believe in things like protective custody. I think he has it in his macho head he can keep her safe."

"I take it you don't put a lot of stock in his abilities?"

"No," I said. "He's all talk. Nancy's worried, so she left school early, and I set her up with a GPS tracker."

"You mention I'd be sitting on her?"

I leaned forward again. The chair wobbled too much the longer I reclined. How did people use these every day? "No. I'm sure she won't see you, anyway. What I did gave her some peace of mind."

"All right," Rollins said. "I'll get on it."

"Thanks." We hung up, and I texted him Nancy's address and where she went to school. Maybe today would be the day we got one right.

* * *

RICH TOSSED a stack of index cards onto his desk and scowled at them. "This is crazy," he muttered as he sat.

"What's going on?" I asked.

"We setup a hotline this morning. Anyone with any information about Violet or any of the other girls is encouraged to call. Apparently, quite a few people took the encouragement to heart."

"Is there a reward?"

"If Violet is found as the result of a tip, yes," Rich said. "There's some more legalese in there, but you get the idea."

"If lawyers are involved, it's already ruined." He snorted and nodded in assent. "The problem is people will call about any blonde teenaged girl they see. They'll hope it's Violet, and they can collect the reward."

Rich picked up the cards, fanned them out, and spiked them back onto his desk. "Probably what's happening. King is getting a stack, too. I think some of the uniforms are involved."

"Wow."

"We have to investigate anything seeming like a reasonable tip." He rocked his head back and forth, clearly trying to parrot someone. "O'Malley."

"I'm surprised he's looking for someone whose family didn't make a donation," I said.

"He's not so bad." Rich held up a card. "Here's one from a psychic. You believe this shit?"

"Sadly, I do. Maybe I should go to Crackpots R Us and pick up a divining rod."

Rich worked through his stack while I looked online for any signs of Violet. Her parents were all over the local news, begging anyone with knowledge of their daughter to come forward. It drew the predictable mix of sympathy and mockery in local forums, Facebook groups, and subreddits. Actual clues to the girl's whereabouts were nonexistent, however. By the time I looked up from my unproductive search, King had joined us and conducted his own follow-ups.

"What a crock of shit," he said, slamming the receiver back into the base.

"I know," I said. "I can't believe you guys still have landline phones."

He glared at me for a moment. "People see a blonde girl, and they call the tip line. No chance any of these are Violet. I just talked to some asshole who admitted he reported three girls because they were the right age and had the right hair color."

"It's a waste of time."

From down the hall, Leon Sharpe bellowed for the three of us to come into his temporary office. We packed into the place, and I was the one who lost the game of musical chairs. "I just got a call from the county." Sharpe paused and sighed before continuing. "They got a report about a blonde girl." My stomach clenched.

"Dead?" Rich asked after a few seconds of silence.

"Yeah," Sharpe said. I'd never heard his voice so quiet.

"Violet?"

"She fits the description." He handed Rich a piece of paper. "Get to Timonium. County will wait for you."

We left Sharpe's office in silence, walked to the car, and got underway without saying anything. No words remained. We knew we'd failed again.

"It may not be her," King said after we'd been on the road for a few minutes.

"It's Violet," I said.

"How do you know?"

"Because nothing has gone right. Whoever this is started out a step ahead of us, and they've only widened the lead."

King frowned and fell silent. No one said anything else the rest of the drive.

* * *

TIMONIUM IS NESTLED in Baltimore County between Towson and Hunt Valley. It's probably most famous for the fairgrounds which house the state fair each year and for John Hanson College. We pulled into a shopping center on York Road. It sat amid a professional building across the street and restaurants on either side. Rich swung the car behind the buildings where we followed the flashing lights to the crime scene.

Detective Sergeant Gonzalez, whom I'd worked with a few times, waited for us on the other side of the yellow tape. He stood with another detective and a phalanx of uniformed officers. We all knew each other from prior cases, so we skipped the introductions and jurisdictional pissings and got down to it. "Call came in about a half-hour ago," Gonzalez said. Three officers stood around a dumpster situated behind a Giant Foods store. "One of the employees found her."

"He still around?" King asked.

"We sent *her* home. Took her statement, but she was really shaken up. I didn't see the need to keep her here."

Rich frowned but didn't say anything. I sided with Gonzalez. If they already took her statement, there seemed little point in keeping a traumatized witness around. She wouldn't want to rehash her story for us. We all approached the dumpster. A blonde girl's body was visible through the small blue metal sliding door. She lay face-down amid a bunch of black and clear trash bags.

"ME come yet?" Rich said.

Gonzalez shook his head. "On his way. We've photographed the scene and done some basic forensics."

I peered over the top of the bin. The body looked to be the right size for Violet. The hair—a shade darker blonde than the other girls—also matched. Like the rest of the victims, the young woman had been shot once in the back of the head. I wondered if she would have a needle mark on one of her arms.

The medical examiner arrived a couple minutes later. He was a tall, burly man who looked like he could wrangle a corpse under each arm. Gonzalez and some of the county contingent conferred with him. I nosed around the area. Every business had a rear door, but large dumpsters like this one were scattered about. I noticed cameras above some of the doors and summoned Rich with a jerk of my head. He followed my eyes. "I'm sure Gonzalez is on it," he said.

"I'm sure he is, too. He probably sent uniforms to talk to anyone in the other business and request security footage."

"They'll probably have it soon, then."

"What if we could get it sooner?"

Rich stared at me. "You're suggesting hacking the camera system?"

"Of course not," I said. "I would hack the Wi-Fi network on which the camera system resides."

"You're . . . I don't know if there's a word for it."

"I think 'awesome' will do nicely." I took out my phone. It was a recent Android model untraceable to me with the factory operating system replaced by something more specialized. I cycled through mobiles a couple times a year as faster models came out. I fired up a wireless network exploitation tool. "Try to join their network a few times," I told Rich.

He took out his mobile. The back door read *Alice's Boutique* in faded stencil letters. Rich tapped on his screen a few times. My app sniffed the traffic and analyzed it. After about a minute, Rich asked, "You have enough?"

"Probably," I said. "I'm going to presume someone who owns a small shop like this isn't too keen on security."

"Sadly, you're probably right." Rich walked away to rejoin his fellow cops as they watched a small crew remove the body from the bin. A couple minutes later, my program provided me with the password to join the wireless network. I was right—Alice used the very simple *trinkets* and expected it to suffice.

Once on her network, I quickly found the camera system. It opened in a browser window and prompted me for credentials. I entered Alice for the user with the same password, and it let me in right away. From there, I spent a few minutes deducing the menu and how to access footage. The camera would show any vehicle or person passing by it, and its angle suggested it might see something stopped in front of Giant's dumpster. I accessed the live feed and confirmed this when the cops standing in the alley appeared.

I reviewed the earlier footage, pausing each time something drove past. The fourth time proved the charm. The playback was not in color, but the van in it looked white. It stopped, and then two men got out and walked to the rear. They reappeared a moment later carrying a large object between them. It looked like a body wrapped in plastic. One set the corpse down while the other kept watch. A moment later, they heaved Violet into the bin, took the plastic roll with them, and left.

They came into the frame by Giant, but drove past the boutique on their way out. I paused the video at the best shot of their license plate I could find, took a screenshot, and texted it to Rich and King. *Let's run this. We don't need to share it with the county yet.* I rejoined the group as the ME went over a few things. He mentioned a small puncture wound on the inside of the left elbow.

"What kind of needle do you think it is?" I asked.

"Thick," he answered curtly.

"What would someone inject with it?"

The ME shook his head. "I don't think it's for injections. I think it's for drawing blood."

I'd considered the possibility earlier, but we never went anywhere with it. We all presumed the other girls had been drugged and kidnapped or kept sedated while held captive. Having a likely suspect focused my thoughts. Drawing blood provided an easy and reliable avenue for DNA testing. Especially for someone who owned a business capable of performing it.

Like Shauna Sullivan.

CHAPTER 25

RICH, KING, AND I HUDDLED AS THE COUNTY'S MEDICAL examiner finished. "You don't want to share this with them?" Rich asked in a tone like he accused me of murdering the mayor.

"No. It's our case."

"The crime happened in the county."

"Good," I said. "You and Gonzalez go draw up an agreement about who can go where and investigate what. And while you're getting everything signed in triplicate, I'll catch a killer."

"You still think it's the Sullivan woman?" King said.

"More than ever. You heard the ME. The girls had blood drawn. We should've kept going with this when we thought of it. Who do we know who's already on the radar and owns a facility which could handle the DNA testing?"

"Fine," King said, raising his hands. "How are we going to divide it up?"

"C.T. and I will look into Shauna Sullivan," Rich said. "You ride with Gonzalez and talk to the family." King nodded and walked toward the county contingent. Rich and I climbed into another BPD Charger.

"We can run the plate from here," I suggested. Rich looked at the image on his phone. He moved his fingers apart. "Zooming in isn't going to help."

"I know. You've gone on your pixellation rant before."

"Good to know you're paying attention," I said.

"Frequency of exposure," Rich said. He squinted at the photo. "I can't make out the first character on the plate."

"I couldn't, either."

He tapped on the keyboard, logging into the mobile terminal mounted in the front of all BPD vehicles. It chewed up some of my space in the passenger seat, especially when Rich swiveled it toward me. "Run your search while we drive."

I scooted toward the door as best I could. "Now I see why the BPD has weight standards," I said. "A fat cop couldn't sit up here with this thing." I'd never used a system like it before, but it was intuitive enough, especially to someone who already knows how to work a computer. I found the license plate search, entered characters with a wildcard at the beginning, and pressed Enter.

The program told me my parameters were wrong. I double-checked the letters and numbers we could see; I'd entered them correctly. "What's the wildcard character?" I asked.

"What did you use?"

"An asterisk."

"I don't know," Rich said. "I couldn't tell you the last time I used the terminal to run a plate."

I rolled my eyes, tried a pound sign, and got the same results. An ampersand turned out to be the winner. Several years ago, Maryland plates became less predictable in their formatting. A letter or number could appear anywhere on the tag regardless of what kind of vehicle it was affixed to. The missing first character thus represented thirty-six possible combinations.

Not all were in use. The system spat out seventeen results. It included vehicle type in the output, so I could filter out sedans and coupes. Of the seventeen on the screen, four were vans. One was black, which left two white and a silver. I leaned toward the former based on the colorless footage. Clicking on an entry brought up the registration details.

The second white van belonged to Sullivan BioGenesis.

"It's hers," I said.

"Why don't we pay her a visit?" Rich said.

"Sometimes, I like the way you think."

"Only sometimes?"

"It's confined to the occasions we agree," I said.

WE DROVE to Bel Air in Harford County, about thirty-five minutes northeast of Baltimore. Along the way, Rich called Captain Casey Norton, and he agreed to meet us there and solve the jurisdictional issue. Bel Air is an interesting city. My parents remember when it was mostly farmland. Its agricultural part still exists, but you have to look harder to find it. Pockets of civilization and consumerism are surrounded by cow pastures. The combination might make it the quintessential suburban town.

Rich took a side road off of Maryland Route 24, and we came to a nondescript two-story brick building. In the lobby, a blank board encased in glass hung on the wall. In the past, it probably served to inform guests which business or doctor occupied which suite. Now, Sullivan BioGenesis owned the place. I Googled it on the drive here; they bought it out of receivership a year ago.

Norton waited for us inside the glass doors to the company's main suite. The young woman behind the reception desk eyed us as she examined our credentials. Baby blues flicked among the three of us. "You don't look like a cop," she said as her gaze settled on me.

"Thank you." She smiled. "Someone has to bring the charm and good looks. It's my gift . . . and my curse."

Rich and Norton both rolled their eyes as the receptionist giggled. She was pretty, though her behavior made her seem a bit ditzy. I couldn't help notice the long blonde hair which made her resemble all the dead girls on a superficial level. Maybe Shauna Sullivan tested her DNA earlier, and whatever the results indicated spared this young woman a bullet to the head.

Think of the devil, and she shall appear. Shauna entered the reception area. She wore a white lab coat with her name embroidered on it. Large glasses enveloped her face but couldn't hide her lack of happiness at seeing us. "I'll take them back, Rachel. Thanks." We followed her down a maze of glass-walled corridors to her office. Rich and I snagged the two guest seats, forcing Norton to stand. "You can get another chair from the conference room. It's next door." He wheeled an identical model in and sat to Rich's right.

"Thank you for seeing us," Norton said. "We're part of an interagency investigation."

"I hope I can help," Shauna said.

"It's really cool your company owns the building," I said. This elicited a small smile. "As a woman in STEM, you've probably faced a lot of obstacles. This must be satisfying."

"It is. I'm sure you didn't come here to discuss my success, though. It hardly seems worthy of a . . . what did you call it? An interagency investigation?"

On the ride over, Rich and I strategized about how much to reveal. If Shauna Sullivan was indeed the woman behind the kidnappings and murders, we couldn't simply tell her everything we knew. We decided to focus mostly on the old D&S sale, and Norton agreed to our tactic over the phone call. I liked it in principle, but I also knew Shauna wouldn't be able to tell us much. As usual, I stood ready to improvise. "We keep coming back to your father getting bought out of D&S," Norton said. "There's not a lot of information on it. You were a teenager when it happened, correct?" Shauna bobbed her head in confirmation. "What can you tell us?"

"Like you said, I was in my teens. I wasn't a businesswoman. My father told me a little about the company, but he didn't go into a ton of detail. I know we liked Vincent Davenport and his family, and this changed with the buyout."

"So your father and Davenport didn't split amicably?" Rich asked.

"No. I don't think one partner paying the other to go away can ever avoid being acrimonious."

"How is your father, by the way?" I said, interrupting Rich's questions. I felt his eyes on me but didn't look at him.

"He's . . . as well as can be expected," Shauna said.

"I hope your research is able to help him."

"Thank you."

"Miss Sullivan," Norton said, "do you think anything illegal was happening at D&S at the time?"

"If it was, I didn't hear about it."

Rich and Norton droned on about the seventeen-year-old business transaction. I busied myself with looking around the office. The wall facing the main corridor was glass, but the others were covered in wood paneling. My first renovation would have been pulling it down and setting it ablaze. On the wall behind her desk, Shauna displayed three degrees. She earned a bachelor's and a master's in molecular biology from Johns Hopkins and an MBA from the University of Maryland.

At a lull in the conversation, I said, "If I wanted to get my DNA tested, how long would it take?"

Shauna gave me a quizzical look. "I'm not sure I understand the question. What kind of testing?"

"Those Ancestry commercials interest me. Then I read some other company turned over DNA records to the police, and they used the data to catch a serial killer. I'd like this kind of testing, but I'd also like it paired with a functional privacy policy."

"They're conducting a different kind of test than what we usually perform," Shauna said. "We don't do that."

"If you did, though, how long would it take?"

She shrugged. "This is a guess, but I would say . . . maybe two or three days?"

"You're much faster than they are," I said. "Maybe you can start doing the kinds of tests they do."

"I'll think about it," Shauna said in a tone suggesting she would do nothing of the sort.

We ended the interview a minute later. Shauna walked us back to the reception area. "Lots of offices," I said to Rachel. "You could probably sleep here, and no one would notice."

"People crash here occasionally," she said. "There's a small lab at the north end of the building with a few cots in it. It's nice to have for bad storms or just long nights."

The three of us bid Rachel farewell and headed back to our cars. "What the heck were you doing?" Rich asked once we were back in the parking lot.

"If you want me to follow a script," I said, "you should hand me one. Be ready for extensive edits."

"We agreed what we would talk about."

"You weren't getting anywhere. Someone needed to mix things up and build a little rapport."

"Now you're an interview expert," Norton said.

"I'm good with people," I said. "Instead of good cop, bad cop, we did boring cops, charming PI."

Rich leaned against the Charger and crossed his arms. "Did you learn anything?"

"Sure. Did you?" He didn't say anything.

"Why don't you share with the class?" Norton said.

"We now know Shauna could turn a DNA test around in two or three days. It fits our timeline, but now we know."

"We could presume it already."

"I'm sure judges and juries are swayed by presumptions at murder trials," I said. "Who needs facts and evidence?"

"Is this all you learned?" Rich said.

"No. You heard the receptionist say they can sleep people in one of the old labs." Norton spread his hands. "Do I need to draw you a fucking map?"

"You think they're keeping the girls there?"

"It's possible."

"During the business week?" Norton said.

"You got a better theory?" I asked.

"Not yet," he said.

"Then let's get one."

* * *

"I HOPE she doesn't think we're onto her," Rich said as we drove back. We'd ridden in silence for miles, but once we left I-83 for the Baltimore Beltway, he got chatty again.

"How would she?"

"You asking her about turning around a DNA test might be a pretty big clue."

"I don't think so," I said. "I couched it pretty well. It let her talk about her company, which she's obviously proud of, rather than some old buyout she doesn't know much about."

"And your little chat with the receptionist?" Rich said.

"You seriously think she's going to run and tell Shauna what I said?"

"I guess we need to hope she doesn't."

"She won't," I said. Rich didn't say anything, and neither did I. I felt glad for the silence now. Talking to Rich sometimes proved exasperating. He probably felt the same way about me, but I was right, and he was wrong. His black-and-white outlook on things probably served him well in much of his work. A lot happened in the gray, however, and its various shades was where I came in.

We arrived back at the precinct. I told Rich I'd prefer to work from my own office. He didn't object. I drove there and accessed the BPD's resources as if I were sitting at one of their desks. Maybe no one would mind if I chose to work remotely for however much longer this task force lasted. I hoped its continued existence would be brief for a plethora of reasons.

My phone vibrated in my pocket. Rollins. By now, Nancy's school day should be wrapping up . . . unless something terrible happened. "She didn't come out of work," he said when I picked up.

I shut my eyes tight and rubbed the bridge of my nose. "What happened?"

"She went in on schedule. I popped in once to see if she was there, and she was. Everything looked normal. She should've left ten minutes ago. No sign of her."

"Is there a school bus waiting?"

"No," Rollins said. "It looks like the kids are on their own once they're done here."

"It must be near her house, then," I said.

"Not too far. I've seen a couple buses . . . but none of the yellow kind."

"It's only been ten minutes, right?"

"You're injecting way too much optimism into this."

He was right. I needed to. Whatever these murders were about, I'd hoped they stopped with Violet as the last dead girl. "I guess I am. I'll call Rich, and we'll go there. Can you hang around there for a little while and see if she comes out?"

"I'll text you if she does."

"Thanks." I hung up and called Rich. He didn't sound

pleased to hear from me. "I think Nancy Meyers was just kidnapped."

"What? How do you know?"

"I asked Rollins to tail her throughout the day."

Rich sighed into the phone. "You can't do things like this, you know."

"What?" I asked. "Try to protect people from getting abducted and killed?"

"No . . . arrange your own surveillance. She should've had police protection."

"Yes. She should've. But her idiot father said no, so I improvised. This is giving us a headstart on the investigation."

"How do we know--"

"Rich," I broke in, "you can go with me to where she works. If you'd rather sit at your desk and be sanctimonious, then piss off. I'll go myself, and I'll do it without you. It would be better than listening to your Dudley Do-Right lectures nonstop."

Silence ruled the day for a few seconds before Rich answered. "Fine. I guess the case is getting to me, too. Where does she work?"

"I'll text you the address," I said.

"Great." He hung up. I fired off the message. As I got into my car, I once again hoped Rollins would tell me she came out after working a little late. My phone remained disappointingly silent on the drive.

* * *

NANCY PARTICIPATED in a work-study program through her high school. She did basic data entry and other tasks for a medical supply company according to the paunchy middle manager who spoke to Rich and me. He flip-flopped between being more concerned about Nancy and about what a police presence at the business might look like. Rich must've known I was about to ream him out because he glanced at me and shook his head. For now, I would comply.

I checked my phone. Nancy's tracker should have registered in the app. As far as I could tell, its last location had been right here, but it currently sent no beacon. Did the kidnappers find it? Rich didn't know about it, and I held off on telling him. The building featured a lot of metal, so the issue could have been interference. It probably wasn't, but I kept waiting for even a small a break in the case. Maybe we would get one before Nancy turned up somewhere with a hole in the back of her head.

The manager—whose name I didn't catch and didn't bother asking about again—took us to where Nancy worked. She sat in a small cubicle. Unadorned gray fabric walls stared back at her. What a depressing way to spend a few hours. A monitor, keyboard, and mouse sat atop the desk, and a small tower PC below it. The screen was dark. I jiggled the mouse, and the Windows login appeared. Nancy must have been finished with her shift. "She work with anyone?" I said.

"She's alone in here on Fridays," the paunchy supervisor said.

"You let a high school girl work by herself?"

"Nancy's great. We trust her."

"It's not about trust," Rich said. "This goes to employee security. Any cameras?" I'd already scanned the ceiling and didn't see any obvious ones.

"Not in here. We only keep them around the supplies . . . so the warehouse and loading dock."

"Any other ways out of here besides the dock or the front door?" I said.

"Yes," the manager said. "They're both at the east section of the building, so there's another exit at the end of the western hallway."

"With no camera?" He offered a sheepish nod.

Rich told the guy he didn't need to stick around, and he took the hint. Neither of us saw anything in the area. "Another medical-related company," I said.

"Could be part of the pattern," Rich said. "As much as I'm not into coincidences, it could be one of those, too. I think the girls' other factors are the important ones."

We left the moribund cube area and crept down the corridor toward the side exit. "You still think Shauna and her old man are hunting for an illegitimate daughter?"

He nodded. "What else could it be?"

"We should have seen it sooner."

"What do you mean?"

"The bigger connection," I said. "School internships end around the same time as proms and graduations. It just seems like we missed something big."

"We didn't know the mothers all worked at D&S when they were in school," Rich said.

"We did at some point. It should've been a logical inference."

"Look . . . sometimes, you go blind to these things. This case has seen a lot of activity. We've been back on our heels from the start. Things are going to slip through."

"I guess," I said. "One of Sullivan's interns must've gotten pregnant. Either he only found out recently, or he only started to care once he saw mortality speeding toward him."

"Or his daughter cared," Rich pointed out. "If the old man suddenly has another heir, she loses a lot in the inheritance."

"Good point."

We neared the end of the hallway. I saw a sparkle from somewhere off to the side. The necklace I gave Nancy lay on the floor, the amber smashed and in pieces. The internal electronics didn't fare any better. "This was hers," I said as I crouched beside it.

"They took her this way, then," Rich said.

"Now we need to figure out where they went from here."

CHAPTER 26

WHILE RICH RETURNED TO THE PRECINCT TO WORK Nancy's disappearance with King and Norton, I begged off and went back to my office. The words of Rachel the receptionist played in my head. *There's a small lab at the north end of the building with a few cots in it.* Shauna Sullivan could be keeping Nancy Meyers onsite at her company. She could have stashed all the girls there.

I called Rollins, who picked up right away. "Want to take a drive to Bel Air?"

"We looking for a missing girl?" he said.

"Yeah. I want to see if they're keeping her in the labs."

"It'll be dark soon. By now, I'm sure all the workers have cleared out."

Sullivan BioGenesis would have a good security system. It wasn't a place where I could pick the lock and nose around unobserved. "You have any kind of thermal imaging equipment?" I asked.

"Sure," Rollins said. "Q issues some to all the double-ohs."

"Very funny, Mister Bond."

"I have some, but it's not going to help. You watch too many movies. Thermal scopes can't see through walls."

"Shit."

"Best we could do," he said, "is see something on the other side causing a heat difference."

"Like what?" I asked.

"Hot water running, maybe? If they're trying to keep the girl alive, they can't just throw her in a room for three days."

"I guess it'll have to do." We arranged for Rollins to pick me up at my house, and we'd head to Bel Air from there. The limitations of infrared technology disappointed me. Even if we saw evidence of hot water in use, it wouldn't mean someone held Nancy captive inside. Though why someone would need it after working hours on a Friday was a worthwhile question. I grabbed a directional microphone from my home office before we left.

Rollins swung by a few minutes later, and we left for Sullivan BioGenesis. "I figure we can use the scope first," he said. "If it picks up anything, I'll see if I can have a look."

"Good." I held up the mike. "We can try to listen with this, too. Even if the scope doesn't pick up anything. We might hear a conversation."

"Or a scream."

"No one will let me be even a little optimistic," I said.

About a half-hour later, Rollins eased his truck onto the parking lot of Shauna's business. All the cars were gone, and only two company vans remained. I couldn't see light coming from any of the windows. "Think anyone's here?" he said.

"Unless somebody stayed behind to babysit Nancy, I doubt it. Let's drive to the west end. That's where the receptionist said they had a few cots setup."

The asphalt ended at the front of the building, and Rollins' tires crunched over gravel as we drove to the western side. Rollins got out of the truck and looked through his scope. He spent a few minutes examining the first and second floors in turn, walking closer to the building a couple times as he did. At the end, he shook his head. "I'm not getting anything. Nothing in there is giving off enough heat."

I got out and rested the directional microphone on the hood of the truck. I angled it toward the second story and gave it a few minutes. Nothing. I moved it down so it could pick up sounds from ground level. We didn't even hear any static. "You think getting closer would help?" Rollins asked.

"Probably not," I said, "but I'll feel like an ass if I don't try." I did, and the results were the same. "If someone's in there, they're doing a good job of being quiet."

"The girl could be drugged and asleep."

"Maybe," I said, "but we can't break into the building on a small chance."

"I never thought I'd hear you advocating a responsible approach," Rollins said.

I packed up the microphone. "I must be getting old."

* * *

WHEN I ARRIVED at police headquarters, Rich and King were headed out. "We're going to hit the streets," King said. "Talk to a few people, hope we get a lead."

"You stay here," Rich told me, cutting off my question before I could ask it. "See if you can find anything in common among the disappearances."

I thought his idea was a poor use of my limited time and considerable talents, but they hustled into a car, and I didn't have a chance to object. I walked inside and sat at the desk I'd been using. Leon Sharpe wandered out and saw me. "Thought we might've chased you off."

"Were you trying to?"

"Of course not," he said. "Just haven't seen a lot of you recently."

I nodded. "I've been working out of my office. It's easier to be there sometimes."

Sharpe sat on the corner of the desk. Its wooden leg groaned under him. There was no definition of "fat" which encompassed Captain Sharpe, but two hundred seventy pounds of muscle and attitude was enough to strain a lot of furniture, especially the kind purchased by cities with strict budgets. "You and Rich getting along?"

"About like we always do," I said.

My evaluation made Sharpe smirk. He understood my relationship with Rich. "We're glad to have you working with us on this."

"Thanks, Leon."

"Sure." He stood, and the desk practically sighed in relief. "Now get cracking."

Exactly how I should crack eluded me. Rich wanted me to find anything in common beyond the obvious factors. My grand plan to track Nancy in the event she disappeared got ground beneath the heel of someone's boot. The only factors I could think of were the apparent ones—age, appearance, mothers' ages, and the obvious connection to the Sullivan family we should've seen before.

There were others, however. The girls who participated in school work-study programs toiled away in the medical field—a pharmacy, nursing home, and supplier. These were places someone with a proper credential from a company like Sullivan BioGenesis could gain access to. In a building full of doctors, no one will question one more person in a white lab coat.

I could break into those businesses and see if they issued any documentation to one of Shauna's employees. It would take time, however, and I'd need to do it from my office and not BPD headquarters. Complicating this was HIPAA, the American health records privacy law. If my intrusion were detected, the companies I breached could be on the hook for piles of money in fines. While I felt confident I could get in and out undetected, I also didn't want to bankrupt an innocent business if the challenge proved harder than I thought.

Sometimes, the old-fashioned method works best. I first called the pharmacy in Cumberland. Being a small business in a remote county, I figured the odds were low they'd even heard of Sullivan BioGenesis, and a thirty-second conversation proved this theory correct. Next, I tried Graceful Meadows Nursing Home.

I turned my back on the rest of the squadroom when the receptionist answered. "This is Detective Ferguson with the Baltimore Police Department." I'd pretended to be Rich on a couple occasions before. Besides having the same last name, we sounded similar over the phone. Besides, I was a private detective sitting in BPD headquarters. As my lies went, this one bottomed out on the list.

"What can I do for you, Detective?"

"We're still investigating Miss Graham's disappearance." I paused and hoped for a sympathetic word there but got nothing. "I was wondering if you could help me with a certain aspect."

"I'll do what I can," she said.

"Has your facility issued any credentials to employees of Sullivan BioGenesis?" I hoped she wouldn't transfer me to Curran, the security chief. Dealing with him once had been enough.

"Mister Curran approves those, but I can check in the system for you. Guests always have to register with me when they arrive."

"Thank you," I said both for her willingness to help and ability to do so without bringing Curran into the process. Her keyboard clicked and clacked over the phone. "I see one person from that company . . . Jeremy Green."

"Do your records show Mister Green's role?"

"He's listed as a clinical technician."

"Which is . . . what, exactly?" I said.

"It seems to mean a lot of things these days," she said. "It's supposed to refer to someone from a company who can help with their equipment while it's in use."

"From your tone, I gather it's used a bit liberally."

"Yes."

"Did Mister Green meet the term's qualifications?" I asked.

"I don't know. You'd have to ask the people he worked with. I just make sure he signs in and collects his ID."

"Speaking of checking him in—did you on the day Violet Graham went missing?"

"I did," she said. "You don't think—"

"It's too early to tell. Thanks for your help."

"You're welcome, Detective," she said and hung up.

A call to the medical supply company where Nancy worked revealed the same information. Jeremy Green, listed as a clinical technician, was issued a credential a couple hours before Nancy Meyers got hustled out the unwatched side entrance. The woman on the other end mentioned Green had also been there the prior day. The timing would allow him to learn the lay of the land, including which doors to use if he wanted to avoid the security system.

Sullivan BioGenesis' website listed Green as a technical manager, a nebulous term potentially covering a wide variety of duties. His LinkedIn page showed no job history before his current gig. Facebook, however, conveyed no job history, but pictures displayed Green's love of working out and taking selfies in front of gym mirrors.

It didn't disqualify him as a technical manager, but it definitely marked him as someone who could strong-arm a high school girl out of a building. I perused his friends list and discovered the smiling visage of Abe McLelland.

Green didn't look like any of the goons I'd encountered so far. I got the feeling I'd be seeing him soon enough.

* * *

ARMED with the knowledge Abe and Shauna were sharing at least one goon, I went hunting for other commonalities. The law firm didn't publish an employee roster online, but Green was no attorney and seemed ill-suited to the subtleties of investigation. The two companies had no employees in common and were located two municipalities apart.

I focused on Shauna and Abe. The former owned a condo near her business in Bel Air, while the young lawyer lived in a small townhouse in Baltimore County. They were certainly close enough to make a relationship work. Neither possessed any other properties I could find. Keith Sullivan lived in the fancy area of Fallston, not far from his daughter. The house would be big enough to stash a kidnapped girl. Doing it in a residential neighborhood, however, introduced all sorts of risks. It didn't feel right.

My problem came in finding a place which did. Rollins and I eliminated Sullivan BioGenesis. McLelland's law office wasn't configured for overnight guests. There must have been a place I didn't uncover yet, and I was at a loss for how to find it. I took my work offline and called Melinda. "I'm hoping you can tell me something about Shauna Sullivan."

"You're still looking into her?" she said.

I briefly filled her in on the events and discoveries of the last few days. "They must be hiding this girl at a place I don't know about," I continued. "It's not obvious from any of my research. Do you remember someplace else Shauna and her father would have gone?"

Melinda took a deep breath. "I was pretty young when the split happened."

"I know. I'm not sure who else I can ask right now, though."

The line went quiet. After several seconds of silence, Melinda said, "Shauna was in to horses. I think her parents had a farm somewhere." Before I could ask the obvious follow-up, she added, "I don't know where. We lived in Baltimore at the time. It was a bit of a drive. I remember . . . thinking it was in the county.
"

Her lack of details didn't tell me much, though they might allow me to narrow the place down. "Thanks, Melinda." I considered adding the fact her father lied to me about the great corporate schism and probably hindered the investigation. She didn't need to be involved in his part of it, though. My gripe was with her asshole father, and I'd make it known to him before all was said and done.

"I hope it helped."

"It did," I said, and I ended the call. I dialed my parents next, and my father answered. They knew a lot of people with money in Baltimore, and the Sullivans definitely counted. "Dad, I hope you can help me with some information."

"You mean I might help with one of your cases?"

"Yes. Let's not get you fitted for a badge and gun yet, though. This should be pretty simple."

"All right. Go ahead."

I provided an abridged version of the case's events and my current suspicions. "I don't know how well you knew the Sullivans back in the day, but I need to know if there's any non-obvious place Keith and Shauna could be hiding a missing girl. Probably in the county somewhere."

"I think Keith's wife was into horses," my father said. "I remember taking Samantha somewhere when she'd just started high school." My late sister would be about the same age as

Shauna Sullivan if she'd survived. "It was in Harford County somewhere. Hmm." He fell silent for a few seconds. "Churchville, maybe?"

I'd never heard of it, but Google knew all about it. "Thanks, Dad. Looks promising."

"Let us know how it turns out."

"I will." We bade each other adieu and hung up. Churchville sat near Bel Air and was known for being more rural and—as its name suggested—packing in many houses of worship. A terrain view on Google Maps showed plenty of farmland. I remembered Brittany O'Connor's autopsy showed a few pieces of hay in her shorts.

I kept digging. Keith Sullivan was a widower, and his late wife Andrea joined the choir invisible a decade ago. She'd never divorced him, and I wondered if she knew why Vincent Davenport handed her husband a pile of cash and told him to get lost. I combed through old property records. Andrea Carroll brought a horse farm to the marriage when she tied the knot with Keith Sullivan. When she died, the deed reverted to their trust. It was why I couldn't find it under Keith or Shauna—neither technically owned it.

But it remained in the family so to speak. The satellite view revealed a large house, plenty of land for animals, and a sizable barn. These buildings could be where all the girls had been held and where Nancy Meyers currently awaited a grim fate.

I picked up my phone.

CHAPTER 27

I returned to BPD headquarters. Rich and King sat in a small meeting room on the main floor. I joined them. The table could accommodate a dozen people. Whiteboards encircled the room, and someone taped photos of the farm grounds onto several of them. Leon Sharpe strode in a minute later, and Casey Norton entered behind him. "Nice of you to join us again," King said to the state police captain.

"I'm just here to claim the glory for my agency," he said as he sank onto one of the surprisingly comfortable chairs.

"I've already done it," I told him. "You see the results of my handiwork all over this room."

"You hung the whiteboards?" he said with a smirk, and I smiled and pointed at him in recognition of the good zinger.

"Let's get down to business," Sharpe said, and his booming, authoritative voice would brook no silliness or backtalk. "You all can see these photos. They're satellite views of a property in Churchville. We think Nancy Meyers is there now, and all the other girls were kept there before her."

"Sheriff's Office up there want in?" Rich asked.

"They're willing to support our operation," Sharpe said. "Major Tompkins with the MSP and I already hashed it out with them. The task force has the lead. Locals are there to do everything else." He pointed at Rich. "You're up."

Rich stood and replaced Sharpe at the nearest whiteboard. "The entrance is here, off Route One-Thirty-Six. It's past a bunch of this new construction. The driveway splits—left goes to the residence, and right leads to a freestanding garage." He pointed to what looked like another narrow road. "There's also a walking path here. It's probably wide enough for a bike or an ATV, and they could store those in the garage. It takes you to what looks like a large barn."

"Which is where they're probably keeping Nancy," I said.

"It's speculation, but it's sound. I don't think they'd keep her in the house."

"How many bad guys we anticipating?" Norton asked.

"Unknown," Rich said. "Between Shauna Sullivan and Abe McLelland, they have the resources to assemble a good crew. It doesn't mean they're always on the grounds, though. I would say anywhere from four to ten."

King pointed at the maps. "Lot of trees around. Easy to sneak onto the property. I guess we're trying to be quiet once we're there?"

"Yes," Rich said. "We'd like to do this without raising an alarm. Who knows what they'll do to Nancy if they see a bunch of cops sneaking around?"

"A bunch of cops and one handsome private investigator," I said. Rich rolled his eyes. "When do we roll out?"

"It's already dark," Rich said, "so as soon as we all gear up. You ready to go?"

"Spot me a vest?" I asked.

"Is it all right if it says you're with the police?" Rich grinned. He knew how I'd feel about it and enjoyed the moment.

"Can I wear it inside out?"

"No," he said.

"I guess beggars can't be choosers," I said.

"Good."

* * *

A HALF-HOUR LATER, our van turned out of the BPD's parking lot and began the trek to Churchville. King drove, with Rich sitting up front and me in the second row. Norton took his state police car. I wore a loaner bullet-resistant vest which falsely advertised my affiliation with the Baltimore police. Before we rolled out, I hunted around the building for a can of spray paint but came up empty. Hopefully, this would be the worst indignity I suffered tonight.

Rich conferred with the Harford County Sheriff's Office as we drew closer. A church sat off the road immediately before the house's driveway on the other side of a thicket of trees. We could emerge onto the property without being detected if we did it right. Once clear of the leaves and branches, much of the rest of the property was wide open, however. Staying unseen would be more difficult.

A few minutes later, King killed the lights and swung the van onto the church parking lot. A half-dozen HCSO cars waited for us with two deputies standing outside of each. Norton pulled up beside us. "Weapons check," Rich said before we exited the van. I brought my .45 with seven rounds in the mag and one in the pipe. Everything looked good. My vest was affixed properly. I took a deep breath. Rich, King, and Norton were professionals. Times like this drove it home. I was the amateur who got to come along, and I needed to pull my weight.

Norton and Rich conferred with the locals. A bunch of pointing and nodding ensued. A couple minutes later, the pair returned to carry the word to us mere mortals. "They're going to leave two cars here in case anyone makes a break through the trees," Norton said. "The rest will be stationed near the driveway across the road, two pointing in each direction."

"Sounds good," I said as if I participated in farm raids every week.

Rich gave me a radio, microphone, and earpiece. "We're all on the same frequency. I've already set it. Try to whisper if you can."

"This isn't my first rodeo."

"I know," Rich said. "I don't want it to be your last."

"Me, either." I slipped the earpiece in, then clipped the mike onto my collar and the main unit to my belt. Not only did my vest proclaim my membership with the BPD, but now I was geared up exactly like everyone else. My sense of uniqueness cringed.

My cousin eyed the knife on my hip. "You trying for the Crocodile Dundee look?"

"I think I'm missing the hat and accent."

"I'm surprised you've heard of it."

"I like old movies," I said.

Rich frowned. Norton and King laughed. "I don't know why you bother," Norton said.

"Stealth doesn't mean you have to stab someone," Rich said.

"I've clearly logged more *Call of Duty* and *Assassin's Creed* hours than you."

Like any defeated man, Rich sighed and shook his head. "Let's get ready to roll. Comms check."

We all tested our mikes and earpieces, and everything worked. The trees loomed ahead. Darkness lay on the other side. I could only see a few scattered lights on the farmhouse grounds. At Rich's direction, we waited among the branches for our eyes to adjust to the lack of light. Once our vision acclimated, Rich made hand gestures indicating who would go where. We were near the road and the top of the driveway. Norton went straight ahead; Rich, King, and I fanned out at varying angles to the right.

I hugged the tree line, moving from trunk to trunk and staying behind cover as much as I could. Despite the occasional light, darkness bathed the property. Low fences—probably for animal pens—lay somewhere to my left. In the distance, if I walked a straight line, I would arrive at the barn. It was where I wanted to end up. Maybe I'd get lucky, and the goons patrolling the grounds would cooperate and not be nearby.

"One down." I heard Rich's harsh whisper in my ear. If only we knew how many remained. I stepped out from behind a tree when I saw someone. He was clad in black from head to toe and wore a pistol on his right hip. He kept low and edged through the thicket. On the other side, two cars and four deputies waited. They'd left the lights off, but they weren't invisible. It appeared this fellow noticed them.

He reached for his belt. My hand fell to my .45. The man pulled something off his left hip.

It was a walkie-talkie.

CHAPTER 28

THE GUY STOOD ABOUT FIFTEEN YARDS FROM ME. DESPITE being in the middle of a thicket, I had a clear line of sight to him. I couldn't let him radio his friends and tell everyone the jig was up. The locals stood ready to rush to our aid, but what a desperate Abe or Shauna—or a ruthless Jeremy Green—would do to Nancy Meyers before making a run for it was the big unknown.

My options were few. I wouldn't--couldn't--shoot someone reaching for a walkie-talkie. Throwing the knife wasn't an option, either, mostly because I lacked the skill to do it well. I could yell and get his attention, but how much more would I attract in the process? I glanced around on the ground and found a length of branch.

I grabbed it and heaved it in his general direction. While it soared through the night air, I advanced as quietly as I could. The stick landed somewhere to the goon's left. He'd raised the walkie-talkie to his mouth but turned to look at the noise. I quickened my pace. He moved to check out whatever made the sound. I was a few paces away.

Something must have given me away because he pivoted back toward me. His eyes widened, and he raised his hand again. I threw a punch. He blocked it. I stayed on the attack to keep him off the comms, and it worked. My blows were meant more to distract him than do damage, but one slipped through and caught him in the jaw. While he cleared the cobwebs, I knocked the two-way radio out of his hand and kicked it into the brush.

My foe's eyes flicked to it for an instant before turning back toward me. Anger creased his face as he went on the attack, and I played defense. "Where's the girl?" I whispered as we sparred. He didn't answer. After a quick flurry, he pivoted away and drew a knife from his belt. His next attack was a swing aimed at my throat, which I stepped back and avoided. He followed up faster than I expected, taking a wild slash at my midsection. I jack-knifed out of the way but not enough. The blade gashed my vest, and pain rose from my stomach behind it. The corner of my assailant's mouth curled upward.

"Fucking pig," he said in a gravelly voice, swinging the weapon again. I've never liked fighting opponents who have knives. One lucky swing is all it takes. The blade itself—while obviously sharp enough to slice Kevlar—was only about four inches long, so it didn't add a lot to his reach. I could either try to stay outside it—a tactic at which I was only batting .500 so far—or move in and engage him in close quarters where slashing isn't a factor.

I chose the latter. After ducking under a swing aimed at my face, I pressed forward, catching his forearm as it came back. He shifted the blade and tried to cut me with it. I moved my arm fully underneath his. It cost me a little power, but it kept me from taking another knife wound. The one in my midsection already burned. This guy was about my size and didn't overpower me. He shifted his weight and tried using leverage to stab me.

I headbutted him between the eyes. His grip weakened as he rocked backwards. I broke the hold and kicked at his hand, dislodging the knife and sending it spiraling to the ground. His eyes went to the pistol on my hip, and he frowned. Going for the knife wasn't an option. "Now we can beat each other senseless like gentlemen," I said, keeping my voice low. "Or you can tell me where the girl is."

"Fuck you, pig," he said, and he came at me again.

"It was the only vest they had." I turned aside a couple wild punches. This fellow was not the typical goon I encountered. Those guys were brawny and used to ending fights with a single punch. Once they expended some effort, they slowed considerably, and the result was then inevitable. Not so much with my current foe. He showed no signs of tiring.

"Another down," I heard in my ear. It sounded like King this time.

We went back and forth with me mostly playing defense and looking for an opening. I'd grown accustomed to the rhythm when my opponent surprised me, grabbing my wrist instead of simply blocking a punch. He spun me around before I could react and locked me in a chokehold. I grabbed for his head, but he moved it away before I could do anything. Breathing became a challenge. I needed to get this guy off of me. I swung an elbow behind me. It found the mark, and the hold slackened for an instant, but he didn't let go. I tried it again and got the same result.

Black spots appeared in the edges of my vision. A large tree stood a few feet in front of me. I moved my feet, spinning us both around and then pushed off hard and went backwards as quickly as I could manage. We slammed into the trunk. The impact rocked me even through my opponent's body. He maintained the hold, however. I took a couple steps forward and put whatever strength I had left into another run at the tree. He released his grip on my neck.

I fell forward as I heard my foe slump over near the tree. He groaned as I filled my lungs with precious oxygen. We both got back to our feet and moved toward one another. His punches lacked the zip they'd had before. I turned a couple aside and hit my assailant hard in the midsection. The impact bent him in half, allowing me to wallop him in the face. To his credit, he didn't go down. I moved behind him and applied the same chokehold he used on me.

He struggled, but between getting run into the tree twice and the other blows he took, there wasn't much behind it. A few seconds later, he passed out, and I let him fall to the forest floor. "One down in the woods," I said. "I think he was about to radio his friends." I took his pistol and inspected it. It was a standard-issue 9MM Baretta with a full magazine. A perfectly good weapon. Once I'd reset its safety, I tucked it into the back of my waistband.

"Good work," Rich said.

"Another one down," Norton announced. "I'm headed toward the house."

"I'm going to the barn," I said. "I don't see anyone else blocking me."

"Be careful," Rich said. "You want me to come along?"

"I think I'll be all right. Just come running if you hear any gunshots."

I padded toward the smaller structure and eyed it from the edge of the thicket. It could pass for a house, being two stories and larger than plenty of homes I'd seen over the years. Before I could make a move, I heard a radio crackle behind me. "Jake, are you there? How are things in the woods? Over."

I moved back toward my fallen foe. The same call came in again. If someone radioed all the men patrolling the grounds, they'd soon discover something was amiss. I found the walkie-talkie next to a stray branch, pushed the talk button, and answered in my best scratchy voice. "All clear. Over."

A few seconds of silence passed before the person at the other end responded. "Roger."

I pressed my fingers to the slash wound, and they came back with some red smeared on them. Not too bad. I'd need some stitches later, but I could finish this. I carried the device with me in case someone tracked Jake's movements. When I reached the edge of the trees again, I set it down and once more studied the barn. A small door faced me. The opposite side would feature the larger entry used for moving animals to and fro. No one patrolled the perimeter. Lights shone from the upstairs window and around the edges of the door.

This must be where they kept Nancy prisoner. I stayed low and advanced.

* * *

I reached the back of the barn. Even with my ear to the door, I couldn't hear anything inside. I stayed in my crouch and padded to one end of the wall. I leaned my head out enough to peek with one eye. No one was there. I did the same at the other side and again saw no one. Hopefully, I wouldn't be stumbling into an ambush.

After a final look over my shoulder told me I remained unobserved, I tested the door. It was locked. I took out my special keyring and got to work. I'd recently bought a snap gun to make lock picking easier and faster, but given the tactical needs of our scenario, I didn't bring it. The old-fashioned way would be good enough tonight.

About a minute later, the cylinders lined up. I turned the knob, inched the door open from the side, and waited. Neither a goon nor a hail of bullets came my way. I created an opening exactly wide enough for me to slip inside. An old tractor sat to my right, and I crouched beside it. A couple lights were on through-out. While it felt good to be able to see better, I knew the advantage came with the downside of being more visible to any members of the strong-arm crew.

I'd been in a couple barns as a kid; the present one was bigger but laid out mostly the same. It also smelled a lot better with the main aromas being dirt and hay. I wondered when a horse last stayed here. A wide center aisle allowed access to stalls on either side. Hay and dirt served as the floor. A second level could be accessed via a ladder at the opposite end where the more traditional barn door was. This would be the way to get animals and farm equipment in and out.

I drew my .45 and checked the stalls. The closest two were empty, which made sense. Why put the prisoner so close to the exit? In the next one on the left side, a girl lay face-down on an air mattress. The middle of her back rose and fell in a classic sign of life, and I released a breath I didn't know I'd been holding. Now to get her out of here without drawing any attention. "Nancy," I whispered. She didn't stir. "Nancy." I put a little more volume into this one, balancing the need to wake her up with the desire to not attract undue notice.

She rubbed her face and sat up. She looked around confused and seeing me didn't help. I put up my hands before she said something and gave us away. "I'm here to get you to safety. We need to be quiet, though."

She nodded. "There's a guy around somewhere," she said, keeping her voice so low I struggled to hear.

Whoever put her in the stall locked it. It was a simple mechanism—perhaps not so for a horse, but a person on the wrong side of it could unlatch it quite easily. Nancy did this, and I cringed as metal slid over metal. I hoped it wouldn't be loud enough to raise the alarm.

It was. "Hey!" A burly man with a gun emerged from the last stall on the right. "Who the hell are you?" He pointed his weapon at me, and I was glad to return the favor. With my left arm, I nudged Nancy behind me.

"I'm taking her out of here," I said.

"The hell you are."

"You're not enough to stop me."

I heard footsteps from the second level. Another man appeared, descending the ladder quickly and jumping onto the hay rather than bother with the final few steps. As soon as he landed, a pistol appeared in his right hand. "How about two of us?" he said with a sneer.

"What is this, the party barn?" I could activate the mike I wore and make sure Rich and crew heard me. The situation could go off the rails, however, if three cops stormed the place. For now, I would confine the task force's involvement to me alone.

"You gonna tell us who you are?" the first one asked. "You don't look like a cop."

"I'm glad you noticed," I said, "but it's not a good time. We need to be going."

"She ain't going anywhere."

"Why?" I said. "Can she open the Chamber of Secrets? Is she the heir of Slytherin?" They both gaped at me. "How about the heir of Sullivan?"

"Maybe," the second guy said. "None of the others were."

I studied these two men. Both were at least my height and built like they spent most of their time lifting weights and guzzling protein shakes. The one closer to me had blond hair and looked like the younger of the two. The man who dropped down from the second story wore his dark hair slicked back, and black eyes peered at us from a hard face. If I needed to pick one of this pair to be the killer, it would be him. The more I looked at him, the more I noticed his strong resemblance to Jeremy Green. I wondered if he'd pulled the trigger on all the prior girls who got shot in the backs of their heads.

I couldn't let the same thing happen to Nancy.

"Let me tell you how this is gonna go," Green said. "You're gonna put your gun down. Ricky there is gonna take it from you. Then, you'll tell us why you're here and who you're with. Once you do, I promise to kill you quick."

"I have a better idea," I said. "Why don't you go fuck yourself, and I'll leave with the girl?"

"You ain't making it out of here."

"I'll take your bet, Mister Technical Consultant."

Green smirked, confirming his identity. I felt Nancy fidget behind me. None of my bravado meant anything if she ended up dead. At least she was tough enough not to bolt for the back door. Panic would end poorly for all involved—especially me, as I'd get shot before her. "You should put the gun down," Ricky said. "We got you two to one."

"Basic math," I said. "I'm impressed. If you outnumbered me eleven to one, would you need to take your shoes off to count?"

"Look, asshole," Green said, "set your gun down. This ain't a hero moment for you whether you're a cop or not."

If I complied, we were dead. I certainly was. Who knew what fate would befall Nancy after an aborted rescue attempt? Following a string of needless murders, I couldn't let the same thing happen to her. Ricky was right, however—they held the advantage.

Then I remembered taking the other goon's gun in the woods.

I would never be confused for a marksman, but I was a pretty good shot, especially at close range. I didn't relish the idea of our lives resting on a gun I'd never fired before. Still, these two didn't know I carried it at the small of my back. I only needed to get a chance to use it. Ricky stood to my right about twenty feet away. His hard-faced colleague was about fifteen feet farther away and pretty much dead even with me. We would form a very squat triangle if someone drew the lines between us.

"All right," I said, and I inched to the right. I felt Nancy move behind me. If I did this slowly enough, they might not notice. Getting the two of them lined up might buy us a second, which could be enough time to get the drop on Ricky. He would also screen us from Green's direct fire. It wasn't the best plan I'd ever concocted, but I didn't have another one ready to go. "I'll put my gun down. I don't want you to hurt the girl, though."

"She's safe for now," Green said. "Least until the test results come back." A sinister smile passed over his face. He'd definitely been the one to pull the trigger on the other girls. I kept edging to the right an inch at a time. So far, neither of the men holding guns on us had adjusted.

"I guess you won't trade me for her?"

"Wouldn't if I could. She's a more valuable hostage than you if shit goes south."

"You ain't a cop," Ricky added.

I shifted the .45 to a two-finger grip as I took a final tiny step. The three of us were now standing in a row—four if I counted Nancy behind me. "I'll toss it down," I said, and I let it go. It kicked up a bit of dirt as it landed. I moved my left hand in front of my face and turned slightly toward Nancy. "Move when I do," I whispered as quietly as I could. I didn't risk turning far enough to see her, so I had to hope she heard me. The tactic wouldn't work a second time. I needed an alternative. When she met me to get the necklace, Nancy ditched her Spanish class. I hoped neither of the gringos staring us down knew much.

"Ricky, take the gun," Green said. Ricky stuffed his own pistol into his waistband and started toward us. He held the line, which was good. The discarded .45 lay to my right. I needed to act before he veered off and broke the arrangement.

When he'd passed the halfway mark, I bent my knees,

exhaled a breath, and drew the pistol from the back of my jeans. Ricky fumbled for his own, but I squeezed off a shot and hit him in the right side of the chest. He staggered back a step and fell.

Before he hit the ground, I dove to the left and said, "*A tu izquierda*" so Nancy would, too. Ricky hit the dirt. Green's eyes widened. A shot blasted from his gun. I heard it shred the air as it passed over me. I landed on the barn floor and pulled the trigger as quickly as I could. The first couple shots whizzed over his head and allowed him to return fire. The next nine or so slammed into his torso, and I kept it up until the slide locked back.

Green stumbled backwards. His gun fell from his hand. Blood ran from multiple 9-millimeter holes in his body as he pitched forward and lay still.

Rich's voice barked in my ear. "I said, what's going on in the barn?"

"Two down," I said as I walked to Ricky. He held his left hand over the wound. Blood seeped between his fingers. Pain screwed up his face. I kicked his weapon away, even though he didn't look to be in any condition to reach for it. "One's still alive." I turned and looked at Nancy. She lay on her side, eyes wide, glancing between the goons and me. Moonlight dotted the ground through the holes where Green fired over us. "Nancy and I are all right."

"We'll get an ambulance," he said. "I'm coming your way."

I walked to where Nancy lay and crouched beside her. She sat up and wrapped her arms around me. "Thank you," she said through tears. "Thank you. I don't know how you found me."

"Hard work and brilliance," I said. "What happened to the necklace? We found it in pieces."

After taking a minute to compose herself, Nancy answered. "They wanded me. You know . . . like those things at the airport?"

"Clever of them." Shauna and Abe ran a sophisticated operation. I guess kidnapping and murdering potential heirs to the family fortune required it.

"Can I go home?" Nancy asked.

"Soon," I said. "We have a few things to wrap up here first."

She looked past me to Ricky, who still lay on the barn floor. "Will he be all right?"

I shrugged. "Out of my hands."

Rich came through the back door with his pistol leading the way. "We're good," I said. I cocked my head toward Ricky. "He'll need the ambulance."

"The locals called for one." Rich holstered his weapon and crouched by the fallen goon. "He's going into shock." He stood, retrieved a blanket from the wall, and covered Ricky. "Paramedics will be here soon." Rich looked at the other one, who lay dead near the ladder, his body twisted at an awkward angle. "Jesus. You did a number on this one."

"I'm pretty sure he's the one who killed the other girls," I said. "Meet Jeremy Green."

A siren sounded in the distance. "Sounds like the ambulance is close. King and Norton should be in the house by now. Let's wrap this up."

"Yes," I said, "let's."

CHAPTER 29

Following an initial round of questioning, Nancy insisted on leaving the barn via the front door. Rich and I escorted her out, and once she stepped into the night air, she inhaled it deeply before continuing. We walked around the structure and took the path toward the main house. Local deputies swarmed the grounds, and three handcuffed men got led to waiting vehicles. I knew more arrests would be forthcoming.

Norton waited for us on the porch. "They're all in there. The old man, Shauna, and her boyfriend."

"You don't need to do this part," I said to Nancy. "The deputies can take you back to your father."

She shook her head. "I want to see the son of a bitch who had me kidnapped."

Rich jerked his head to the side, and I joined him for a sidebar a few paces away. "You're not going to indulge her," he said.

"Why not?"

He fixed me with one of his patented serious stares. "She's seventeen. Put her in a car and get her out of here."

"No," I said. "She's been through a lot. If she wants to see this through, I'm not going to stop her."

"Have you forgotten she's seventeen?" Rich said.

"How could I? You've mentioned it twice now." I held up my hand to preempt Rich's objection. "First of all, it's ridiculous we're talking about her when she's fifteen feet away. Second, I don't care if she's a minor in the eyes of the law. She's old enough to decide something like this for herself, and I'm not going to take the choice away from her." A brief staredown ensued before Rich offered a slight nod.

"Fine," he grumbled. "King said the same thing."

"I always knew he was smart."

"He did pick a great partner."

I smiled. We rejoined the others. "Are we ready now?" Norton asked.

"Yes," Nancy said before Rich or I could.

The front door opened into a tiled foyer. Cherry hardwood extended ahead into a corridor and to the right where it spilled into a living room. I expected to see everyone gathered there, but it was empty apart from a single sofa and coffee table. "We're upstairs," King called from the second floor. The steps were covered in a soft cream carpet which continued on the upper level.

Everyone sat or stood in the master bedroom. King, accompanied by two of Harford County's finest, watched over the seated forms of Abe McLelland and Shauna Sullivan. Keith Sullivan lay in a large hospital bed, a couple of machines and an IV bag connected to him by various tubes and wires. He breathed with the assistance of oxygen piped into his nostrils. His right hand twitched involuntarily under the blanket. "Hi, Shauna," I said. "Hi, Abe. What a surprise to run into you here."

"My father is dying," Shauna said, apparently believing none of us could see the obvious.

"In light of recent events, you'll forgive me for withholding my sympathies."

She glared at me. Abe stood and promptly got pushed back into his chair by a deputy. "I'm a lawyer!" he said, and I imagined it was not for the first time. Attorneys love to be sure everyone knows what they do for a living regardless of the situation. "You can't keep us here."

"So you've told us, Counselor," King said. "Given Mister Sullivan's condition, we're having a chat here before we drive back to Baltimore. I know you were Mirandized because I did it. Now, shut up."

Abe pouted like the teacher told him he couldn't play with his favorite toy during class. Norton walked to the foot of the bed. Keith Sullivan looked at him but offered no other reaction. "What do you have to say about all this?"

Sullivan's voice came out raspy and weak. "No comment."

"Given your condition," Norton said, "you're unlikely to be convicted and put in prison. Was this elaborate scheme your idea?"

"Fuck you," Sullivan said.

"The silver tongue must fade with age," I said. Sullivan glared at me. "Unless money was the only reason the interns slept with you."

The old man had nothing else to say. A deputy listened to some garbled words over his radio before reporting all the goons were rounded up. "Let's take this party somewhere else, then," Norton said. He addressed one of the deputies. "You'll keep someone at the house?"

"Yes, sir."

"Good. Let's go."

Nancy climbed into the van with Rich, King, and me. She and I sat in the second row. Once we were underway down Route 136, Rich half-turned to face us. "You'll need to get checked out," he told Nancy.

"I'm fine," she said.

"Not negotiable. You got to see the man who set all this in motion. I . . . hope it helps in some way. We need to make sure you've been treated well, though, so you're going to get checked out at a hospital. I'll have an officer drive you once we're back at headquarters."

"Fine," Nancy said in a resigned voice. She turned away from Rich and looked out the window.

My cousin turned to me. "You're not looking so hot, either."

"I'm OK," I said, though I instinctively touched the slash wound across my stomach. Despite getting the cut a while ago, my fingers still came away with some red on them.

"You sure you're up for this?" Rich said.

"I'll live. When we're done, I'll get it looked at." Rich frowned like he didn't believe me on either count, but he didn't press the issue. I wiped my hand on my vest. Let the BPD pay for the cleaning.

Nancy shot me a worried look. I gave her a smile and a thumbs-up. It didn't seem to put her at ease. I turned away and watched trees and million-dollar houses zoom by.

WE ARRIVED AT BPD HEADQUARTERS. Two things happened as soon as we walked through the doors: Rich directed a female uniformed officer to take Nancy to the hospital, and Abe shouted for a lawyer. Rich left Shauna and Abe in an interrogation room with the latter reminding us every so often he was, in fact, an attorney and demanded representation. After a few rounds of the same refrain, Rich poked his head into the room. "We called your lawyer, you mouthy prick." He closed the door and walked away.

King and Norton grilled a pair of goons in another room. Leon Sharpe summoned Rich and me to his office. "Sounds like everything is in order," he said once we were all seated.

"Getting there," Rich said. "We'll need to take a run at Shauna and Abe once his lawyer gets here."

"Harford County's working on their part of the reporting. They'll have it to us as soon as they can."

"We're holding these two, right?"

"Sure," Sharpe said, and he punctuated it with a nod. "I just talked to the state's attorney. She wasn't thrilled to be woken up, but we had a nice conversation about charges. We'll hold them. No fancy lawyer is getting these two out of here anytime soon."

"I wonder if Abe's using his father," I said.

Rich shook his head. "Some young hotshot. I've heard the name before."

"Probably for the best. Confessing to a long list of crimes in front of your dad must be difficult."

"Speaking from experience?" Rich asked with an amused smirk.

"I only confess to one sin at a time," I said. "It gives us more to talk about later."

After a few minutes, Abe's attorney arrived. He looked to be in his mid-thirties, and despite being summoned to police headquarters in the wee hours, he wore a sharp suit. He also decided a neckbeard was a good idea, and our paths diverged at this point. I couldn't understand how a judge could take him seriously when his facial hair suggested he should be sweeping and mopping the courtroom, not arguing the law in it.

They conferred for a while. Neckbeard emerged and approached Rich, Sharpe, and me. "Joshua Cohen. I'm representing Mister McLelland and Miss Sullivan."

"Mister Cohen, we need to talk to your clients," Sharpe said.

The lawyer had the audacity to chuckle. "You think you can hold them?"

Sharpe's eyes narrowed. For a second, I thought he might try to stuff Cohen into the closest trash can, a feat I would pay good money to witness. "I spoke to the state's attorney. Your clients are being charged with several counts each of kidnapping, forced imprisonment, murder, and conspiracy to commit murder. Five girls are dead because of what they did, and we saved the sixth tonight. Why the hell do you think I couldn't hold them?"

Cohen swallowed hard and offered an awkward smile. "Gotta open the negotiation by shooting for the moon, right?" Sharpe continued staring at him. "Um . . . I think we're . . . uh, ready to talk now."

"Good," Sharpe said through clenched teeth. The three of us walked into the interview room. Cohen came in last, closing the door behind himself. When he turned back around, he looked two shades paler than when he first arrived. He sat next to his clients. Sharpe and Rich took the opposite seats. Five chairs in the small space already made for cozy confines, so I stood off to the side. The slash wound in my gut burned no matter how I leaned.

"My clients are ready to answer questions."

"Good," Rich said. "Let's open with the obvious one—why?"

No one offered a reply. Cohen looked at the two assholes beside him and spread his hands. Shauna scowled, and Abe stared at the table. We waited them out. The only person here who may not have possessed a firm grasp on the proceedings was Shauna, and her reticence seemed likely to carry her through.

After a couple minutes of silence, Sharpe said, "This is your opportunity to make your sentences a little less hellish. Five families are looking for closure. I'm sure the state's attorney would like to see progress made."

His suggestion did not spur a wave of confession. We fell into silence with them. Shauna broke it a couple minutes later. "You know who my father is?" We all nodded. "He used to cheat on my mother. She accepted it. Said it was part of living with such a powerful man." She snorted and shook her head. "When I was old enough to know what was going on, I thought it was wrong. But he was my dad, you know? What was I gonna do about it?

"Then, a few years later, we hear rumors he's fucking the interns at work. His mistresses had all been grown women up to this point. Now he's going after high-school girls? That was the breaking point for Mom. She said she would leave him. He told her he'd stop."

"Did he?" Sharpe asked.

"Yeah, but not on his own. Mom didn't trust him, so she went to Vincent Davenport. He was appalled, but he couldn't just get rid of my dad. They were partners. They built the company together."

"Then, the buyout happened," I said.

"Yeah. Under normal circumstances, Dad probably could've held out for more. Davenport knew he had him by the balls, though. We took the offer, and he was gone."

"We knew most of this already," Rich said.

"Aren't you all so smart?" Abe muttered.

"Yes," I said. "It's why we caught you."

Abe went back to scowling at the table. I got the impression he was on board with the plan but didn't put in any of the work. More money for Shauna meant more money for him, and it made a fine arrangement. Shauna—maybe with some input from her father—did the legwork, so she laid it out for us while her boyfriend sulked like the spoiled child he was.

Shauna continued after a short pause. "My mom left him. The high school thing was too much for her. Even she had her breaking point. Once she died, my dad was the only parent I had left. So we patched things up. That was about a year before he got diagnosed with Parkinson's. He'd had cancer in there, too, so it's been a pretty rough time. You saw how he is." Her eyes glistened, and she wiped at them with her sleeve.

"Anyway, we've known for a while the end was in sight. Not

long ago, I heard one of the girls he . . . slept with back then had a baby about nine months later."

"How did you find out?" Sharpe asked.

"I've got a good biotech company," Shauna said. "People tell me things."

"Just not who it was."

She shook her head. "All we knew was the baby was a girl born at Saint Joseph's around a certain time, and the birth records wouldn't list any names. I didn't even know that was possible, but there we were. We saw several candidates, so we started working through them."

Rich leaned forward at this. "I want to establish your process here. You'd find a girl who might have been the one on the anonymous birth certificate, and you'd kidnap her."

"Sort of," she said.

"Do we need to go into this?" Cohen broke in, reminding everyone he still wasted his share of oxygen in the room. "I think my clients have been very forthcoming already."

Sharpe stared at him. I couldn't see it from my angle, but I'd been on the receiving end before. Cohen blanched again and put his hands up in surrender. "Please continue, Miss Sullivan," the captain said.

"Like I was about to say, we didn't do the kidnapping." She flicked a finger between herself and Abe. "I farmed that out to someone at my company." Her admission meant the late Jeremy Green was a legitimate employee. "He took care of the dirty work. Once we had the girl, we drew blood and did a full DNA test. If it wasn't a match . . . well, we couldn't have her talking."

"So Green killed them?" I said.

"You found Jeremy?"

"Yes. And shortly after, I shot him about ten times."

Shauna's brows pulled down into a deep frown. Sharpe

smirked. Cohen and Abe continued to sit at the table in a contest to see who was the most useless. By virtue of being paid for his negligible contribution, Cohen enjoyed a narrow lead in the dubious race. "Miss Sullivan?" Sharpe prompted when she remained quiet.

"Yeah." Shauna sighed. She looked noticeably more tired than when the interview began. I sympathized. "Jeremy handled getting rid of the girls. We'd find the next one and do it again."

"What would you do if you found an heir?" Rich asked. I'd been wondering the same, and he beat me to the question.

"Abe and I talked about this," she said, though her boyfriend didn't even look up at the mention of his name. "We'd offer her a sum of money to walk away and stay quiet about everything. She'd renounce any claim to inheritance, the Sullivan name . . . all of it."

"If she were to accept?"

"We'd pay her the money."

Rich looked up from writing a note. "If she declined?"

"Then, Jeremy would deal with it," Shauna said.

"By killing your own half-sister?" Sharpe asked. They probably needed this on the record, or some asshole like Cohen would try to get the charges tossed.

"Yes."

No one said anything for a minute. We were all tired. The adrenaline of the fight and the shootout had long since left my system, and I'd been dragging for a while. Now, I felt like I was running on fumes. "I think we have what we need for now," Sharpe said. "We're going to book you. You'll be arraigned soon."

"I'll be there," Cohen said.

Sharpe stood and glared down at him. "How nice for you." He left the room.

"I'm going home," I said to Rich. "It's been a hell of a night."

"But a good one," he said.

I looked at the other side of the table. There sat two people whose lives were in a ruin of their own making, along with a lawyer too dumb to know he was out of his depth. "For some of us, at least," I said.

CHAPTER 30

After stopping at a 24-hour clinic for stitches, I pulled onto my parking pad and took a deep breath. Weariness had long since settled in. My curiosity as to what Shauna and Abe did got me through the interview. Now, I felt like I wanted to sleep for the next two days. I got out of the car, trudged into the house, and dragged my way upstairs. Despite my best efforts to be quiet, Gloria woke up when I entered the bedroom.

She flashed a sleepy smile. It was the most adorable thing I'd seen in a while. "You look tired." Her just-awakened voice sounded deep and sexy. "Come to bed."

I took her hand and squeezed it. "Give me a couple minutes." I kept my word, returning with minty breath and clad in a pair of shorts and a T-shirt. I slipped in beside Gloria, and she rolled over to drape an arm atop my chest. "Is it finally over?"

"Yeah." I told her what went down from the raid on the Harford County farm to the interrogation of Abe and Shauna. She gripped me tightly when I talked about my rescue of Nancy in the barn. "The police have everyone they need now. They'll make the case."

"It sounds so scary." Gloria shifted and rested her head on my chest. "You got shot at." Her fingers lingered just above my patched-up wound.

"You should see the other guy," I said. Then, I remembered I emptied the magazine into him. "On second thought, you probably shouldn't."

"This was a dangerous case."

"I'm glad it's over. Losing Ashleigh was tough." With everything piling up since, it felt like weeks ago, but I knew it was far more recent. The sting still hadn't gone away. Some part of me pumped rounds into Jeremy Green after the first few decided his fate because of what he did to Ashleigh. I'd never before lost a client in such a way, and I didn't care to repeat the experience.

"You tired?" Gloria said.

"Extremely."

"OK. Let's get some rest, then."

I fell asleep in a matter of seconds. Gloria remained snuggled against me. At some point after dawn, she woke me up. "You could've died." She tugged at my shirt and traced her finger below my stitches. "I really need to be with you right now."

Despite my lingering weariness, I didn't object.

* * *

WE SLEPT UNTIL TEN-THIRTY. I still felt tired as I disentangled myself from Gloria and crawled out of bed. I walked downstairs, brewed a pot of coffee strong enough to pour itself, and worked on breakfast. I didn't feel especially creative, so I sufficed with toast and yogurt, accompanied by three mugs of steaming java. I felt human again afterward. Gloria came downstairs a short while later, and I whipped up the same for her.

"What's on your agenda for today?" she said as she sipped her second cup of coffee.

"I want to see how Nancy is doing. Physically, I think she's fine. She went through a lot, though . . . plus, she could've gotten shot in the barn."

"You think she's still in the hospital?"

"Maybe. I'll ask Rich if he knows anything." I fired off a quick text to my cousin. "I also want to talk with Vincent Davenport at some point."

"Why?"

"He could've told me the truth earlier," I said. "I'd asked him about the Sullivan buyout, and he fed me the corporate spin. If I knew what really happened, we might have wrapped it up sooner."

"Maybe Nancy never gets kidnapped if you do," Gloria said.

I nodded. "Or maybe Violet doesn't have to die."

Gloria frowned as she regarded her mug. "I wish he would've told you the truth."

"Me, too. You still want to do work for this asshole?"

She considered my question for a few seconds. "I'll have to think about it. I know you've never cared for him, but I didn't see that side of him. He was always good to me, and the fundraisers we did helped a lot of people."

"But now you're starting to see he might be a slimeball after all," I said.

"I wouldn't call him that." Gloria pursed her lips. "It bothers me, though. If he'd been forthright with you, it could've made a difference."

"It's your decision. I'll support whatever you decide."

Gloria grabbed my hand and squeezed it. "Even if I say I want to continue working with him?"

"So long as you don't mind my snarky commentary."

"It's part of your charm," she said.

"It's most of my charm," I said, and we enjoyed a laugh. My phone buzzed on the kitchen table. Rich texted back. *She's still at Mercy, though she's supposed to be discharged soon.* "I'd better get to the hospital. I'd like to see how she is before they release her."

I threw more professional clothes on, kissed Gloria goodbye, and drove to Mercy Medical Center. After collecting my visitor's pass, I found Nancy's room on the third floor. She sat upright in bed, and her father occupied the guest chair. Both perked up as I walked in. "C.T.!" Nancy said, scrambling out of bed to wrap me in a tight hug.

"Good to see you, too," I said. The embrace went on longer than I felt comfortable with, but I figured she needed it, so I let her hold on as long as she wanted. Once she released me, I saw her eyes were wet.

"It's great to see you," she said.

Allen stood and extended his hand. I shook it. "Thank you," he said. "I don't know what I'd do without her."

"She leaving today?"

"Yes, thank goodness," Nancy said. "I just want to sleep in my own bed."

"She's physically fine," Allen said. "They're referring us to a therapist."

"Do it," I said, even though my own experience after my sister's death had been unproductive. "You've been through a lot . . . both of you."

"What happens next? The police haven't told us much."

"The people behind all this will get charged with an extended list of crimes. If it turns out to be a typical case, they'll plea some of them down and avoid a long trial. They're going to jail for a long time, though."

"Did that old guy really have sex with my mom?" Nancy said, her lip curled and nose wrinkled.

I shrugged. "I don't know. Did they draw your blood?" She nodded. "They hadn't found out yet, then. She probably worked or interned at D&S in high school and overlapped with Keith Sullivan's . . . period of indiscretion."

"I hope she didn't. He's gross."

"I hope not, too." I bid them adieu, received another long hug from Nancy, and left the room. When I got back to my car, my phone rang.

"It's Jon Swain." Now I realized why the number looked familiar. My chest tightened. "We heard you caught the people responsible."

"Yes," I said. "I'm sorry it wasn't in time for Ashleigh."

"We are, too." He paused. "Karen's still gutted. We both are, really. She's . . . more bitter than I am, I guess."

"She still blames me."

"Yes. I told her she should blame the people who got arrested. She will in time. I wanted to call and thank you, though. You could've walked away from this after . . . what happened. I'm glad you stuck it out."

"If it's any consolation," I said, "I found the man I'm pretty sure killed Ashleigh and the other girls."

"Did you kill him?" Jon asked, a hard edge coming into his voice.

"Yes," I said. "I think I put about ten rounds into him. It was academic after the first two or three, but I felt . . . I needed to empty the magazine."

"For Ashleigh."

"And the other girls." I paused and sighed. Their faces passed in front of my mind's eye. "But mostly for Ashleigh."

We hung up. I spent a couple minutes collecting myself in the car before I drove away.

* * *

AT A RED LIGHT, I flouted Maryland law and Googled something on my phone. Among the hierarchy of sins I've committed, it would rank near the bottom. I looked up Vincent Davenport's campaign headquarters. An article in the *Baltimore Sun* told me and the seventeen other people who still read it about Davenport's newly-opened base of operations in Canton. I drove there and found he'd picked a spot on the water. If his mayoral campaign went into the death spiral I hoped it would, at least he could enjoy the view. Or walk off the pier.

I walked in and was disheartened to find Melinda. She saw me and smiled. "C.T., what are you doing here?" She came over and hugged me.

"Nice to see you, too."

"You know I'm always glad to see you. What brings you by?"

"I was hoping to talk to your father," I said. I figured the conversation wouldn't go well, which is why I wished Melinda were at her own office. Now, she'd be curious about what we said. I wondered if she'd still be glad I dropped by when it came time for me to leave.

"Did you decide to take him up on his offer?" she asked.

"No," I said. Optimism drained from Melinda's face as she no doubt realized I was here on less pleasant business. "There's something else I need to talk to him about."

"He's at the end of the hall." She frowned as I walked away. On one level, I felt glad to see Melinda's concern about her father. Their relationship could be charitably described as complicated. A rift in the family led to her living as a prostitute for five years. I found her, deduced who she really was, and got her out. By then, Daddy Dearest figured a way to come through it all smelling like a rose. Melinda was terrific, and Davenport didn't deserve her. She was glad to have him back, however, and I wouldn't ruin it for her.

I found Davenport sitting behind a desk in a large office. The sight made me recall our first conversation, though he enjoyed a much larger and more needlessly opulent space in his own building. Leases probably frown on marble columns and statues. "Mister Ferguson," he said as he looked up. Something approaching a smile crossed his face. I doubted it would last long.

Davenport was about sixty, and he kept himself in pretty good shape. Some more gray wove through his hair now. I wondered if he stopped coloring it because a focus group told him he'd look more distinctive. He was exactly the type to solicit and follow this advice. Today, he eschewed a suit for a light Polo sweater and a pair of chinos. He stood and came around to shake my hand.

"I think you'll want to close the door," I said. He remained in place and regarded me with a quizzical look. "I'll give you five seconds. Then, I won't be responsible for what your staff thinks of you." Anyone standing close enough would probably be able to hear us, anyway. Davenport stopped gaping long enough to shut the door. He returned to his desk, so I sat, too.

"What's this about?"

"You *asshole*," I said.

"It's a word you've thrown at me before, Mister Ferguson. You'll have to be more specific."

"The Sullivan buyout. You could have told me the truth."

"I did tell—"

"Bullshit! You fed me whatever corporate line your lawyer came up with all those years ago." He opened his mouth to say something, but I held up my hand to cut him off. "I learned what really happened . . . no thanks to you."

"You can see the bad position the company was in," he said, leaning back and folding his hands across his midsection.

"A position you created. Your partner was screwing a bunch of high school girls. You could have told everyone what happened, run him out of town, and been the hero. Instead, you paid him to go away and buried the whole thing."

"Why is this important now?"

"Five girls are dead," I said, pointing at him for emphasis. "If you'd told me the truth when I asked you, I would've put every-thing together sooner. One girl might still be alive, and another never would've been kidnapped."

"All of this because of what Keith did?" Davenport said.

"Apparently, one of the girls got pregnant and had a baby in secret. Your old partner and his daughter went looking for the heir. Shauna didn't want to share her money."

Davenport frowned. "I'd heard Keith was in bad health, but I never thought he'd concoct something like this."

I thought Shauna was the mastermind of the two, but I didn't feel like having this debate. "The point is you should've told me what really happened. Now, you get to live with knowing you could have prevented an innocent girl's death."

Davenport sat up and glared. "You have no way of knowing you could've saved her." I remained quiet; probability would be another debate I didn't want to have. "Why have you come here, Mister Ferguson? To threaten me? To expose this to the press?" He flipped the script by pointing at me. "I'll come after you if you do."

"I'm not going to tell the press," I said. Davenport exhaled a deep breath. "I'm going to tell the families of the girls involved. They'll know exactly what you did and what you could've done. Maybe they'll talk to the media. It'll be up to them. I don't think your image consultants will want you attacking a bunch of grieving families, though. Bad optics."

He took his glasses off, held them near his face, and studied me. "You'd do this?"

"Absolutely."

"Can I talk you out of it?"

"No."

"I'm going to be the next mayor, you know," Davenport said.

"Maybe. I hope your strategy to deal with problems has evolved in seventeen years. You probably can't get rid of the drug dealers by paying them off and telling them to go somewhere else."

"Get out of my office," Davenport said in a quiet voice. I heard the anger come through loud and clear.

"With pleasure." I stood, opened the door, and walked away. I saw Melinda again before I left. A few staffers who looked like they'd barely finished the college year stood nearby.

"How did your chat with Dad go?" she said.

"Melinda, I'm glad you two have a good relationship now," I said. "But your father's a real prick."

I left before she could say anything in his defense.

* * *

LATER, I saw on the local news how McLelland and Katezenberg suspended operations "in light of recent events." Considering the combined age of the older partners topped one-fifty, I figured their doors would stay shut for good. I hoped Elaine the secretary scored a nice severance package. She deserved it, and not only for dealing with me in one of my more petulant moments.

I next thought of Tony Rizzo. He'd used the firm to try and put his name on a revived park somewhere in the city. It always struck me as a weird move. Tony knew which wheels to grease better than anyone in the city. He should be able to get it done with a couple of phone calls, a reminder of who he is, and a veiled threat. Why go through an attorney when it was easier and cheaper not to?

A few minutes later, my phone buzzed. Gabriella Rizzo texted and asked if I could stop by the restaurant. I didn't feel like making the jaunt, so I begged off. She called me right away. "Dad's salty about McLelland going under."

"I'm sure he's not the only one," I said.

"He told me you've been against him a couple times now. What's going on, C.T.?"

"Nothing unusual. Just case work."

"What happened?"

"Five young women got killed," I said. "The junior partner of the firm was one of the people directly responsible. Your father can be bitter all he wants, Gabriella. We both know he won't cross some lines. Ask him where murdering teenaged girls fits in."

She sighed. "All right. He wouldn't stand for killing innocent kids. I didn't know the whole story."

"I hope he still gets his park."

"Me, too," she said, and we hung up. What was going on with my female friends and their fathers? At least I liked Tony most of the time. About an hour later as Gloria and I considered our dinner options, I got the call I'd been expecting.

"Coningsby, this sounds like a dangerous case," my mother said. Her tone carried a mix of pride and worry. I couldn't tell if I was about to get congratulated for closing the case or receive a tongue-lashing because of the risks involved.

"They all have the potential, Mom. Some realize it more than others." I touched my stitches through my shirt.

"I'm serious. Richard tells us you were in a shootout."

I wished Rich wouldn't have such detailed conversations with my parents. They inferred way too much danger from what he told them. "I wouldn't call it a shootout," I said.

"Did you fire your gun?"

"Yes."

"Did someone fire at you?"

"Yes," I said, even though I knew where she was going.

"That's a shootout!"

"I'm fine, Mom. The girl I went there to save is fine, too. The only people who took bullets were the ones who deserved them."

"Are you sure you still want to do this job?" my mother said. "In the beginning, you said you'd do your work online. Your father and I didn't think you'd be trading gunfire in some county barn."

Now, I didn't know if the exchange of bullets or the barn being in Harford county was the worse sin. Conversations with my mother often confused me. "I can't solve all my cases over the computer, Mom. I thought I could at first. There's a lot you can't do online."

"You be careful, Coningsby."

"I will, Mom."

She harrumphed like she didn't believe me. I'm not sure I would've in her place, either. "Be sure you do, dear. Your father and I will wire you the usual amount of money."

"Thanks."

"I don't want to learn about any more gunfights," she said. "And why are we hearing it from Richard and not from you?"

"I don't know," I said. "Would it really make a difference who gave you the blow-by-blow?"

"I suppose not. Maybe you can take an easy case next."

"It's not like I go hunting for the most difficult ones." In truth, a simple case would bore me. I craved a challenge. It would be nice if the next one didn't include getting shot at, however.

"Very well, dear. I hope we'll see you for dinner soon."

"Sure," I said. "I'll bring Gloria, too."

"Perfect. We're always glad to see her."

"I am, too." We hung up. I set my phone back on the coffee table and stared at it to prevent it from buzzing or ringing any further.

Gloria rested her head on my shoulder. "Your mom wants us to come for dinner?"

"Yeah," I said.

"We haven't gone over as often ever since the . . . Samantha thing."

"I know. Can you blame me?"

"I guess not," she said, snuggling into me. "What's for dinner?"

We pored over a few menus. As we did, my phone rang again, showing a number I didn't recognize. I let it go to voicemail. After dealing with the ups and downs—mostly the latter—of this case, I didn't feel like taking another one right away.

There was always tomorrow. Or the next day.

END of Novel #8

HI THERE,

Thanks for coming along on C.T.'s latest adventure. I hope you enjoyed it.

In his next case, C.T. will attempt to solve the one murder he never expected—his own. You can get *In the Blood* at https://books2read.com/ITBCT9.

THE END

Do you like free books? You can get the prequel novella to the C.T. Ferguson mystery series for free. This is unavailable for sale and is exclusive to my readers. Visit https://bit.ly/CTprequel to get your book!

If you enjoyed this novel, I hope you'll leave a review. Even a short writeup makes a difference. Reviews help independent authors get their books discovered by more readers and qualify for promotions. To leave a review, go to the book's sales page, select a star rating, and enter your comments. If you read this book on a tablet or phone, your reading app will likely prompt you to leave a review at the end.

The C.T. Ferguson Crime Novels:

1. The Reluctant Detective
2. The Unknown Devil
3. The Workers of Iniquity
4. Already Guilty
5. Daughters and Sons
6. A March from Innocence

7. Inside Cut
8. The Next Girl
9. In the Blood

While this is the suggested reading sequence, the books can be enjoyed in whatever order you happen upon them.

Connect with me:

For the many ways of finding and reaching me online, please visit https://tomfowlerwrites.com/contact. I'm always happy to talk to readers.

This is a work of fiction. Characters and places are either fictitious or used in a fictitious manner.

"Self-publishing" is something of a misnomer. This book would not have been possible without the contributions of many people.

- The cover design team at 100 Covers.
- My editor extraordinaire, Chase Nottingham.
- My wonderful advance reader team, the Fell Street Irregulars.

www.ingramcontent.com/pod-product-compliance
Lightning Source LLC
Chambersburg PA
CBHW021123190726
48288CB00008B/2472